Derailed

The Obscured Series
Book Three

C. M. BOERS

ISBN:
0-9906452-4-X
ISBN-13: 978-0-9906452-4-5

DEDICATION

I dedicate this book to my husband, who provides for our family with in the most admirable way. If it wasn't for his hard work and support this series would not be possible!

CONTENTS

ACKNOWLEDGMENTS

I have a lot of support in my writing journey, a lot of which comes from family and friends, but the biggest support comes from my readers like you! Thank you all for helping me continue on this amazing journey!

CHAPTER ONE

My feet came down in front of me, one right after the other. Our pace remained slow. I watched the dust rise in small puffs and settle again with each step we took. Heat rose up my back causing me to perspire. My lungs felt heavy. As I tried to gather a deep breath, I felt as if I were underwater. I slid the back of my hand across my forehead to stop the beads of sweat from rolling down my face.

High above my head, trees surrounded me in neat rows. Bursts of sunlight drifted through the spaces between the leaves, casting strange shadows on the ground. Eli trekked ahead of me, close enough for me to touch him, yet he did not respond. Confusion and desperation brimmed at the surface of my patience. Ren seemed to appear out of thin air. He lifted his head toward me in an attempt at a greeting and fell into stride next to Eli, matching Eli's pace. The tree line ended. Eli and Ren continued into the clearing, and I stopped short of it. Someone stepped into view. Who? I couldn't tell.

I squinted as if the sun were causing a glare, but that was far from the problem. Their face was hidden by a gray mist. The mystery person broke into a run and lunged at Ren. Another attacker materialized. Again, his face was obscured. Without warning, his fist connected with Eli's cheekbone. Ren's listless body fell to the ground in a heap. Too much happened at once. My eyes darted back and forth between Ren's attacker and Eli. I stepped back, biting back a scream. Eli tackled the second man. The grinding of gravel under my feet alerted the unrestrained strong-arm to my presence. My heart thumped in my chest. He rushed toward me, and before I realized what was happening, he stood in front of me, his fist headed for . . .

Jolting from sleep, I tried to reorient myself. *My name is Abby Martin. I am in my room. My dream was not real . . . yet. It will be real at some point, but I have time. Time to figure out what it means. Time to stop it . . . maybe.*

I stretched, letting my heart gradually slow to a normal rhythm. My dreams—nightmares, really—had come true twice, each time leading my friends and me into terrifying situations. A few months ago, I would have laughed at anyone who said their nightmares came true, but I guess the movie directors have to get their ideas from somewhere.

Eli, my boyfriend, came from a line of immortal Protectors—yeah, I know my life is weird—and he was supposed to help me with my nightmares, but after his mom was murdered, he blamed me, and we broke up for a while. In the meantime, I convinced or maybe tricked would be more correct, Ren, one of Eli's closest friends, to take me to their elders. I hoped the elders who governed the Protectors could explain my dreams. According to the elders, I was gifted but not immortal, which was something they had never seen before. But they thought I would probably start discovering more 'gifts' as time passed. *Well, I don't want them.*

One elder seemed keen on helping me, but from what I could tell, this wasn't normal—the other two elders seemed perturbed that he had taken such an interest. While I was at it, I made myself available to help catch Eli's mom's killer. The elders put me on a team with four great guys, and once we brought the killers to justice, Eli came back to me. I also gained an ally—the head elder, Edward.

I pushed back the covers, letting the cool air hit my overheated legs. I stretched my arms and sighed. Ah, summer. No school. Free time. Something I had craved for months. Maybe I would settle into normal teenage life again. Maybe. I wouldn't hold my breath.

Lifting myself out of bed, I grabbed the duffle bag that I had yet to unpack from my trip to California and pulled out all the remaining things. I threw my clothes in the laundry before tossing the bag back under my bed. The three little souvenirs I had picked out by the beach made me smile as I laid them on my desk. The first was an ivory seagull wind chime I had bought for my mom. When it spun in the wind, it looked almost like the seagulls were swooping down on the beach. I knew it would remind her of our life in California. The second—a shell necklace—I bought for Bailey. Something about the purple shells made me think of her. And last, for me, a single sand dollar.

Eli was surprised by my choice until I told him about my collection. This would be number four. I only bought sand dollars to mark something special. When I was a baby, my dad bought me one during my first trip to the beach. I still remembered the day he gave it to me, as soon as I was old enough to care for it. He held it out to me wrapped in a dainty handkerchief. Since then I had kept it wrapped up in a very safe place—my underwear drawer. Soon after, I got my second one, the day after my dad bought the sporting goods store. We went to the beach to celebrate with our friends and family. I had made sure to bring money with me, and when nobody was paying attention, I snuck off to buy one. I hid it in my waistband until I got home, hoping I wouldn't break it.

The third I bought with Kelly when I told her I was moving. Tears streamed down my face through the whole transaction. I was sure the lady at the store thought I was crazy. It also marked the start of a new journey, though at the time, it had seemed like the worst thing. I bought one for Kelly too, as a memento to remember me by.

This one, the fourth and hopefully not the last, marked my first trip to California with Eli. A trip I would never forget.

I mulled it over, remembering the highs and lows as I wrapped up the new sand dollar with the others and nestled them back in the hiding spot I had always used. Two weeks in California had passed in the blink of an eye. Beach trips, sunburns, shopping, and lots of time with Kelly. And the romance. I couldn't forget about that. Eli didn't hold back. My favorite night of the whole trip, he surprised me with my favorite Chinese food and a candlelight dinner by the ocean. He laid out a blanket and buried countless glowing candles in the sand that our picnic area gleamed brightly on the dark and desolate beach. He even made me laugh when he tried to use chopsticks—for his sake I was glad he brought plastic silverware, too. To top it off, he bought the most decadent chocolate cake to finish the evening. Of course, there was plenty of star gazing, wave watching, and, of course, a bit of making out. We stayed out until one in the morning. It was the closest I had ever come to wanting to . . . well . . . you know. I still had no idea how he had pulled off such an extravagant gesture. It melted my heart.

Then my mind ventured back to Casey, who had shown up out of the blue on the beach days before the beautiful, romantic evening. What had he been thinking? *Eli isn't who you think he is*, he had said. I had no clue what he was talking about. Eli was the same as he always had been. In fact, he wasn't being shy about pulling all the stops. I wished I had asked him why he had come when I saw him, but I had been too infuriated by his audacity. I just wanted him to leave. In hindsight, that had been stupid. I took the coward's way out instead of pushing to get answers, and then I high-tailed it from him. I didn't see him again during the rest of our trip, but that didn't mean he wasn't occupying my thoughts. It boggled my mind. What would have compelled him to speak out so boldly against Eli?

Eli and I went back to work the day after arriving home, and it felt great being there again. The easy banter between our co-workers returned to normal now that Eli didn't have an ax to grind, and the days went by quickly. Late one night, as I stalked up the stairs after work, I realized that even though I missed California all the time, it was no longer my home. Arizona was, and I didn't mind it anymore.

I yawned. After four straight days of eight-hour shifts, I welcomed my day off.

My shiny silver laptop caught my eye from where it sat perched on my desk, beckoning me to open it. Unable to stop myself, I popped it open and typed *car listings* into the search box. I perused auto listings constantly now, and thanks to Eli, I knew a few things to look for and a few things to avoid. Unfortunately, no convertibles had been listed in my price range. I still held out hope, though—there was still time. My dad was coming to help me shop, and I was counting down the days until he arrived. I crossed off yet another day on my calendar.

Three more days.

"Abby?"

I spun around to see my mom standing in the doorway, her long brown hair pulled back into a ponytail. Her blue eyes captured my attention.

"Yeah?" I asked.

"Are you going to join me for breakfast? I wanted to talk to you about something."

"Ah, okay. I'll be right down," I said, glancing at her again.

She shut the door and was gone as quickly as she had come. I shifted on my feet, hurrying to glance at the newest car listings. When nothing caught my eye, I relented and headed downstairs.

Things between my mom and I had been a little strained. She seemed happy, yet she had become super suspicious about everything I did. Our once-close relationship began to disintegrate, and while I knew it wasn't all my fault, I felt partially responsible, given what my life had transformed into. I had to keep secrets. She would never know even half of what I have been dealing with. To her, immortal beings were fiction. Maybe if she knew the truth, she wouldn't be so hard on me, but chances are she would probably lock me in my room and never let me out.

I hopped down the stairs and bounded into the dining room, where the table was already laid out with eggs, bacon, and biscuits. I threw myself into my seat and dished up.

"Are you off work today?" I asked.

"No, I'm going in late." She smiled.

"I see. So, what did you want to talk about?"

"Well, I'd like to have dinner together tonight."

"Uh, I already have plans with Eli."

"Tomorrow, then? With George. Just the three of us."

I had forgotten about George. He had taken up residence in my kitchen before I left for California, but I hadn't seen him much since I had gotten back.

I wondered why this was a big deal. I had eaten meals with them before, once even at dinner, but Eli had been there too.

"Okay."

"Good," she said.

She looked pleased, as if she had expected me to put up a fight, and I might have if I hadn't been so confused.

"Dress nice. Make sure you're ready to go at six."

I nodded. I finished eating in silence and went straight up to my room when I finished. I grabbed my phone and sent a quick text.

Good morning.

My phone buzzed to life moments later. Eli's name flashed on the screen.

"Hey," I said into the phone.

"Hey yourself."

"What are you doing?" I asked.

"Laying in bed, staring out the window. The sky is very blue today."

I absently wandered to the window to look at the sky, which shimmered a brilliant blue I had long since realized was normal for Arizona. Already high in the sky, the sun cast mirages out in the distance as the heat set in. Our summer temps had already reached the triple digits for weeks and today would be no different. Heat radiated off the glass, so I shut the blinds again to block it out.

"A day off. What are we to do?"

I couldn't help the smile that spread across my face, but I said nothing, knowing he was teasing me.

"Hmm . . . I think something might have gotten my girlfriend's tongue."

I giggled.

"So she is there!" He faked surprise. I could hear him chuckling in the background. "What time am I picking you up?"

"Six?" I asked.

"Okay."

"I'll see you then."

"Bye." He hung up before I could respond.

I held the phone to my chest, smiling to myself like a fool. It had been a month since our explosive reconnection. Before that, Eli had cut off all communication with me as he dealt with—and blamed me for—his mother's death. Thankfully, he had come to his senses. So far, life hadn't slowed down enough for us to just enjoy being together again. But now, without school standing in our way, I anticipated date nights galore. All that started tonight.

My mind drifted back to Casey's accusation that Eli was different. *Different how?* I couldn't stop wondering. I searched for things that were wrong, watching every move he made like I would be able to magically see what Casey was talking about.

I hadn't even told Eli about the conversation with Casey on the beach weeks ago. I felt guilty about it, but I just couldn't bring myself to say anything. He already mistrusted Casey as it was, and I didn't need to give him more ammunition.

After lunch, I went outside to stretch my legs and get the mail. The mailbox sat at the end of the block, so I welcomed the exercise and the warmth of summer after being in the air conditioning, at least for the short walk. I stretched my arms out, letting the sun's rays soak into my skin for a little Vitamin D therapy. After unlocking the box, I pulled out all the mail before locking it again. As I walked back, I browsed through the mail. One piece stopped me dead in my tracks.

A postcard from the Phoenix Zoo—a place that had been the center of good and bad times for me, but few knew it. Five words and I felt like my heart would beat right out of my chest:

SEE HOW EASY IT IS . . .

I glanced around, my skin prickling as if someone were watching me. Pushing the postcard to the bottom of the pile, I rushed the rest of the way home, on edge. I set all the mail on the counter, slipping the postcard out first, and hurried back to my room to mull it over. *How easy what was?*

It didn't make sense. I debated calling Eli right then to tell him about it, but I decided to wait. It didn't seem all that threatening.

As I combed my hair later that afternoon, my mind continued to churn without coming up with any plausible explanation for the note. I threw down the comb with a huff.

Shaking my head, I slid myself into a bright blue maxi dress. It hugged my body in all the right places and flowed down to my ankles. The perfect mix of comfort and sexy. This date also marked the first time I would wear my new necklace, the one Ren had bought me for my birthday. I pulled the delicate chain out of the box and draped the owl pendant around my neck. The owl's blue eyes complemented my dress. I slipped on a pair of white sandals, and I was ready to go.

Eli picked me up a short time later, looking handsome in a button-down shirt. His brilliant blue eyes caught my attention the minute I saw him, just as they had captivated me the first time we met.

"Abby, you look beautiful," he said, taking the time to look me over.

My cheeks warmed under his scrutiny. "Thanks," I said.

"Shall we go?" he asked.

I nodded.

His warm hand rested on my back as we headed to the car, sending shivers down my whole body. Lord, he could set me on fire with just his touch. He opened my car door, and we headed on our way.

I waited until we were in the car to pull out the postcard from my purse and hand it to him. I longed for the night to go on without complication, but I knew I had to tell him. The note unnerved me.

"What's this?" he asked.

"I don't know. It was in my mail today."

He glanced at it, reading it over. His jaw clenched. Then he slid the note into the crack between the seats.

"Let me know if you get any others," he said.

I sat back and mulled it over.

"What do you think it means?" I asked.

"No idea. Let's just forget about it for tonight, okay?"

"All right."

If Eli said not to worry about it, it was probably nothing. I didn't want to freak out and make this into something it wasn't. I did my best to push it out of my mind and hoped it wouldn't resurface.

"If it makes you feel better, I'll see if I can find out who sent it by the postal stamp."

"Thanks," I said, squeezing his hand.

Fondue was on the menu, and my excitement had been building since we decided to go. I adored fondue. I knew it would be hard for me not to stuff myself before the dessert course came, but that was the absolute best part. Maybe they should switch things around and serve dessert first. Now that would be amazing.

A burgundy curtain closed off our booth from the rest of the restaurant. It felt secluded and romantic. I cuddled up to Eli while we waited for the first course—cheese.

His hand drifted from my fingers to the necklace perched on my throat. He caressed the pendant, inspecting the beautiful gold owl, with its striking blue eyes.

"Where did you get this?" he asked.

"Ren," I whispered, remembering the day he had given it to me. Things had been strained between Ren and me ever since the meeting with the elders. Then he had shown up out of the blue on my birthday. It had been so thoughtful. "For my birthday."

"Your birthday. That's right. I missed it."

I nodded.

"I'm sorry. I can't believe I missed it. I'll have to think of a way to make it up to you," he said.

I smiled to myself, thinking of how he might try. "I'd like that."

"Why an owl?" he asked.

"Ren said tawny owls mate for life. I guess he figured that even though things were bad, you and I would be together again someday. I think it was his way of saying you and I are soul mates."

I opened it, showing him the picture of himself inside. A smile touched the corners of his mouth.

"I love it."

He cradled my neck as he leaned in and kissed my neck just above the locket. I reclined back, allowing his lips to brush my neck. My hand gripped his chest as desire filled my body. He pulled me closer and pressed his lips to mine. I savored the taste of him on my lips and teased him with my tongue.

A moment later, the curtain slid open, making us jump. I blushed as we pulled away from each other and turned our attention to the steaming metal bowl in front of us. Our waiter prepared it right at the table. I watched closely, hoping to recreate it at home, though I knew it wouldn't be the same.

The waiter poured in the dark beer first and let it warm, explaining that it was of the highest quality. Next, he put in the cheese. Soon it melded together, looking gooey and delicious.

"There you go. The cheese will continue to melt as it warms. Let me know if you need anything else."

"Thanks," I said as he walked away.

I slid the curtain closed again just before we dug into the cheesy scrumptiousness.

I giggled as Eli dripped cheese across the table. A smile crept over his face.

"That funny, huh?"

I nodded, my smile never leaving my face.

"I bet you'll be messier than me!"

"Oh yeah? What's the winner get?" I asked.

"Oh, you want to wager on it?" He grinned.

"Of course."

"All right. How about this—loser gives the winner a massage?"

"You're on!"

It didn't take long for me to dribble a small amount on the table, despite how careful I was being. I looked at him to see if he had noticed, and his eyes were on me. He looked thoroughly amused.

I made a face. "So, my mom wants me to go to dinner with her and George tomorrow night," I said, changing the subject.

"Oh yeah. That won't be so bad, will it?" he asked, taking in my look of doubt.

I groaned. "No, I suppose not. But there's something off about it. My mom's acting weird."

"What do you mean?"

"This morning, she came up to my room to make sure I came down for breakfast because she wanted to 'talk to me.' I always come down for breakfast. If it was no big deal, why the fuss about it? Normally she would have just said something in passing."

"Hmm . . . I'm sure it's nothing. Maybe you're reading into it."

"Maybe," I said, trying not to be disagreeable, but I knew better. There was something going on, and I wasn't so sure I would like it.

"Don't worry about it," he said.

That was easier said than done.

A few minutes later, I had to admit that Eli knew me well. I had been far messier than he had. I had even tried to hide it a few times without success. Eli just laughed at my misguided attempts. I knew I would lose and end up owing him a massage.

We were halfway through the third course when Eli's phone rang. He checked it and stood up. "I'll be right back."

My eyes followed his back as he walked away, and I couldn't help but wonder who it was. *What would make him leave the table in the middle of our date?*

It was a long time before he returned. My entire plate of meat was gone. I tried to push away my annoyance. *There has to be a good reason.*

"Sorry about that," he said. "Oh, you finished. Ready for dessert?"

"I can wait."

"Nonsense," he said, reaching out of our curtained bubble to flag down the waiter.

"We're ready for the dessert course," he said once the waiter made his way over.

"Absolutely, coming right up," he said.

"You hardly ate any of it," I complained when the waiter had cleared it all away.

"I'm fine," he said.

But I wasn't convinced. He seemed to be trying to speed the night along, making eye contact with the waiter as if to say we were waiting to move on.

Five minutes later, the waiter set the chocolate in front of us, along with a plate filled with strawberries, bananas, pound cake, and rice crispy treats. It was heavenly. I would have gladly devoured a second helping, but my stomach didn't seem to agree. I felt stuffed. The decadence distracted me momentarily from Eli's apparent hurry to end the meal until we finished, and he again rushed the waiter along by asking for the check while he cleaned up the dessert.

"What's wrong?" I asked.

"What? Why would you think something was wrong?" he asked.

"You seem like you're in a hurry to leave."

"Of course not. I'm having a ton of fun with you here." He flashed a smile at me.

He paid the check the second it came and stood up, holding his hand out to help me out of the booth. We didn't speak during the walk to the car, and when we got there, he didn't stop to open my door for me. His gentlemanly ways had become the norm, so it seemed unusual for him to skip it. I felt frustration beginning to surface. *What was with him?*

He drove me straight to my house, even though it was well before my curfew, and walked me to the door.

"Do you want to come in?" I asked when he stopped on the doorstep.

"Nah, I think I'm going to head home. I'm tired."

"Ah, okay. I guess I'll just owe you that massage." I hoped that would bring him back to me from wherever his mind was wandering.

"Uh-huh," he said. From the faraway look on his face, it was clear he wasn't listening anymore.

"Don't forget to tie a cowbell on before bed," I said.

"I won't."

He was on autopilot.

"Eli!" I shouted.

His head whipped in my direction. *At least that got his attention.*

"You aren't even paying attention to me."

"I'm sorry. I'm really tired. I need to go," he said.

"Fine."

He leaned in to hug me and planted a kiss on my cheek. The next moment, he was in his car driving away, leaving me standing on the doorstep, wondering what had just happened.

*   *   *   *

The next afternoon, I stood in front of the mirror, dressed in a knee-length black skirt and a cream-colored top, pondering just what I was in store for. I did my makeup slowly, enjoying that there was no reason to rush. I left my long brown hair down, letting it hang down my back in thick waves.

When I was ready, I waited for my mom in the living room and fingered my pink phone. Other than a few vague texts, I hadn't talked to Eli since he had left in a hurry the night before. I knew something must be going on. I wished he wasn't being so distant. I could use his support tonight, even if it was only through text.

Butterflies filled my stomach. The thought of hanging out with my mom and her boyfriend still didn't sit well with me. It felt so strange that she was dating someone who wasn't my dad. Plus, I hated not knowing why I was being asked to dinner. When the doorbell rang, it surprised me. I had never once heard George ring the doorbell before. He always just seemed to be there.

"Can you grab that, Abby? I'll be right down," Mom called down the stairs.

I groaned and marched to the front door. Swinging it open, I found George in black dress slacks, a dark lavender dress shirt, and a black tie. He held a beautiful bouquet with a colorful assortment of flowers.

"Hey Abby," he said.

"Hi," I responded, stepping away from the door to allow him to enter.

"I'm so glad you can join us tonight."

I nodded, saying nothing. I still had mixed feelings about him and even more so about tonight.

"Hey," Mom chimed in behind me.

She glided forward, reaching up around his neck and kissing his cheek.

"These," he gestured toward the flowers, "are for you." He handed my mom the bouquet.

"Aww! That's so sweet. They're beautiful. Thank you." She blushed when she turned back toward me. That's all it took to make her blush? I rolled my eyes.

"Should we go?" George suggested.

"Are you ready?" Mom asked me.

"Yeah."

We piled into George's luxury car, my mom in front next to George. The inside smelled of new leather and looked surprisingly clean. One might have thought it was a rental car if you didn't know any better. I hadn't expected that. Maybe I had envisioned him as a slob.

After my mom settled into her seat, George's hand wandered over to rest on her knee. I gagged. Knowing they were dating was one thing, but seeing the small gestures of it felt overwhelming. I couldn't help but think of my dad and how, not that long ago, his hand rested there. I shifted my body so I faced out the window instead. This was going to be a long night.

My phone buzzed in my pocket.

Don't stress. I'm here if you need me.

Eli always seemed to know just what I needed to hear to make me feel at ease. I was glad he texted. Maybe he had taken care of whatever had distracted him the night before. I closed my eyes and sucked in a deep breath.

We drove twenty minutes until the streetlights tapered off, and the streets around us held a muted glow. We entered a road that weaved upward toward a restaurant that was nestled into the mountain. I found myself pressed up against the window, trying to get a good look around as George searched for a parking place.

"So Abby, has Eli brought you here yet?" George asked as we got out.

I shook my head and mumbled, "No."

"The view is spectacular," he said.

When we walked inside, George grabbed my mom's hand and pulled her forward. They sat on the floor and disappeared. I closed the distance to the spot they had sat down at and found a slide that plummeted into the dining room. My mom and George were at the base, laughing. My mom glanced up at me, smiling. Her face was flushed. It was the happiest I had seen her in months.

"Come on, Abby," she shouted up to me.

I contemplated using the stairs to my right. I hated that someone I didn't know might see me act silly. I hesitated a moment longer, looking around to see if anyone was watching. Feeling satisfied that nobody had their eyes on me, I sat down, crossing my legs to be ladylike, and pushed off. I coasted down fast, faster than I had expected, and slipped off the edge, landing on my butt with my skirt lifted in the air. I clutched my skirt, shoving it back down. My cheeks flushed, and my eyes darted around the room as I scrambled to my feet.

"You all right?" Mom asked through her laughter.

I nodded. This was already shaping up to be a mess. I had just flashed the whole restaurant, my mom, and her boyfriend. *How embarrassing.*

"Right this way," a hostess said. She seemed to appear out of thin air.

We followed her through the maze of tables.

"Graceful landing," a boy said as I walked by. He appeared to be my age and was dining with his parents.

I glared at him and resisted the urge to punch him in the face.

The hostess seated us at a table, handed us our menus, and disappeared. I held the menu in my hand, hiding my face from the rest of the dining room, willing my blush to dissipate. *No one else saw you fall. No one else saw you fall.*

When the waitress ventured back to our table, we ordered and handed her the menus before she left us alone again.

"So Abby, what do you think?" George asked.

I looked at him, perplexed, "Of?"

He chuckled. "The restaurant."

I looked around.

"Oh, it's nice."

"We've come here a few times. The view outside is something you have to see. I know you'll love it," Mom said.

She looked over at George. A moment passed. I fiddled with my hands in my lap and avoided looking at them.

"So, we wanted to have dinner with you tonight because . . ." Mom hesitated, looking unsure. Her eyes shifted from me to George as if she was asking him for help.

"What your mom is trying to say is that we have decided to become exclusive," George said.

"Okay . . ."

Why was this so important for me to know?

"We wanted you to be the first to know." Mom smiled.

I furrowed my brow. To me, they had been exclusive for weeks now. Why else would he have spent so much time at my house?

"I sort of thought you already were exclusive," I said.

"Well, technically we were, I suppose," Mom said, looking at George. "But the thing is . . . we feel like things have moved quickly for us. It wasn't anything either of us expected."

"Abby," George said, pulling my attention back. "We're planning on moving in together."

My eyes went wide. "What?"

"We haven't made any decisions about when," Mom added.

Like that makes it better. "Move in together?" I whispered. My heart thumped in my chest, drowning out all the commotion around us. The waitress moved in front of me, placing three plates on the table and stopping to look at me. After a few seconds, my mom tapped my shoulder. I blinked a few times as I came back to reality.

"What?" I asked the waitress.

"Do you need anything else?" I could tell she was frustrated with me.

"No. I'm fine, thanks."

She moved away from our table, leaving me with my mom and now soon-to-be housemate.

I stared at my food, hoping to escape the stares from both George and my mom.

"Abby?" Mom asked.

"What?" I glared at her, challenging her to push me. I didn't care how I sounded. What I cared about was having to give up part of my house to this man I hardly knew. It hadn't even been a year since we had moved out here. Her divorce was still fresh!

My mom's eyes fell to her plate as she pushed the food around without taking a bite.

"Abby, we brought you to dinner so that you and I could get to know each other better."

"What if I don't want to get to know you?" I spat.

"Abby!"

I glared at my mom. George wrapped his arm around her and mouthed, "It's fine." I rolled my eyes and looked down at my food. I was done with this night. My phone buzzed, but I ignored it. I wolfed down the majority of my food, letting the silence stretch on.

"May I be excused?" I asked out of habit when I finished.

My mom nodded without looking up from her plate. I threw my napkin on the table and stormed out of the dining room, marching straight to the overlook outside. I was fuming. I sat on the knee-high wall barrier and pulled my knees to my chest.

How could she do this? Didn't she know this was too soon? How could she be ready?

I wanted to scream until I caught sight of the lights of the city below. Even in my rage, I had to admit the view was spectacular. I wished I could enjoy it to its full extent. I couldn't see the moon, but I knew it was rising, the brightness on the horizon tinted the sky. Yet it didn't take away from the luminosity of the stars. Up on the mountain, they looked like little night lights glistening by the millions. The sky seemed to stretch on forever.

A breeze swept through my hair, blowing it into my face. I exhaled slowly, trying to get out the pent-up frustration. Closing my eyes, I sucked in another deep breath.

My phone buzzed again. I grabbed it, checking to see who was texting me, though deep down I already knew it was Eli.

I hope everything is going okay. Let me know if you need me.

Knowing he was there for me calmed me a little.

I shoved my phone back in my pocket. I wasn't feeling so angry anymore. Just exhausted and tired of fighting everything.

CHAPTER TWO

I hadn't heard from Casey in weeks. His silence worried me. After his accusations about Eli, I wasn't sure where our friendship stood.

I held my phone, staring at the buttons. Casey hadn't been off my mind for weeks, yet I had avoided calling him, and he seemed to be avoiding me, too. I hadn't figured out what to say to him, so I sat on my bed, trying to figure it out.

Finally, I decided the magic words weren't ever going to come to me. I pressed his picture and held my breath as the phone rang. When the third ring sounded in my ear, I wondered if he would even answer. It hadn't occurred to me that he might not be ready to talk. After all, I had gotten mad at him and told him to leave that day in California. My stomach filled with nervous flutters as I waited for the final ring.

I jumped when Casey's masculine voice filled my ear. "Hello?"

"H-hi," I stammered.

The phone had rung so many times that I was flustered and unsure what to say. He remained silent for a few moments. I shifted.

"Can we talk?" I asked when I couldn't waste any more time.

He hesitated. This time, I could hear him shuffling around. "I don't know . . . "

"Casey, we need to talk." I hated that my voice sounded like I was pleading with him.

He let out a breath. "Okay. I'll text you when I have time. I'm on assignment right now."

My team was working without me? I knew I had volunteered to help find Elizabeth's killer, and that was done, but I had never thought my time with them was over. I wanted to be on assignment too. I missed all of them—Luke, Brad, Ferdinand, and Casey.

"Abby? You there?"

"Uh, yeah. All right. I'll talk to you then," I said, recovering.

"Bye," he said, and then he was gone.

How could one strange encounter on the beach have strained such a great friendship? Was it fixable? The idea saddened me. The thought of Casey not being my friend hurt. But what he had said hurt too, and I wouldn't forget that.

Casey had come into my life when Eli and I were on the outs, but it was no secret that I had been Eli's girl. No one had prepared me to be thrown into the Protectors' world, where everyone knew me because of Eli. Eli had never mentioned that he was something of a celebrity.

At first, Casey had been interested in all things Eli, asking me questions about him. He almost seemed to look up to him. But his complete flip had me befuddled. *What happened?*

I had to get my mind off it for now, or it would consume me. I lifted my laptop screen to look through the car ads. In an hour's time, there were a hundred new listings. At this rate, I could be at it all day. Unfortunately, little stood out.

A grin broke out across my face. My dad would fly in the next day. It was time to pick my favorites and shop. Over the last year, I had saved up $3,000 on my own, which meant my parents would contribute $3,000 to my car fund. It was more than I could have ever dreamed I would have. It made me hopeful I would end up with a good car. I printed several ads for cars in my price range and hoped that I would love at least one of them.

The next morning, Eli picked me up early to head to the airport to pick up my dad. I had taken the whole weekend off so our time together would be uninterrupted.

We picked my dad up at the arrivals curb and set off again after exchanging quick hugs.

"Well, where to first?" Dad asked once we were rolling down the freeway.

I was getting ready to speak when Eli cut me off. "We're going to find an empty parking lot to make sure Abby can pass her driving test."

My mouth dropped open. "Wait, what?"

"Well, we can't buy you a car if you don't have a license, now can we?" Dad teased. "I know your mom helped you get your permit months ago, and you've driven here and there, but I need to make sure you know what you need to in order to pass the driving test."

I thought back to the few times my mom had taken me driving. She had been a nervous wreck the entire time, gripping her seat belt at her neck at each stop and turn as if she expected it to suddenly clamp down on her. I didn't ask to drive anymore so I didn't have to put her through it. I think seeing her so scared stressed me out more than actually driving. I felt like I had driving down perfectly anyway, but the thought of driving Eli's beautiful, flawless car terrified me. What if I scratched it? Or worse?

My nerves were still rattled as we pulled into a parking lot, which thankfully didn't have a single obstacle, not even those pesky curbs that separate parking places. I had bumped one of those once, and my mom had just about had a panic attack.

Eli came to a stop at the far end of the lot. He stepped out and went straight to the trunk, pulling out numerous orange cones. My dad never even flinched. *The little sneaks. They had planned this.* When had my dad and Eli exchanged numbers?

They arranged the cones around the parking lot. I stood back, watching them work, wondering just what kind of course they were making for me. A few times they stopped to talk for a second, hands pointing, then they would change the cone placement and move on. When they finished, they came back to stand in front of me. Eli held the keys up in front of my face. I hesitated.

"Go on," he said.

"What if I scratch it or something?" I asked. I bit my lip.

Eli turned to his left, then to his right, as if checking out our barren surroundings for the first time. I followed his gaze, and he smiled at me. "I think we're good."

I grinned. "You guys are the best." I took a deep breath to build up my courage. "Okay! Let's do this."

It felt strange to be in the driver's seat of Eli's car, let alone with my dad in the passenger seat.

"Put the top down," Eli called from outside the car.

I pushed the button, and the roof slid out of view, letting in the hot sun but improving my line of sight.

I started the car and put it in gear, and then I looked at my dad. "What do you want me to do?"

"First of all, drive around the parking lot a couple of times to get a feel for how the car handles."

I slowly lifted my foot off the brake. The car began to creep along. My arms trembled as I gripped the steering wheel. I eased my foot onto the gas pedal. The car jolted forward at first, but as I got the feel for the pedal, I went at the right pace. We coasted through the parking lot. My dad only corrected my control twice.

"I've got to say, I'm a little jealous that you get to drive this car," he said.

I giggled to myself. My nerves were beginning to settle as I became more comfortable and confident behind the wheel.

"I think you've got it. Pull in there," he said, gesturing toward the two sets of cones lined up.

I did as he told me and pulled up alongside Eli.

"Looking good," he said, leaning on the door.

I smiled. "Thanks, but you must be talking about the car," I teased.

"It doesn't hurt." He grinned, leaning down to kiss my cheek. "Now, park."

He stepped away and pointed at a section of cones that were set up as a parallel parking spot. I looked at my dad. He smiled and pointed at the same place Eli had.

I groaned. Never once had I tried to parallel park. I had watched my dad do it countless times growing up. He made it look easy most of the time. Once when I was little, my mom took me shopping, and the only parking spaces open were parallel spots. She struggled with it, backing in and out, and she ended up bumping into the car in front of us. She was so embarrassed that she jotted down a quick note and left, abandoning all our plans for the day. I never heard what became of it. My mom never spoke of it again, though I knew she tried to avoid parallel parking as much as possible after that.

When my mom mentioned that I would need to learn how to parallel park, I wasn't surprised she didn't offer to teach me. I had an inkling she wasn't sure how to teach me. Or maybe she was just afraid I would hit something.

I hesitated, feeling unsure. My dad nodded for me to proceed. I lifted my foot off the brake and approached the cones before putting the car into reverse. As I coasted backward, I held my breath. Staring in the rearview, I realized quickly that the angle was all wrong, and there was no way this attempt would work. I stopped, straightened out, and began again. This time, I improved the angle, but when I pulled forward, I felt two loud thumps. Eli erupted in laughter. My face warmed. I had failed again. Over and over, I tried and failed, each time trying to incorporate the tips my dad and Eli were giving me.

Just when I was about to give up, thinking I would never get it, I nailed it. A grin lit up my face. After that, it was like something clicked, and I could do it with ease the first time, every time.

Next, they had me try a three-point turn, and I knew this would be super easy. I stuck it on the first try and grinned at Eli. He ran over to high-five me.

"Great job, Abbs," Dad said. "I think you're ready."

"Are you sure?" I asked.

"I wouldn't say it if it wasn't true." He put his arm around my shoulders and kissed my forehead. "You sure have grown up since you moved out here. I'm so proud of you."

I smiled up at him, grateful for his support.

Eli ran around the parking lot, gathering up all the cones—including the blackened ones I had run over. I climbed into the back seat, being extra careful to make sure I didn't put my shoes on the seats.

An hour later, I sat in the driver's seat of Eli's car for the second time that day. I gripped and ungripped the steering wheel, readjusting the position of my hands at ten and two. *Where was ten and two again?* I shifted the tilt of the mirrors for the third time. This time, there would be unforgiving obstacles—cars and trucks—and an unfamiliar face watching my every move. I took a deep breath just as the driving test administrator sank into the passenger seat next to me. She was still admiring the incredible car.

"I have to say, this is one of the prettiest cars I've ever tested anyone in."

I chuckled. "My boyfriend is a bit trusting to let me use it for my test."

She laughed with me. "I'm sure you'll do fine."

My heart revved to life, pounding against my ribs. I pulled out of the parking lot onto a back street as she directed me. She sat back, watching every move I made, and I felt like a jumbled mess on the inside. On the outside, I hoped it wasn't visible.

"Turn right onto the main road," she said. Her voice, although soothing and quiet, did nothing to calm me.

I hit the turn signal and waited for traffic to clear. My stomach flopped for the third time since the wheels started rolling.

Once I turned out onto the road, the rest of the test went by in a blur, parallel parking and all. When it was over, I stood next to the car, waiting while she wrote on the paper. Minutes ticked by. I shifted on my feet, eagerly waiting for her to tell me if I had passed or failed. She glanced at me over the clipboard. I lifted my eyes to meet hers, but she looked back at the paper and wrote one more thing.

"You need to be more confident in your own ability," she said. The comment caught me off guard. I tilted my head. "Because you passed."

"I did?"

She nodded. "Don't be so surprised." She handed me the form and pointed toward the building. "Go in there to get your picture taken. Congratulations."

I jumped in the air. "Thank you!" Just before I bolted toward the building where my dad and Eli were waiting, she called me back.

"Abby, I almost forgot!" She reached into her pocket and pulled out a folded piece of paper. "A friend of yours approached me when I headed out to start your test and asked me to give this to you. He said he wanted to wish you luck. I didn't want to give it to you before the test so you wouldn't have any distractions." She handed me the paper, and for a second, I couldn't breathe. I held it between my fingers. It was still warm from being in her pocket. When I looked back up to thank her, she had already walked away. I knew this note could only bring bad news.

I unfolded it as if it might bite me. The paper seemed different than I had expected. It was off-white and elegant, with deckled edges I would guess you would find on very old paper. Inside, I found the neatest handwriting I think I had ever seen.

Tell Eli to watch his step. We're watching. Always watching.

I surveyed my surroundings, detecting nothing out of place. Taking a deep breath, I tried to pull myself together. It astonished me how a little piece of paper could turn things around so fast. I couldn't let my dad see me like this. I folded the paper back up, hiding it in my hand, and shook my arms at my sides to calm my jitters. Then with a deep breath, I jogged back to the building and pushed my way through the doors.

I launched myself into Eli's arms the moment I saw him. "I passed," I squealed. Without thinking, I shoved the note into his palm. He closed his hand around it. Confusion only registered on his face for a moment, and then it was gone again. He slid the paper into his pocket, and his eyes searched the room. My dad was never the wiser. Eli set me down, and I threw my arms around my dad's neck next. He gave me a tight squeeze.

"Congrats!" they said in unison.

When we sat down to wait for my license, my dad stepped outside to make a phone call. Eli took the opportunity to pull the paper from his pocket. His eyes moved across it in one swoop. His jaw tightened, and his lips formed a tight line as he crumbled the note, stomped to the trash, and threw it away.

"Where did you get that?" he hissed.

"The test administrator. She said a friend of mine handed it to her just before the test. She didn't give it to me until after."

He slammed himself back into his chair and crossed his arms.

"Who is it from?" I asked.

"Don't worry about it. I'll handle it."

His answer told me he knew exactly whom it was from. This was new. But I knew just by looking at him that I wouldn't be able to push him to tell me. His posture alone told me he had shut down. My dad strolled in seconds later. I plastered a smile on my face.

"Everything okay at the store?" I asked.

"Yeah, everything's fine. Just an inventory question. How many numbers before us?"

"Two more," I said, holding up my ticket.

Eli was silently brooding the rest of the time we sat there. An hour later, we walked out with my license in hand.

"I'm hungry," I confessed.

"Me too!" Dad said.

Eli nodded. "Lunch it is."

When we got in the car, I couldn't wait to tell my mom and Bailey that I had passed the test. I pulled out my phone, snapped a picture of my shiny new license, and sent it to each of them. I smiled to myself looking at it nestled in my hand. *Freedom.*

At lunch, I pulled out the ads I had printed to show to my dad and Eli. In truth, I knew nothing about cars, so I relied on them to get me what I needed. The last thing I needed was a car that would be nothing but problems.

They looked over each ad, nixing a few by saying they cost too much to repair or would have a lot of problems. By the time they had sorted through my list, only two options remained. I felt discouraged. Maybe car shopping wasn't going to be so much fun.

Sensing my disappointment, Eli reached across the table and rested his hand on mine. "Hey, don't worry. We'll find the perfect car for you." He rubbed the back of my hand to reassure me.

He pulled a stack of folded papers out of his back pocket. When he unfolded them, I saw he had been car shopping too. He never ceased to amaze me, always thinking of everything. As I looked over each car, one ad caught my eye. I looked it over, feeling the overwhelming desire to look at this and only this car.

"A convertible," I said under my breath.

"You didn't think I'd forget, did you?" Eli whispered back. It sounded like a question, but I knew it wasn't.

"A convertible? Is that what you want?" Dad asked.

I nodded, smiling.

He chuckled. "I should have known."

We shopped for the next day and a half at private sellers and dealerships, making sure I got the best car we could find. In the end, I drove away with the very convertible Eli had found for me. The 2005 Mitsubishi Spyder Eclipse was more than I could have ever dreamed my first car would be. Its charcoal gray color sparkled in the sun as if I had just driven it off the lot new. And the best part? I had money left over after it was paid for. Dad said that was a good thing since I would still need to register and insure it, expenses I hadn't considered.

* * * *

The feeling of freedom was exhilarating as I drove myself to work for the first time Monday afternoon. No more waiting for rides. No more relying on others. I had my car and my license. No one could ruin my mood. I drove with the top down just because I could, despite the sweltering heat.

Eli wasn't working, but I didn't mind. I was too excited to be on my own for once. I walked in with an extra spring in my step. A four-hour shift would go by fast when I was in this good of a mood and now that every penny I made didn't go to saving for my car, tips seemed that much sweeter.

I breezed around the restaurant, serving tables and making conversation. Either everyone was as happy as me, or I had never noticed how talkative my customers were.

Instead of leaving like normal when my shift ended, I hung out with everyone, eating pizza and chatting until well after nine p.m. Most of the staff lounged around the dining room with me since our last customer left just before I got off.

I loved choosing what I did and when I did it. This was just the beginning of the freedom I had so desperately craved.

My phone buzzed in my pocket. I slipped it out to see who it was. Eli.

Did you get home okay?

It hadn't occurred to me to let anyone know I was staying late at work. I typed a message back.

Hanging out still. I'll be leaving soon.

Before I could even put the phone down, another message popped up.

Why?

He was prying more than usual.

Just talking and eating. I'll text you when I get home.

I didn't know why, but it annoyed me that he was so inquisitive, making me feel like I shouldn't still be there. I shoved my phone back in my pocket, ignoring it when it vibrated again.

Something outside the window caught my eye. I turned to give it my full attention, and my jaw clenched when I saw a man in a ski mask driving a black SUV. He waved at me. A chill ran down my spine. I closed my eyes and shook my head. I had to be seeing things. People did some strange things, but that couldn't have just happened. When I opened my eyes again, there was no sign of the SUV. I must have been more tired than I thought. My eyes must be playing tricks on me.

A few minutes later, the conversation slowed, and I decided to go home. I finished the last of my pizza and said my goodbyes before heading to my car. My car. I loved the sound of that.

I pushed the unlock button, and the flashing headlights captivated me. They looked almost like they were saying hello. I reached for the door handle, but just before I grabbed it, a man's voice startled me.

"Abby?"

I dropped my keys as my hand went to my chest. My heart slammed so hard it was almost painful. I whirled around and jumped back at the same time.

When my eyes met Casey's, I let out a relieved breath.

"Oh my gosh, Casey! Don't do that to me."

A wave of the shakes seized my body as I glanced around to find my lost keys. I hated the way adrenaline affected me. I felt like a blubbering girl.

"Sorry. You got a car?" he asked.

I turned back toward my new obsession and nodded, a smile overcoming my nerves. "Want to go for a spin?"

"Will I survive?" he teased.

My mouth dropped open. "Of course! I'm a great driver!"

I crouched down to the ground to find my keys, but it was hard to see anything in the dark. I fumbled in my purse for my phone, but Casey motioned for me to move out of the way.

"Let me."

He bent down, coming up seconds later with my keys in his hand.

"Thanks," I said.

Sometimes I wished I shared the Protectors' uncanny ability to see in the dark.

He walked to the other side of the car and climbed in. I put the top down, letting the beautiful sky above mesmerize me. Then I pulled out my phone to send a quick message to my mom, letting her know I wasn't coming straight home. My curfew wasn't until eleven, but I figured I should let her know what was up since Eli had been worried about my whereabouts.

"Where to?" I asked, turning to Casey.

"Take me somewhere you want to go," he said. "This car is really something. Congrats!"

"Thanks."

I don't know why, but it meant a lot that he liked it.

I thought for a moment. *Where could we go?* Then an idea hit me. A smirk spread across my face, and I backed out of my parking spot.

"I'm glad you came by," I said.

"Are you?" he asked. "I wasn't so sure you'd want to see me."

"Of course I do!"

I wanted to see his face, but I didn't dare look away from the road. He fell silent, and I could sense the rift between us widening again. I bit my lip, hoping we could move past this.

As I drove, I focused on the road and the time seemed to slip away. Soon, I pulled into a parking spot next to a large castle. I put the car in park and glanced at Casey.

"Mini golf," he said, grinning.

"That was a fun night," I said.

"It was."

I took off my seat belt and turned toward him.

"What's going on?" I asked.

"What do you mean?"

I took a deep breath, mustering all my courage.

"You showed up in California, out of the blue telling me my boyfriend is dangerous. And I haven't heard from you since. What's going on?"

He turned his attention to the window.

"Casey?"

"I didn't think you wanted to talk to me."

"Why?"

"You told me to leave, and you were so mad. I crossed a line."

"That doesn't mean our friendship is over."

He fell silent.

"I need to know what's going on, though."

"I can't tell you," he said without looking at me.

"Why?"

"I just can't."

"Well, then what am I supposed to do?" I asked.

"Trust me," he whispered.

This wasn't the first time a Protector had told me to "trust them." Eli had once been that Protector. Back when I had no clue what a Protector was, he warned me to stay away from Pete. He had been right all along, but I hadn't listened to him, and that had blown up in my face. Now here I sat, torn between two people I trusted with my life, and yet I was being asked to choose. *How could I?* Eli was my boyfriend. He knew me better than I knew myself sometimes. On the other hand, Casey was my best friend and had been there for me when Eli hadn't.

Casey grabbed my hand, pulling me from my thoughts, his fingers traced over the back.

"Abby, there's something going on. I don't even know all of it, but you can't trust him. He's changed, and he's up to something."

"Nothing has changed. He's the same as he's always been."

"It's an act. It is. You have to believe me," he pleaded.

Frustration filled me. My hands flew to my face as I tried to rub the tension out of my temples.

"What is with you Protectors? Why do you always expect me to just trust whatever you tell me?" I fumed.

"What?" he asked, his voice filled with confusion.

"Nothing," I huffed.

"No. What?"

I hesitated, stewing in my irritation. Then I recounted how I had met Eli and his warning that Pete was bad news. That he had expected me to trust him at first, but when he realized I wouldn't, he made up a story. He had thought it would spook me away from Pete, but instead, it drew me in like a moth to a flame. Ultimately, it ended in disaster. I realized how bad the story made me look and that it wasn't in my best interest not to trust Casey.

"I see," he said when I finished.

"You see? That's it?"

"What do you want from me? I won't make up some lie to make you stay away from Eli. Don't you see how wrong that is? How could you trust someone who lies to you?"

"He was trying to protect me, as he was assigned to do. And I never asked you to lie. I want the truth."

"I can't give you that."

"Then I guess talking is pointless."

I turned the key, and the engine roared to life. Without waiting, I shifted into gear and headed back. I sped out of the parking lot squealing the tires. We remained silent for most of the fifteen minutes it took to get back to work. When I turned into the parking lot and spotted his car, I pulled up next to it.

"Abby, you know I'd tell you if I could. You have no idea how hard this is for me."

"Actually, I don't know that," I spat. "So much for being a team."

"We are a team."

I glared at him. "Teams don't have secrets." I turned back to the road in front of me, ready to leave. "Bye."

He hesitated as he opened his door and climbed out. "Please don't shut me out." He closed the door but held his ground as he stared at me.

"You've already shut me out. This is your doing." And with that, I sped away without a second glance.

I pulled into my driveway, still frustrated. When I flipped down the visor to inspect myself in the mirror, something fell into my lap. I switched on the dome light and grabbed it. My hand shook. It was a postcard from Papago Park. I took a deep breath and flipped it over.

FOR ME TO GET TO YOU.

I dropped the note on the seat next to me, grabbed my things, and rushed inside. I hated this. The unexpected reminders that this wasn't over cropped up whenever things seemed to be going well. Whoever kept sending these notes wanted to torture me, and it was working . . . far too well.

In my room, I threw my things on the bed and grabbed my phone. I typed out a text and sent it to Eli.

I ignored the note. A lot of good it did!

Grabbing my pajamas, I headed for a nice soak in the tub. I had gone from carefree to irritated to surprised to terrified, and now I was just done. I didn't want to deal with anything, and for the next thirty minutes, I intended to relax. I switched my phone to silent and slid into the tub.

* * * *

"I can't believe you ignored my calls!" Eli's face might as well have been bright red.

"I told you. I turned my ringer off. I didn't expect you to show up."

I stood on the front step, shifting my weight from foot to foot in nothing but my bathrobe, which I had thrown on when my mom said Eli was at the door.

"Where's the note?"

I listlessly lifted my hand to point at my car.

"What does it even matter? Whoever it is has already made it clear they can get to me whenever they want."

Eli swung around and grabbed my hands.

"Do you think I can't protect you?" he asked.

"I didn't say that."

"Then what are you saying?"

"I'm just saying you didn't seem concerned about the first note, and now one's shown up in my *locked* car."

"I might have acted like it was nothing, but that's not how I felt. I've been looking into it the best I can. I just didn't want you to worry."

"Well, it didn't work," I said.

"Obviously. I'm sorry. Let me handle these, and try not to think about them, okay?"

I nodded.

"Now go back inside and relax."

He swatted my butt as I went inside. I turned to giggle at him, but he was already walking away.

CHAPTER THREE

It had been weeks since Bailey and I had hung out, so we planned a girls' day that weekend. We were far overdue. I missed her. Shopping was just what we needed to unwind and catch up. All the drama with Eli and Casey—I couldn't seem to escape it. But with Bailey, things were sure to be good.

I was leaving my house, fumbling for my keys, when I heard a sound behind me. I was just about to turn around when someone touched my shoulder. I jumped, spinning around with my fists clenched. *What was it about people sneaking up on me?* When my eyes focused, a familiar face stared back at me.

"Vince?" I clutched my chest to avoid hunching over as adrenaline coursed through my body. I hoped that one day I wouldn't respond in such an over-the-top way when I was startled. Or better yet, maybe people would stop sneaking up on me altogether. I never knew who it could be anymore, and I hadn't expected Vince.

"Hello Abby," he said.

I hadn't spoken to Vince since his wife, Eli's mother, was murdered. Even though there was an ancient feud between Vince and the killer, Vince still blamed me on some level. Yet, to the killers, I had just been a pawn in the revenge games they were playing.

"What are you doing here?"

He had given me the cold shoulder all this time, and it hurt. Before Elizabeth's death, I had come to think of Vince as a second father since my dad wasn't around. He had looked out for me and even saved my life once. But then he dropped me like a hot cake and hadn't looked back. Nothing could have prepared me for that betrayal.

"I felt like we needed to talk," he said.

"What is there to talk about?"

His eyes flickered, and he set his mouth in a grim line.

"I wanted to come tell you I don't harbor any ill feelings toward you," he said.

I crossed my arms and narrowed my eyes. "You have a funny way of showing it."

"I may have taken longer to realize it than my son did, but we're on the same page now. I'm sorry for letting my emotions decide otherwise."

His crystal blue eyes stared into mine, waiting for a response. I wanted to run away from those eyes. I didn't know what to say. Part of me wanted to accept his apology and go back to the relationship we had shared before Elizabeth's death. But part of me wanted to scream at him, stomp away, and leave him to feel a portion of what I had felt at his betrayal. Instead of doing anything, I froze. After the long, awkward silence dragged on, Vince spoke again.

"I understand if you need some time to think."

At that, he turned and walked away.

My mind raced. Had Eli known Vince was coming? He had never mentioned it. Maybe if there had been some notice, I would have had a response and wouldn't have just sat there with a dumb look on my face. Now that I wasn't on the spot, I wished I had told him how bad he had made me feel. I wished I had told him I didn't know if I could ever trust him again.

Within minutes, I pulled up to Bailey's house. Just as I climbed out of my car, she emerged from her front door.

"Hey Abby!" she squealed. "I'm so glad we're hanging out!"

"Me too. Feels like it's been forever!" I gestured toward my new car as if I were a model showing it off. "So . . . what do ya think?"

"Wow! It's really pretty," she said, grinning.

"Isn't it? I never thought I'd get anything so nice," I admitted.

"Can we put the top down?"

For the first time since buying my new car, I had left my house without even thinking about putting the top down. Vince had thrown me for a loop.

"Absolutely," I said, hoping my confusion didn't register on my face.

In the car, I had set a wrapped box on Bailey's seat. She almost sat on it.

"What's this?" she asked, holding it up.

"It's for you."

"For me? What is it?" She tore into the wrapping.

Inside lay the purple shell necklace I had bought for her in California.

"It's so pretty!"

"I saw it one day when Eli and I were shopping at the beach in California. It made me think of you."

"That's so sweet!"

I helped her put it on, and as it turned out, it matched her outfit.

"I love it," she said as she looked in the mirror.

When we got to the mall, I could still feel Vince's presence nagging at the back of my mind. I tried my best to ignore it as we walked, exchanging stories from the past few weeks. Every. Little. Detail.

As Bailey recounted how Ryan had made her mad the previous week for falling asleep and not calling her when they were supposed to go out, I couldn't make myself understand why it was such a big deal. Disappointing, yes, but to still be dwelling on it? It was then that I realized how our lives had diverged. My priorities were much different. It had been obvious that I was changing, yet I had chosen to ignore the signs. I felt disinterested in everything that seemed important to her. I tried to squash my boredom without success.

"Hello! Earth to Abby! Where are you today?" she asked, snapping me from my thoughts.

"I don't know. I guess I'm just out of it."

In truth, the realization that I didn't seem to fit in anymore disheartened me. Making friends had come so easily after I moved from California, but I never guessed it would slip through my fingers. Not that I was totally alone. I had Ren and Eli. They were my friends. And, of course, my team, though I hadn't spoken to any of them in weeks, and I no longer knew where I stood with them. That didn't help.

A couple hours later, I dropped Bailey off and put the convertible top up. I wasn't in the mood for my hair to blow in the wind. I wanted normal teenage girl problems like Bailey.

As I glanced in my rearview mirror, I spotted an all-black SUV trailing a little closer to my bumper than I would have liked. I was glad my turn was coming up so I could get away from the jerk, but when I turned into my neighborhood, the SUV followed. It struck me funny, but I continued on. The image of the man in the ski mask flashed in my mind. I felt on edge. I tried to rationalize it. *They could live anywhere in my neighborhood.* When they followed me onto my street, my pulse quickened. *Are they following me?* I turned into my driveway, cringing, hoping they would keep going. The SUV didn't even slow down as it sped past my house. I let out a deep breath and chastised myself for being so paranoid. The man in the ski mask was a figment of my overactive imagination. Nobody was following me. It was a silly thought. *Though given what I had been through the last few months, it wasn't that big of a stretch.*

Once I was inside, I called Eli.

"Hey. How was the mall?" he asked.

"It was okay." My voice remained unenthusiastic. I cut right to the chase. "Did you know your dad was coming to talk to me?"

"What?"

"Your dad. He stopped by to talk to me. Did you know he was coming?" I realized I sounded angry and accusing, but given the bond we shared—Eli could feel what I felt at any moment—it didn't matter what I sounded like. He knew better.

"No," he said. "I didn't know. What did he say?"

"Can you come over?" I asked. "We can talk about it."

He hesitated. I could hear him rustling around in the background and wondered what he was up to. "All right. I'll be there in a few."

The line went dead in my ear. I was excited to see him. I ran downstairs and pulled out a glass pan to whip us up some dessert as a surprise—a delicious Oreo cookie crust filled with vanilla cream pudding and topped with more Oreos. My mouth watered as I set it in the fridge.

My hands felt chilled, so I went out the front door and sat on the porch to wait for Eli. The warmth of the Arizona summer thawed my fingers. I pulled out my phone to play silly a game while I waited.

"That must be some game," Eli said.

I jumped. He was standing in front of me with his arms crossed like he had been there a while.

"Hey, how long have you been standing there?"

"Long enough," he said.

"I can't believe I didn't hear you."

"Not a good thing," he said, looking concerned.

"It's fine," I said, brushing it off. "I'm glad you're here."

I gave him a hug and let him in the house. We sat down together on the couch to talk.

"Let's hear it. What happened?" Eli asked.

He listened as I told him about the conversation with his dad, including that I had said nothing and Vince left without a response.

"So, what are you going to do?" he asked.

Eli's phone chimed, and he pulled it from his pocket. He fiddled with it.

"I don't know what I should do. After all, I forgave you, and you felt the same way. You were even mean. Vince just ignored me."

Was he texting?

I stared at him. He continued to play with his phone. "And you had an elephant standing on your foot."

"Uh-huh," he said.

"Eli, you aren't even listening to me."

"I am," he said, his gaze meeting my eyes.

"What did I just say?" I demanded.

"I'm sorry," he said. "Go on."

He set his phone beside him on the couch and folded his hands in his lap.

"What do you think I should do?" I asked.

He looked me straight in the eyes. "I think you should forgive him. If he apologized to you, he means it. He doesn't take that lightly."

I had a feeling he would tell me to forgive him. Why was it so hard to make amends with Vince, yet so easy with Eli? Eli had been harsher on me than Vince. He had said some hurtful things.

"Can you give me his phone number?" I grumbled.

"Let me give you a little advice. If you want to accept my dad's apology, don't do it over the phone."

"Why?"

"I'm surprised you haven't noticed that the Protectors are old-fashioned. We don't handle that sort of thing over the phone."

He was wrong. I had noticed they were old-fashioned. It was one of the things I loved about the Protectors I knew, the good ones anyway. I had even thought that about Pete before he went crazy on me. I just hadn't thought of the phone as a problem.

"Okay."

"You can go see him tomorrow. Tonight you're mine." He reached over and pulled me close. "But we do need to talk about your awareness of your surroundings."

"I know, I know. I'll be more careful. Promise."

I really didn't want to get into this. I wanted to just have time with Eli when we weren't talking about problems. Time we were just together.

I leaned into him, looking into his eyes, our lips only inches apart. I moved forward but stopped and pulled away ever so slightly, teasing him. Before I knew what was happening, Eli had pounced on me, pinning me to the couch. His lips covered mine greedily, but I matched his hunger as the kiss deepened. He pinned my arms to my sides as I tried to wrap them around his neck. A smile crept to my lips. Before long, I was giggling like a schoolgirl, breaking our kiss. Eli's eyes lifted to mine, confusion etched into the creases of his forehead.

"What's so funny?" he asked. I could see a hint of amusement on his face.

I giggled again. "I made you kiss me," I said in a sing-song voice.

A smirk tugged at the corners of his lips, but I could tell he was fighting it. His lips brushed my ear. "I'd gladly kiss you any day of the week," he whispered, sending shivers down one side of my body. Goosebumps rose to attention covering that half of my body. Desire filled me. I reached up, holding his face between my hands and staring into his eyes. I lifted my head to meet his and kissed him. My hands wandered down his strong shoulders, pulling him closer as I rested my head back on the couch. His muscles flexed with every movement. Warmth spread through my body. Eli's smokin' hot self was on top of me, of all people. *How did I get so lucky?* Eli eventually pulled away. When his eyes met mine again, he smiled from ear to ear.

"I think I like this game," he said.

"What?" I demanded.

"The tables reversed quickly, didn't they?" he teased.

Warmth spread across my face. He laid one finger on my forehead and slid it down my face. My eyes fluttered closed. Nose. Eyes. Cheeks. His finger traced my jawline just before sliding down my neck to my chest. I could feel him caress the bumps of my sternum. He stopped just above my cleavage. Right when I was getting nervous. He lifted his finger from my chest and kissed each of my closed eyes.

The front door opened and slammed shut.

"Abby, I'm home! I brought Chinese food." My mom's voice was getting louder with each word. "I hope you're . . ."

Eli jumped off me, throwing himself a foot away from me on the couch. I righted myself and was smoothing my shirt when she entered the room, the smell of the food following close behind her. My mouth watered.

" . . . hungry." Her eyes landed on Eli. "Ah, hi Eli. I didn't know you were here. Would you like to stay for dinner? There's plenty."

"I'd like that," Eli said.

He was so good at acting like nothing was amiss. I, on the other hand, felt frazzled. I was sure anyone could read what had happened on my face.

Eli winked at me when my mom headed to the dining room, and I had to stifle my laughter. We had almost been caught in a very compromising position. Surely Mom would not have approved. I stood and began to follow her, but Eli's arms shot around me, pulling me back into his chest. He released one hand and gathered my hair moving it to the side. His lips found the back of my neck first. I sucked in a breath. He trailed kisses all along my neck until my knees felt weak. If not for his arm holding me, I was sure I would have collapsed on the floor. Ever so softly he grazed his teeth across my tender skin sending a shiver cascading down my body. I trembled involuntarily only for a second, and then his mouth was gone. Swiftly he pulled away and smacked my butt, bringing me back to reality in a snap. The strength returned to my legs. I stood frozen in place. Eli walked around me, looking far too proud of himself.

"What's wrong? Aren't you coming?" He grinned.

Two could play at this game.

"Absolutely nothing," I smirked and brushed past him.

We ate dinner together, just the three of us. It was really nice to have the time to enjoy something as normal as this.

"Oh! Save room! I made dessert," I said in the middle of dinner.

"Oooh, what did you make?" Mom asked. Her eyes lit up like a kid on Christmas.

"The Oreo one," I grinned, knowing it was one of her favorites.

"Oh, Eli you are in for a treat. That's one of her best desserts."

Eli looked at me. "Can't wait." He licked his lips. Something about the way he was looking at me made my mouth go dry. His intense eyes stared into mine. The smallest grin played on one side of his mouth. My cheeks felt like they were on fire. I had to force my eyes to look away. He was playing dangerously.

After dessert, Eli and I went for a walk. He held my hand, but he wasn't fooling me. I knew he still had his game face on. I was determined to make the first move. As we rounded the corner, out of view of my house, I backed myself against a brick wall, pulling him along with me. He leaned into me, his head at my neck. I could feel him inhaling, breathing me in. I smiled to myself. I leaned in, kissed his neck, and ran my hands down from his shoulders. Goosebumps rose on his arms despite the heat around us. The connection between us was so strong I was beginning to feel weak in the knees again.

"What are you doing to me?" he asked.

That snapped me out of my blissful trap. I had him wrapped around my finger. I smirked, looped my fingers around his and started walking again like nothing had happened. He shook his head, rubbing his forehead.

"You are far too good at this!" he bellowed.

He lunged from behind me and tickled my sides until I dropped to the ground. He knelt over me, tickling me more.

Then he stopped. "Give up?" he asked.

"Never!"

His tickle attack resumed.

"Okay! Okay!"

"Okay what?" he asked, leaning his ear toward me.

"I give!"

"No more games?" he asked.

"Not today."

He eyed me as if he was trying to decide if he could believe me.

"All right," he said.

He grabbed my hand and leaned back on his heels, pulling us both up off the ground. He took my hand again, and off we went.

When we got back to my house, Eli went home. I headed to the living room where my mom had put on a movie. Hanging out with her was exactly what I needed, even if I was still upset she planned to move her boyfriend in with us after dating him for only a few months. Soon I would have to share her.

"Eli went home already?" she asked.

"Yeah."

"Good," she said. "Now we can spend some time together."

She reached over and rested her hand on top of my arm.

We enjoyed a quiet evening without interruption. Even my mom seemed more at ease when we headed up to bed later that night.

The next morning, my phone rang while I was cleaning my room. The caller ID said, *Unavailable.* I had a suspicion who it might be. My heart beat faster with anticipation, wondering what he wanted.

"Hello?"

"Hello, Abby," Edward's rich voice purred.

"Hi," I said.

"I was calling to let you know that I've called a meeting with the team. Does four o'clock work for you?" he asked.

"I have to work at five."

"That's fine. We will meet at the coffeehouse like before. It shouldn't take long."

"All right."

"Great. I look forward to seeing you."

I put my phone down and contemplated what the meeting might be about. My mind churned.

Later that afternoon, I spotted Edward as I stepped through the doors of the coffeehouse. He sat at the center table with three members of my team, Brad, Luke, and Ferdinand. I felt nervous meeting with them. Casey was absent, and I wondered where he was. *Did Edward know that Casey and I had a falling out? Would he be upset with us?*

"Abby, I'm so glad you could join us today," Edward said. A round of nods followed from the rest of my team. Casey stepped through the door moments after I did. I was relieved to see him, but clearly he was not happy to see me. He sank into one of the two available seats and folded his arms across his chest. He never even made eye contact with me. I had never seen such attitude from him. He had always been so mellow. This new side of him confused me. *Was it because of me? Or because of this meeting?* I couldn't help but feel like it was me.

I turned my attention back to Edward and sat down, wiping my sweaty palms on my black work pants. I hoped nobody noticed.

"So?" I said, waiting for Edward to get started.

"You may all be wondering why I've asked you to come, but I kept it quiet because I'm not sure two individuals in particular would have come otherwise."

I groaned inwardly. This was about Casey and me. What else could it be about? There weren't any other problems within this group. I stared at my hands, feeling like everyone was staring at me.

"It has been brought to my attention that there were hurt feelings over being excluded from the team assignments."

Oh god. My face flushed. I looked at Edward. Then I looked at Casey, who was staring out the window. I could tell he didn't want to be here.

I *had* been feeling left out, but Casey had been the only one I had let that slip to. *Why would he tell Edward?* Anger filled me. I felt betrayed that he ratted me out. I never even meant to tell him. It had just come out because I was upset.

"You are all part of this team," Edward continued. "There is no reason why anyone should feel left out." He turned to me. "Currently, the guys are working on an assignment that you cannot be a part of, *but* that does not give them the right to ignore you." He looked at each of them.

I groaned. "It's fine," I said, interrupting him. "I'm fine."

Edward leaned back in his chair and crossed his arms. I wondered if I had made him mad. He was a hard man to read.

After a few moments of awkward silence, he spoke. "All right." He looked around our circle. "Any other matters that need attention?"

We shook our heads in unison. Edward made eye contact with each of us before he spoke again.

"I would like to speak with Casey before he leaves, but the rest of you are free to go." He turned his attention to me, singling me out once again. "Thank you for coming, Abby. It was so good to see you again. Remember, if you have any problems or questions, anything at all, you let me know, okay?"

I knew for certain my face was bright red. I could feel the heat of the blood rushing to my face. I nodded and escaped out the door. I was more than relieved to be out of that meeting. That conversation had been stifling. I hoped none of them were mad at me because it seemed I had just gotten them in trouble.

Luke, Ferdinand, and Brad were right behind me. I took a deep breath and turned to face them once we were a short distance from the door. They all had grins on their faces. I was more confused than ever.

"Aww! You missed us!" Luke said.

"You know you could have just called," Brad teased.

Ferdinand said nothing but swooped me up in a bear hug.

"I thought you guys were going to be mad at me," I said. "Edward seemed angry."

"Nah, he's a teddy bear." Ferdinand smiled.

"I'm so glad, and yes, I've missed you guys." I stuck my tongue out at Luke.

"Better watch who you stick that out at," Luke said. "I might just have to grab it."

"I dare you to try!"

"So, do you want to go do something?" Ferdinand asked.

"I have to work," I said.

"Bummer."

"Yeah . . ."

I was so relieved that they weren't mad at me. I hoped this meant I would get to see them more. Now if I could just get a few minutes with Casey, things might start to look up. I watched and waited while the guys chatted. I didn't want to miss him, and I had my doubts he would seek me out.

Casey

I despised being kept behind like being punished in high school detention. Edward was furious with me. His temper had been flaring since California. *Did he really think I needed him on my case?* I was hard enough on myself.

"When I said to keep close to her, I didn't mean to make her mad a second time and then distance yourself," Edward growled.

"I have *not* distanced myself! She just thinks I have."

"Watch her. Protect her. You know as well as I do that she is in danger, and if you don't do your job, we all know what could happen. Get back in her good graces, *ASAP*."

I longed to be close to her again, but I would fix things my way, on my terms. Not like this. Not because Edward made me. Edward's fascination with Abby bothered me, and my suspicion wasn't driven by irrational jealousy. There was something off about the way he focused on her. I hated it. He was so invested in this gift of hers. I couldn't fathom why, and he wasn't talking.

"Fine!" I stormed out. I couldn't bear his scowl for another moment.

The guys stood around Abby. I caught her eye and hesitated. Looking into her curious face, my nerves set in, and I bolted. I ignored the hurt expression on her face. Now was not the time. I jumped in my car and sped away.

CHAPTER FOUR

After a fitful night of sleep, worrying about Casey, I shot straight out
of bed. I brushed the sweat from my face and threw off the blankets that
felt as if they confined me. My heart beat against my chest. The glinting of
the railroad tracks haunted my thoughts, even after I woke. I hated waking
up that way. I closed my eyes and tried to calm myself, breathing deeply.
When I opened my eyes again, I felt better. I got out of bed on shaky legs
and opened the blinds. For a long time, I stared out the window at nothing.
I hated my nightmares. They made me feel so alone. No one else
understood how much they took away from me, how much they frightened
me. How much time I spent dwelling on them. Let alone the sleepless
nights I spent worrying.

I wondered if any of the Protectors felt this way about their gifts. I
couldn't imagine Eli disliking his ability. He could bring someone to their
knees in pain with just his thoughts. It came in really handy when someone
wouldn't take a hint. If I had to be gifted, why couldn't I have had
something cool like that? Then I wouldn't have to worry so much. I didn't
feel like precognitive dreams would ever be useful.

I bent down and picked up my discarded clothes from the night
before. I went through my pockets and pulled out the tips I had earned
during my shift. *My smallest haul yet.* My heart just hadn't been in it. After
Casey had bolted from the meeting, I had gone to work wondering why.
Why didn't he come talk to me?

These Protectors kept me on my toes. From Eli's emotional spiral
after losing his mom and his strange absentee behavior to Casey's weird
accusations and sudden distance. My head spun.

I had been disappointed with Eli. Once we got back from California, I had been so excited to go on dates and explore new places with him. Not that it hadn't happened at all. In fact, when he was present, he was amazing—better than ever. But we had seen each other less often than I had envisioned, and often he seemed distant, like his mind was drifting elsewhere. Not to mention the strange texts and phone calls. Was Casey right? After his warning, I wondered if I might be paranoid. Maybe even looking for things to nitpick. Eli wasn't dangerous, of course, but I had to know what was going on. That night, I decided, it was time to find out.

Later, Eli took me out to dinner. Once we ordered our food, he seemed to drift away from me again. I stared at him, watching his eyes flicker here and there, looking everywhere but at me. I tried to keep my frustration at bay.

"So," I said. He shifted to look at me. "Is there something on your mind?"

"What? No. Why?" He seemed defensive and taken aback by my question.

"You seem distracted," I said.

He shrugged.

"In fact, you've seemed distracted quite a few times since we've been back," I added. My hands began to sweat under the table as I anticipated his delayed response.

"What are you talking about?" A frown appeared on his face.

"You just seem like you're . . . somewhere else half the time. I just thought you might want to talk about it," I said.

"I have no idea what you're talking about."

"Okay," I said. I glanced at the table, unable to make myself look him in the eye. I hadn't expected him to get so offended by my question.

The tension at our table was intense. When the waitress delivered our food, she talked animatedly to us, and I tried to hide my unease. Finally, she left, and I let out the breath I had been holding.

We remained silent as we dug into the scrumptious chicken parmesan. Just when I thought neither of us would speak the rest of the meal, Eli broke his silence.

"I'm having trouble coping." His voice was so muted that I almost didn't hear him.

I reached across the table and put my hand over his, letting him know I was there for him.

"It's been a lot harder losing my mom than I ever imagined," he said.

"I'm sorry. Is there anything I can do?"

He shook his head. The sadness in his eyes pulled at my heart. I had known there was a valid explanation, but now I wished I hadn't brought it up. Our night wouldn't have had to turn south.

"Forget it."

He lifted his eyes again, and the sadness disappeared, leaving nothing behind to suggest anything was amiss. It puzzled me that one minute he looked so forlorn, and moments later he seemed fine. Why couldn't I be so shielded? Instead, I felt like my emotions were on display for everyone to see.

*   *   *   *

I had been looking forward to this week. We planned a double date with Bailey and Ryan at a theme park called Coasters N' More. Eli and Ryan had been there, but Bailey and I hadn't. I looked forward to seeing what Arizona had to offer in the theme park department. And this Saturday, Bailey was throwing a pool party. It was sure to be a fun week.

After Bailey and I had talked about not seeing many people from school over the summer, she took it upon herself to get everyone together at a mid-summer pool party. I looked forward to catching up with everyone.

Bailey's in-ground pool had always seemed inviting, yet I hadn't been for a swim in it yet. Somehow my hectic schedule never allowed for it. I almost always forgot she even had a pool, even though I had lived in Kelly's pool back in California.

A couple days earlier, I had pulled out all my swimsuits. They were either body gloves for surfing or faded from overuse. When I concluded that none of them were salvageable, Eli and I made plans to go shopping for a new one. That was before our last date, which had been disastrous, but we never broke our plans. Though we had talked here and there since then, we hadn't even seen each other at work. It had been abnormally quiet between us.

The doorbell rang right on time. I knew to expect Eli's punctuality. I grabbed my keys and headed for the door. My anxiety took over for a moment, and I checked the peep hole before I opened the door, just to make sure. I smiled when I saw Eli standing there, waiting, and I whipped open the door, still grinning.

"I'm driving," I said.

I breezed past him, a grin on my face, half-jogging to my car. I jumped in, turned the key, and put the top down before he could object. He walked around the car and stood in front of the passenger door, looking down at it and then back at me.

"But I always drive."

I giggled.

"Not today!"

I patted the passenger seat and shot him a sly grin. I was playing with him, and he knew it. He let a half smile slip onto his face before he opened the door and climbed in.

"Don't get used this," he said.

"Oh, I will," I teased.

We coasted down the road with the wind in our hair, the setting sun giving us a small reprieve from the heat, though I still found myself dripping with sweat after only three blocks. I put the top up. Eli snickered.

"What?" I retorted.

"Nothing."

I glared at him.

"You're funny. That's all," he said.

I shook my head.

At the mall, we browsed a few stores before I found anything I liked, and I ended up in the dressing room with ten swimsuits to try on. The pile almost overwhelmed me, but Eli insisted that if I didn't take them all in, I would regret it when I had to track them all down again. And that proved to be true after the first five were a bust.

I felt comfortable enough to show Eli the sixth one. I stepped out of the dressing room in a red, white, and blue striped bikini, my hands clutched over my midriff. Eli waved his hand in the air in a shooing motion. I rolled my eyes and moved my hands away, revealing my stomach.

"I like that one," he said.

"You don't think it's a bit much?" I asked.

"No. Absolutely not."

I wasn't convinced. I felt like I stood out. I put the striped one into the 'maybe' pile and slipped into a crimson tankini. When I stepped out of the dressing room, I didn't feel the need to cover myself in the crowded store, since it wasn't revealing.

Almost immediately, Eli shook his head.

"No?" I asked.

"Definite no."

"Why?" I asked.

"Really?"

The expression on his face told me it should be obvious. I looked in the mirror again, trying to figure it out. I shrugged.

"It looks like something a soccer mom would wear."

I glanced down at it and couldn't disagree. That must have been what I disliked about it but hadn't been able to put my finger on. I turned back to the dressing room and tossed it into the mounting 'no' pile.

The next time I stepped out of the dressing room, I felt confident in an all-black bikini with a skort bottom. It covered my butt fully, making me feel more modest, but with a bikini top so I didn't look like a soccer mom.

Eli's face lit up. "I like that one a lot."

"Me too," I said.

When I changed into a turquoise bikini, my confidence still ran high. I strutted my stuff, modeling the heck out of it.

Eli's eyebrows lifted. I could tell he instantly approved of this one, and my little act only helped sell it. By the time I turned to head back into the dressing room, he was doubled over.

I looked at myself in my mirror and couldn't hold back a giddy laugh. I did a little strut in the dressing room before I felt silly and tried on the last two. Neither worked, and I didn't bother to ask Eli what he thought. I loaded up the hangers with all of the suits and discarded the ones I hated before heading back to Eli with my three favorites in tow. Eli plucked the turquoise one from the bunch.

"This one," he said.

"Really?"

"Yes."

"Are you sure?"

He nodded.

I took one more look at it. "If you say so."

I set the other two down and went straight to the register to pay.

"I'm hungry," I announced when I found Eli again in the men's clothes section.

"Me too."

He took my hand, and off we went to the food court. It felt good to enjoy a normal date after the last disaster. I wasn't even going to try to broach that subject for fear of ruining the day.

"Sit. I'll go get us food," Eli said.

So there I sat, waiting and wondering what food he might tempt me with. I watched people walk by with steaming plates of pizza, Chinese, and Mexican. My mouth watered in response. The longer I sat, the hungrier I became. My stomach groaned.

Hoping to distract myself from my appetite, I averted my attention to the bungee trampolines in the center of the food court. It amazed me that none of the bouncing kids hit the ceiling. It seemed like they got so close, especially when the operators grabbed their feet and flung them higher than they could dream of jumping. I zoned out, watching them go up and down, and when Eli returned I didn't notice he was there until he tapped me on the shoulder.

"Sorry, I guess I zoned out looking at the trampolines."

I looked down and found a steaming bread bowl of broccoli cheese soup. My stomach growled.

"Yum!" I said.

Eli smiled. "You like?"

I nodded, grabbing the spoon. "I do."

The soup slid down my throat, enveloping my stomach in a warm blanket of deliciousness. I savored each bite, watching Eli blow on steaming spoonfuls of his chicken tortilla soup. I could smell a hint of its spice from across the table.

"Have you ever done that?" Eli asked.

"What? The trampoline bungee?"

He nodded.

"Nope. Can't say I've ever wanted to."

"Really? How come? I think they look like a ton of fun."

I shrugged. "I'm not much for heights. At least not when it comes to flying around without much control."

"I think we should do it." A sparkle glistened in his eyes, one that I could tell meant he was about to get his way.

I shook my head, though my face betrayed me, a grin appearing at the corners of my mouth.

"You want to. I can tell," he said. "You can't hide that grin from me."

"My grin doesn't mean I want to," I protested, shaking my head again. "I think we're too big anyway."

"We're not too big." He squinted as he looked over the rules. It only took him a moment before he smiled again. "There, it says up to two hundred pounds. Last time I checked, you didn't weight two hundred pounds. Now you have no excuse."

I gave him a sheepish look. "Would you believe I suddenly gained a bunch of weight?"

"No." He looked at me sideways. "So that means you're going to do it."

"It does?" I asked.

"Yep!"

His playful side was out, and his worry faded away, pushed to the back of his mind. That didn't happen often. As I sat there, finishing the last of my food, staring at his eager face, I decided it couldn't be that bad. If it made him this happy, I would be glad to oblige, despite my apprehensive stomach's protests.

"Fine. I'll do it," I said.

Eli smiled from ear to ear and jumped up, forgetting the last of his lunch. He dragged me over to the line and paid for us both.

Before I knew it, the operator was strapping me into the waist and leg straps and spouting out the rules. I glanced over at Eli. He gave me two thumbs up as I stepped up onto the trampoline, each springy step bouncing me without even trying. I looked down, my body wobbly. I tried not to lose my balance and flip forward while the man let the harness raise me up. Grabbing the harness at my sides for support, I looked at Eli. He stepped on the trampoline, completely engrossed in the experience. His giddy excitement was obvious, and I had to laugh. He acted like a big kid as he took little jumps at first, then jumped as high as he could. I envied his ability to throw caution to the wind, so I took his cue and sprang up in the air. I went higher and higher each time. I even got brave and did a somersault in the air. When the harness lowered for me to get off, I was disappointed.

I hopped down off the trampoline and turned my ankle, falling to my knees.

"Ow!" I howled.

Eli was at my side in seconds. He and the ride operator hoisted me to my feet.

"Are you okay?" Eli asked.

"Yeah, I'm fine." I chuckled. "I guess I'm just a bit clumsy. That was awesome!" I said as I limped out of the gate.

"It was, wasn't it? I knew you would like it."

"I even did a flip!"

"Really? I didn't even think to try that!"

"Next time," I said.

I smiled at him. I loved the way he helped me be adventurous in ways I may never have dared. He reminded me of my dad in some ways, and that was one of them. I had always looked at the trampoline as a thing for children. Now I looked forward to the next opportunity to try it out.

"Ready to head home?" he asked.

He grabbed my hand.

"Yes, let's go."

Later that afternoon, we were sitting in Eli's room. Eli was distracted and thoroughly engrossed in the TV, but it didn't change my mind. I needed to know what was going on. I had been thinking about it for weeks. This time, I wouldn't let him brush it off.

"Can we talk?" I asked.

Eli reached for the remote and shut off his TV.

"About what?" He turned his full attention to me.

"Are we okay?" I asked.

"Of course. Why?"

"You've just seemed so . . . randomly preoccupied lately. And the texts and calls-"

"We're back to this again?"

I was beginning to lose my nerve.

"Well, I know we've talked about this before-"

"Yes, we've talked about this before, *numerous times!*" Eli said, cutting me off. He stood up and paced the floor.

"I know, I just feel like something is off. You seem like you aren't there all the time, and I feel like it's more than your mom's passing."

"Maybe I'm not, but it has *nothing* to do with you! I'm still dealing with things of my own you know." He rested his hands on his dresser, looking away. Letting out a huge breath, he said, "I think you should leave."

He might as well have punched me in the stomach. His five little words sucked out all the air from my body. I had hoped not to start something again, though deep down I had known there would be a tiff. I had hoped he would come to his senses and open up to me. Maybe even explained what the mysterious calls and texts were about. But he ended the conversation, and that was that.

I stood, frustrated. "Fine. I'll see you later."

Grabbing my purse, I walked out of Eli's room, fuming. I got in my car and threw it into drive. I had nowhere to go, so for the first time in my life, I just drove. I drove until the sun set and my gas gauge brushed 'E.' I turned back and finally decided where I needed to go. The mall. After a quick stop at the gas station, I was back on track.

I pressed the lock button on my key ring. As I put my keys away, goosebumps rose on my arms. The feeling of being watched washed over me. I glanced around, searching the shadows, finding nothing. Just in case, I rushed into the mall, hoping I hadn't missed something.

Bailey stood behind the counter, ringing up a customer, when she spotted me walking in. I waited off to the side for her to finish up.

"Hey," she said. "What's up?"

"Eli and I had a fight."

"Yuck. Hold on." She made her way back toward the counter and whispered something to a woman who stood behind it. The woman looked at me skeptically but nodded. I felt like I was being put under a microscope as I stood there. I avoided eye contact and stared at my shoes.

"My boss said I could take my dinner break. Come on!" She grabbed my arm and off we went. Once we were out of earshot, Bailey pushed me to talk. "Okay, spill. What happened?"

"Well, he's been so distant lately. Like he's not all there when we're together. Most of the time it's been because of his phone. He'll get a call or text and then disappear mentally. I've tried to talk to him about it a few times, and he always brushes me off. This time, I was more direct."

"Distant how?"

"I don't know. Like sometimes when I'm talking to him I feel like he's not even listening. Other times he just seems like he's spaced out, like he's thinking or something."

"Do you think there's someone else?" Bailey asked.

"No. I don't think it's that. I don't get that vibe from him. He says he's still working past losing his mom."

"Oh," she said.

Bailey ordered food, and we sat down in the food court.

"Want some?" she asked.

I shook my head. "What do you mean 'Oh'?"

"Nothing."

"No, what?" I asked.

She hesitated, looking at me like she was trying to decide if she should say something.

"Well, do you think maybe that might be true? I mean it seems logical that he's still struggling with it. That could make someone seem distant, and it doesn't just go away over night."

"I guess it may be part of it. I just feel like there is more to it."

"Maybe you're reading too much into his phone activity. Maybe the texts and phone calls are from his dad. I'm sure he's struggling too."

I nodded.

"Everything will work out. Don't worry. Just give him some time. Trust me." Her exuberant energy made it hard not to be joyous with her, despite the dark cloud hanging over me.

She finished eating her chicken sandwich while I stole a few of her fries.

"Ryan is going on vacation with his family next week." She pouted.

"That's right. I remember him talking about it."

"Yeah." She sighed.

"We should plan a sleepover for while he's gone," I suggested. "Sounds like we both could use a distraction."

"You would want to?" she asked.

"Of course. Why wouldn't I?"

"I don't know. It seems like you're always so busy, like all the time."

A twinge of guilt twisted my stomach. "We can do pedicures and order pizza. Maybe even bake brownies."

"That sounds great," she said, sounding excited again. She glanced at her phone and jumped up. "Sorry, I've got to get back to work. I'll call you later?"

"Yep."

She bent down and hugged me before she bounded away. I turned my attention back to the tray in front of me. Lazily, I munched on the remaining fries and watched the people around me. Eventually, I grabbed the tray and tossed its contents in the trash.

When I got home, Eli was waiting for me. I walked right past him on my way up to the house, ignoring his puppy dog eyes. I left the door open behind me so he could follow me in. He spoke a few times, but I didn't respond. Tossing my things by the stairs, I went straight to the backyard and sat down.

"Why are you here?" I asked once he shut the door behind him.

"You were right," he said.

"What?" I asked, crossing my arms across my chest and staring him down.

"You were right. I have been distant. I'm sorry. I overreacted."

"Ya think?"

"I guess I'm just not working through things as well as I thought."

"I can't help you if you don't let me in. I'm also not going to sit back and ignore it."

"I know."

"You have to talk to me," I said.

"I'll try from now on. Forgive me?"

I considered it for a moment, letting him sweat a little.

"Yes."

He reached over and took hold of my hand, brushing it with his thumb.

"You're the best," he said, smiling.

"That's right! Never forget it!" I said, a grin spreading across my face.

CHAPTER FIVE

Thursday morning, I found myself overwhelmed with excitement. Eli and I were headed to Coasters N' More with Bailey and Ryan. The idea of checking out a new nook of Arizona thrilled me to no end. Add in the theme park element, and I felt like a kid headed to a candy store.

Eli was due at my house any minute, and then we were going to Bailey's to pick up Ryan and her. It amazed me we didn't do more things as a group like this.

A knock on my door startled me, and I jabbed my eyeliner into my eye.

I sighed. "Come in."

"Are you ready?" Eli asked.

I whipped around with tears in my eyes. I had expected it to be my mom.

"Oh! I didn't know you were here." I gave him a bear hug before I grabbed my things. "I was just finishing my makeup."

"Then I guess my timing is perfect," he said. "Are you okay?"

"Oh. Yeah, just poked myself in the eye."

I smiled as we left my room with Eli's arm draped around my shoulders. He brushed his lips against my ear, sending a shiver down my whole body. It didn't get much better than that.

After picking up Bailey and Ryan, we had a thirty-minute drive to Coasters N' More. Our buzzing excitement seemed to double as we got closer.

"I vote we do the biggest roller coaster first," I said.

Ryan groaned.

"What?" Bailey asked.

"I don't do roller coasters."

"What?" I shouted.

"Oww, Abby," Eli said, holding his ear.

"Sorry," I whispered.

"It's all right," Ryan said. "I'll just wait at the bottom."

"That's no fun!" I pouted.

"How did I not know this?" Bailey asked.

"Well, it's not like I announce it to everyone. I mean, how often do we go to a theme park? Really, it's fine. I'll have fun watching."

"Don't worry, ladies. I'll go with you. Roller coasters are my thing," Eli said. "You kind of have to have *cojones* to enjoy them."

My mouth fell open, and the car went silent. *Did he really just say that?* I glared at him. What was this, a contest? Who could be the manlier man? I could smack him.

After his offhand comment, no one dared to speak. I watched the cars go by, puzzled at what had gotten into Eli. I wondered if he had something against Ryan. If he did, it would be news to me. In the past, they had seemed to be friendly. Did he have a problem with Ryan because of his history with Bailey? Did he still have feelings for her? The green monster showed its ugly face. I didn't like the thought of him being upset about another guy dating his ex.

After we paid for our tickets, I pulled Eli to the side.

"What the heck was that?" I whispered, but my voice sounded irritated and harsh.

"What do you mean?" Eli asked.

"Seriously? You have to have cojones to like roller coasters? What was that?"

"Nothing." He shuffled his feet, kicking at a pebble.

"Do you have a problem with Ryan?"

"No! Of course not," he said.

"Well, then what?"

Eli sighed and brushed his hands through his hair. It was getting long these days. It brushed the tops of his eyes. *When had it gotten so long?* He never let his hair grow that long. How had I not noticed?

"You're right. It was harsh. Guess I was just in a bad mood. I'll apologize," he said.

"Thank you."

"I'm sorry if I made you uncomfortable."

I wrapped my arms around his neck, and he pulled me in tight. And with that, the green monster retreated.

I slipped out of Eli's arms as Bailey and Ryan approached us.

"Want to come to the bathroom with me?" I asked Bailey.

"Okay."

We linked our arms, and off we went.

Bailey leaned into me as soon as we were out of earshot. "Is Eli mad at

Ryan?"

"No, everything is fine. He was in a mood or something. I pulled you away so they could talk."

"Oh! Good! We were a little worried."

Bailey and I spent extra time primping in the bathroom, checking our hair and makeup to waste time. Five minutes later, we headed out of the bathroom, hoping all was resolved.

"Are we ready?" I asked the guys, eyeing Eli.

"All good," Ryan said, beaming.

I smiled. "Good. That," I pointed to a looping coaster, "ride is calling my name."

"Let's go," Bailey squealed, grabbing Ryan's hand.

Eli, Bailey, and I rushed into the short line. After boarding the ride, we whipped back and forth and upside down. In what felt like seconds, it was over. We were giggling when we found Ryan at the bottom.

"How was it?" he asked.

"Awesome!" I said.

"Want to go on the swinging pirate ship?" Bailey asked him.

"Sure."

I loved the pirate ship. It swung so high it felt like we might go all the way over. The view from the top was spectacular, but it could only be seen for a second before we went into free fall, the tickle in my stomach made me squeal.

I gripped Eli's arm as we soared back and forth until the ship slowed to a stop.

"We have to go on that again after the sun sets," I said to Eli as we got off.

"Why?" he asked. He slung his arm around my shoulder.

"That view! Gosh, can you imagine it when the city is all lit up at night?"

"You're right. It'll be amazing," he said, kissing the top of my head. "We'll make that our last stop."

We bounced from ride to ride until lunchtime, when we decided to fill up on the finest junk food we could find at the concession counter. We shared nachos, a jumbo pretzel, popcorn, and fries.

"Mmmm, this is so good. I never get these jumbo pretzels," Bailey said.

"Oh gosh, these are one of my favorite snack foods," I said.

"I'm in heaven!" Bailey giggled.

"Me too. These nachos are really good, too."

Eli and Ryan sat back with grins on their faces as we talked about the food and stuffed our faces.

"What are those grins for?" I asked.

"Oh nothing," Eli said, his grin grew to spread across his entire face.

I pushed him over. "What?"

"We just enjoyed watching you guys enjoy your food, that's all."

I eyed him skeptically. I turned my attention to Ryan. My eyes took in his super short black hair, tanned skin, and brown eyes. I could see why Bailey liked him. He was cute and fun, and he treated her well.

"So Ryan, what do you like to do when you aren't with Bailey?" I asked.

"Um . . . I like to build things," he said, looking down and fiddling with his hands.

"Build things? Like what do you build?" I asked.

"Shelves mostly, but I've built tables and chairs too."

"Ever built any other type of furniture? I built a bed frame for my parents once," Eli said.

"Nothing big like that, but I've been wanting to try building a bunk bed."

"Maybe we should build one together," Eli suggested.

"Yeah, that'd be cool. It would be nice to pick your brain about the design you used for the bed you made."

Bailey looked at me and made a face. I was glad we were on the same page—build talk was boring. She and I tuned out the guys' conversation when they started discussing the tools that might be helpful, and soon after, all the food was gone. Then we got back to the rides. A few times throughout the day, we split up, and Eli and I stayed on the roller coaster.

"It's too bad Ryan doesn't like roller coasters," I said, snuggling up to Eli just before we got on the roller coaster for the sixth time in a row.

"Yeah, they're missing out," he said.

He pressed his lips to my forehead and held them there. He seemed to disappear again, but I didn't have time to read into it before the ride operator motioned us forward.

When we met back up, we rode the bumper boats, and I got splashed so much that my shirt was soaked. I had never felt more grateful that I wasn't wearing white.

When the sun set, we headed back to the swinging pirate ship. I snuggled close to Eli as the cool breeze hit my face. We slowly began to rise and fall. I shivered—hours later, I still felt damp from the bumper boats. Bailey and Ryan sat on the opposite side of the ship. I stole a glance at them and smiled to myself. They looked so happy together.

With each swoop, we got higher and higher until we had the view I had been waiting for. Thousands of lights gleamed in the city. I could see the headlights of the passing cars below and streetlights that, from this height, looked like flashlights streaking across the sky. We whipped back toward the ground before we swung up again for another glimpse of the view. We had just seconds to get a good look before we were whisked away again. After a few minutes, we slowed to a stop, and the operator ushered us off so the next group could rush on. *The perfect end to a day at the park! So exciting and romantic.*

We piled into Eli's car and headed to the closest steakhouse. Eli's hand found mine as he drove. I smiled at how happy such a simple gesture made me feel and relaxed against the seat, resting my aching body.

I craved real food after the junk food that had fueled me all day. I glanced at the time on my phone and hoped there wouldn't be a long wait. It should be past the normal dinner rush. As we pulled into the parking lot and I counted the empty parking spots, I felt confident we wouldn't wait long.

Moments after the hostess greeted us, we were seated. The hostess got our drink order while the waitress was busy. I gulped down the first glass of strawberry lemonade.

"Geez, thirsty much?" Bailey asked.

I giggled. "I guess so."

"So, what's the biggest steak they have?" Ryan said as he opened the menu.

"Hungry much?" I teased.

"I guess so," he said, looking me in the eye with a grin on his face.

"Mmmm, a six oz. is plenty for me as long as it comes with a salad and their baked potato soup." My mouth watered just thinking about it.

"Ooh! Yum, I want that too," Bailey said.

"What are you going to get?" I asked Eli.

"Why, steak of course!"

The waitress came by and took our order, then left us to talk again. I glanced over at Bailey and Ryan as they whispered to each other, and I couldn't help but smile again at how cute they were. I was so happy that Bailey had found someone who made her happy. I leaned into Eli and closed my eyes, breathing in his intoxicating scent.

"I'm getting my license," Bailey said, breaking the silence.

"Really?" I asked.

"Yep! My dad's been teaching me to drive on the weekends."

"That's awesome," Eli said. "Do you plan on getting a car soon?"

"I'm hoping to. I have a little money saved," she said.

"If you need help looking, let me know," Eli said.

"Oh yeah! Seriously, Bailey, he found my car for me," I said.

"You'd help me?"

"Of course. Why wouldn't I?" Eli asked. He looked perplexed.

"I don't know." She blushed.

I could guess the reason behind her hesitation. I had felt the same way that morning. Eli had satisfied me on that subject before I had even had to voice my concern. It made me glad I hadn't asked. I would have looked like a jealous girlfriend, and that was not me. I linked my hand in his and rested our intertwined hands on his leg.

"I'd be glad to help," Eli said.

"I would really appreciate it. My dad isn't what you would call mechanically inclined." She cringed.

"Just let me know when," Eli said.

Our salads looked delicious, spotted with cherry tomatoes and croutons. Eli and Ryan looked like the salads might bite. I picked up a fork and played clueless.

"Want some?" I asked Eli, putting it as close to his mouth as I could.

"Eww, get that crap away from me," he said, batting my hand away.

I giggled. "It's good for you."

"Not if I throw it up it isn't!"

At that, all four of us bent over laughing. After we settled down, the table fell silent apart from the sound of our forks clinking against the salad bowls.

"I'm so excited for Saturday," Bailey said, pushing her empty bowl away.

"Me too! I even got a new swimsuit last weekend."

"Ooh! I can't wait to see it."

Seconds after I polished off my salad, our waitress came out, carrying a tray with our food.

"Finally some sustenance!" Eli commended the waitress as if he had been starved all day.

It didn't take long for us to empty our plates. Bailey and I excused ourselves to the bathroom at the very same time as if we had planned it.

"Today was so fun," she gushed when we were alone.

"It was," I said as I thought back to the dips and turns of the rides.

"We should play mini golf next time. That course looked cool."

"Yeah."

"Hey, are you okay?" Bailey asked.

I dried my hands as I glanced in the mirror. "Of course, why?"

"You seem out of it."

"I guess I am. I'm tired." And for once, it was the truth.

"It's been a long day."

I brought my face close to the mirror. My eyes were drooping, and the dark circles under them hadn't been there that morning. I pulled on them as if they might stretch and disappear.

"I think I need to go to bed." I laughed. "These are not a welcome addition to my face!"

Bailey giggled. "Not me! I'm so amped up from today I don't think I'll be able to sleep. Best date ever!"

I had to agree with her there. It had been a great day.

I fell asleep on the way home. I didn't even remember dropping Bailey and Ryan off. I woke to Eli carrying me up the stairs to my bedroom.

"What are you doing?" I mumbled.

"Putting you to bed, silly." His husky voice rattled in his chest.

"You could have woken me up," I said.

"Nah, I like carrying you to bed. You're cute when you sleep." He winked at me, or at least I think that's what I saw with my blurred vision.

A sheepish grin spread across my face, and my cheeks felt warm. I let my eyes close.

"Oh, don't go getting embarrassed on me! Being cute isn't something to be embarrassed about. Now the drool spot on my shirt might be a little more in that direction." He grinned.

My eyes shot open. "Oh my god." My hand flew to my mouth, wiping the dab of drool at the corner of my mouth. "Oh, yuck."

He chuckled, and it vibrated through his chest. "It's not a big deal. I was just teasing."

"Speak for yourself!"

His chest rumbled again. Now that I was awake, I helped out by opening my door, and Eli kicked it the rest of the way open.

"Well, there is a bonus to you being awake now." He paused, stopping next to my bed. "It doesn't matter how gently I put you down." A wicked grin spread across his face seconds before he launched me into the air. I shrieked as I landed on the bed. I sprung up and down on the mattress for a moment and giggled when Eli flopped down on top of me, his back to mine.

"Man, did you know your bed is lumpy?" he asked.

He smacked at my legs and pushed on my back as if he was trying to make himself comfortable.

"You weigh as much as an ox!" I groaned through my laughter.

"Oh come on, I don't weigh that much," he said as he slid off me to lie next to me on the bed. "So did you have a good day?"

"Yes, the best."

"Good. I gotta jet." He rolled to his side, kissed me on my forehead, and rolled off the bed. "See ya later, sweetie. Sweet dreams."

He shut the door behind himself. I sighed and got out of bed. After changing, I grabbed my laptop and shut off the light before I hopped back under my covers. The bright light from the screen cast awkward shadows on my walls. I turned on a comedy and settled in. Relaxing into my pillow, I stretched out on the bed and absorbed myself in the fantasy world on the screen.

The next morning, a loud *thud* startled me awake. I stretched and leaned over the bed to see my laptop splayed on the floor.

"Oops . . ." I mumbled to myself.

I wiped the drool from my cheek and hung off the bed to lift my laptop off the floor. Then I slid out of bed and threw on my slippers. George was alone in the kitchen when I walked in.

"Morning," he said.

I mumbled incoherently in my sleepy haze.

"Your mom will be down in a few minutes," he said.

She wasn't up yet? Why was George here then? Eww. Never mind. Why did I even go there? I shook my head, trying to get rid of those thoughts.

I pulled out the pancake mix and made pancakes. I even made enough for George and my mom. When I finished, I piled them up on a plate and went into the dining room. George was drinking his coffee while he read the newspaper.

"I made you guys some pancakes," I said.

"That's really sweet of you. Thanks."

I nodded and left the room, carrying my own plate. I brought my breakfast into the living room to chow down in front of the TV. When I came back in to rinse my plate, my mom was in the kitchen, pouring her first cup of coffee.

"Morning," I said. "I made pancakes. They're in the dining room with George."

"Thanks, honey," she said.

I ran up to my room and decided it was time I pampered myself. I gave myself a manicure and pedicure while I listened to music. Then I grabbed a book I had been wanting to read. Sprawling out carefully so as not to smudge my nails, I propped it open and let the words flow into my mind.

A little while later, a knock sounded on my door.

"Abby?" Mom said as she popped her head into my room.

"Yeah?" I said, turning my attention to her.

"I wanted to talk to you a minute." She sat down on my bed and motioned for me to join her.

Uh-oh. What was this about? All my senses roared to life.

"What's going on?" My heart thundered with worry.

"Do you remember when we took you to dinner and discussed George moving in?"

Discussed? That's not how I remember it.

"Yes . . ." I hesitated.

I didn't like where this was going. I hated the idea of him moving in.

"Well, we've decided to go ahead and do that next weekend."

She danced around the words *move him in* as if she couldn't say it to me. I seethed.

"*Next weekend?* Why does it have to be so soon?" I was shocked that it was actually happening. It hadn't been more than two weeks since that disastrous dinner overlooking the city.

"George's lease is ending. He planned to extend it a few months, but we talked about it and decided there was no reason to wait."

"Don't you guys think this is kind of sudden?"

"Honey, sometimes these things happen suddenly. Your father and I happened suddenly too," she said.

I cast her a sideways glance.

"The best things in life happen that way sometimes. You just have to learn to embrace it."

"What if I don't want to embrace this?" I grumbled.

"I know this is hard for you, but I hope you'll understand that he makes me happy."

"I know." I covered my face and sighed, rubbing my eyes to avoid eye contact.

"I have a favor to ask."

I spread my two middle fingers apart to peer through them at her. *There's more?*

"George and I need help moving him in. We thought maybe you and Eli would give up next Saturday to help us in exchange for pizza?"

"Mooom . . ."

"I know, I know, not fun at all, but we could really use the help."

I narrowed my eyes at her.

She put her hands together. "Pretty please?"

"Fine."

"Great! Thanks!"

She got up and left the room as if she worried I might change my mind.

"Welcome," I mumbled after she left the room.

This news put a damper on my mood. Now all I wanted was to sit on the couch and do nothing.

CHAPTER SIX

I slipped into my new bikini and looked in the mirror. I had to agree that it flattered my skin tone. I threw a dress over it and pulled my hair into a messy bun. Wet stringy hair was not a look I wanted to rock at a party.

Party day meant time to let loose a little, or so I hoped. Grabbing my oversized beach bag, I headed out the door. Eli had offered to pick me up, but I turned him down since Bailey had asked me to come over early to help set up.

On my way, I stopped at a bakery to pick up two dozen cupcakes for dessert. I set the treats on the seat beside me and hoped they wouldn't tip over as I drove.

I texted Bailey when I parked in front of her house.

I'm here.

She bounded out of the house in full Bailey fashion, squealing as she ran.

"Here," I said, handing her the cupcakes before I grabbed my bag out of the backseat.

Her eyes went wide. "Mmmm!"

"I know! I had to fight the urge to pull over and eat one before I got here."

"I say we eat one now," Bailey said. "Our secret."

I smirked. "There are perks to helping set up, aren't there?"

We each grabbed a chocolate cupcake and stuffed our faces.

"Oh my, these are sinful." Bailey closed her eyes as she took the second bite. "I might have to hide some of these for after the party!"

"Do it!"

I peeked outside. The pool sparkled in the late morning sun. I couldn't wait to glide weightlessly through the water. Around the pool, Bailey had set up three tables.

"Everything looks great," I said. "What do you need help with?"

"The food," she sighed.

She walked to the fridge and pulled out fruit, veggies, sour cream, cheese, mayo, and lunchmeat.

"I dread this part. It takes forever. We need to make sandwiches," she said, pointing to the croissants on the opposite counter, "a veggie tray, and a fruit tray."

"Don't worry! We'll get it knocked out quick with both of us working."

Slowly, the trays came together, and soon I switched gears. I mixed up the dip and poured the salsa into a serving container. Then we assembled the sandwiches. By the time we finished, we only had minutes to spare. We laid everything out, utilizing the entire kitchen island, and put out a cooler with drinks, ice, and cups. Then we stood back and looked at our work.

My stomach grumbled.

"What was that?" Bailey asked. She eyed me, her face amused.

"I guess that cupcake wasn't enough. I'm hungry!"

"Eat. I'm going to run upstairs and change. Mind listening for the door?" she asked.

"Sure."

"Thanks."

Bailey's dad hadn't shown his face once since I had been there, and I wondered if he was even around until he strutted in, looking over the spread.

"Looks like I took a break at the right time," he said.

"Sure did, we just finished," I said.

"You two did a good job setting up."

"Thanks!"

"I think I'll make myself a plate before all the food gets eaten," he said.

"Me too!" I said, showing him my half-made plate. "I'm starved."

He popped a grape into his mouth, then continued on past the fruits and veggies and went straight for the sandwiches and chips. *Typical.*

"So, who is coming to this shindig?" he asked.

"Umm . . . I'm not entirely sure. Me and Eli for sure, but Bailey didn't really tell me who all she invited."

I felt silly for not being able to answer that question better. I should have known at least a few people who were coming. I took a big bite of my sandwich, hoping to squash the tension I felt in the silence. Then I looked around, avoiding eye contact.

"You and Eli are an item, aren't you?" he asked. His tone seemed friendly and curious, yet my guard went up. I remembered Bailey saying her dad didn't like Eli, but I still didn't know why. *Would he have a problem with*

Eli being here?

"Yes. Why?" I asked, throwing caution to the wind and letting my curiosity get the better of me. I wanted to know what he had against Eli.

The doorbell rang.

"The party guests await. Best not to keep them waiting," he said before walking away, heading into his office and shutting the door.

I sighed. *Guess I'm not getting an answer.* I walked to the door and swung it open. Breanne stood there, smiling at me in a huge black sunhat and bikini top with jean shorts. Her hair was pulled to the side and loosely braided. She looked so beachy.

"Hey!" I said. "You look pretty!"

"Thanks! Where's Bailey?" she asked as she gave me a hug.

"Upstairs. She's getting ready." I led her into the kitchen. "Help yourself." I motioned to the spread of food as if it were my house.

Bailey popped into the room.

"Sorry! Just had to put some finishing touches on."

The doorbell rang again. Moments later, Ren followed Bailey in. He waved but immediately began talking to Breanne. I sat down at the counter in front of the food. I loved parties, but I couldn't strike up a conversation, even if I were with my friends. Even if I had been good at it, I would have been thrown off my game by my strange conversation with Bailey's dad. It didn't sit well with me. Maybe it was nothing, and I had read too much into it. It wouldn't be the first time.

The repeated ring of the doorbell faded into the background. I hardly noticed it after the first few times.

When Eli walked in, the rest of the room seemed to disappear. His longer-than-normal hair was undone. It looked just a little bit messy, but heck if it wasn't sexy. His eyes fell on me first, and he smiled. My breath hitched in my throat. His icy blue eyes sparkled in the light that flooded in from outside.

He greeted a few people as he made his way to me. He came to my side, wrapping his arm around me and bending over to kiss my cheek.

"Hey sweets. Why are you sitting here all by your lonesome?"

"I was just thinking," I said.

"At a party? No, no, no. Come on," he said, pulling me out of the chair.

I let him lead me toward Ren and a few of our other friends. Ren's presence calmed me, so I stood between him and Eli.

I could have easily fallen into the conversation around me, but I didn't. I continued on in my silence and nodded at the right times. All I wanted to do was sneak away and ask Bailey's dad why he wanted to know if I was dating Eli. *What was it to him?*

I shook it off. I had to get my mind on something else. I had been looking forward to this party too much to let someone's opinion put a damper on it. Especially Bailey's dad, who I hardly even knew.

Everyone made their way into the backyard. It took only a few moments for water to start flying, with Bailey shrieking at the center of the action. I giggled as a boy threw Alexis across the pool. She belly flopped when she landed.

I lifted my dress over my head and laid it on a lounge chair, hoping it didn't get soaked. The water felt glorious when I dipped my toes in. I plunged to the second step and sat down on the first, fighting the overwhelming urge to throw myself into the water and swim laps. There were far too many bodies to dodge in the pool.

I enjoyed watching the chaos unfold in front of me with a silly grin on my face. Bailey noticed me on the sidelines and swam over.

"Are you having fun?" she asked.

"I am."

"Then why do you look like someone killed your cat?" she asked.

"Now that's morbid!" I said, sticking my tongue out.

"Well, that's what you look like! Everything okay with you and Eli?"

I turned to Eli, and he seemed to be having a good time.

"Yeah, why?"

"I don't know. He's just been looking at you strangely today," she said.

"What do you mean?"

"I don't know. Like he's glaring at you. With you looking so glum, I thought maybe you were fighting, but maybe I just misunderstood his look."

I nodded, looking at Eli, who was laughing with Mason.

"Come on! Have some fun!" She splashed me and darted away, inviting me to join her, Breanne, and Alexis, who were hitting a beach ball back and forth.

"I'm just going to get a drink first," I called out to her.

She made a pouty face at me as I stood to walk into the house. I breezed my way past Ren and *almost* made it by Eli. He grabbed my waist, spun me around, and dipped me. After a moment, he righted me again, pulling my body against his.

"You look amazing in that suit," he whispered.

I blushed. "Thanks."

Then he kissed me, just a quick peck on the lips. "Where ya going?"

"Getting a drink. I'll be right back."

He clutched my hand and spun me out. I surprised myself by keeping my balance and staying on my feet as I twirled away from him and toward the door to the kitchen. I stumbled a few steps and grabbed the door for balance. I turned back toward him and smiled. He winked before turning back to his discussion with Ren and Zach.

Nothing seemed amiss. Bailey must have been mistaken.

From the second I walked into the kitchen, I regretted not grabbing my dress. The chill of the air conditioning sent a shiver through me. Goosebumps peppered my skin. I rushed to the cups, dropped in a few ice cubes, and poured myself some soda. I was setting the two-liter back on the counter when a noise behind me startled me. I bumped my cup, spilling all my soda on the floor.

"*Shoot!*"

I turned around to see who had scared me. Bailey's dad stood in the doorway of his office. I gave him a timid smile and rushed to get the towel hanging on the stove handle.

"Sorry, I didn't mean to scare you."

I sighed. "It's fine."

I tossed the towel onto the spill and cleaned it up off the floor in my bikini. It couldn't get much more embarrassing than that. I kept my head down and heard him shuffle to the other side of the counter, then turn on the faucet. Moments later, he appeared in front of me, holding a damp towel out to me.

"Thanks," I said.

I graciously took it. I had no idea where they kept any of the other towels, and the hand towel I had grabbed wouldn't have cleaned up the entire mess.

Once I was done, I stood and pointed at the wet towels in my hand.

"You can toss them in the garage. Anywhere is fine. I'll take care of them later."

I did as he said and then returned to my empty cup and started over. Ice then soda. Bailey's dad still stood on the other side of the counter, supervising the party outside.

One question kept running through my head. *What did he have against Eli?* I wanted to ask him, but I hadn't been able to work up the courage.

Austen came inside to grab a piece of watermelon, making me feel awkward standing there alone with Bailey's dad. When Austen headed back to the pool, I bit my lip. I wouldn't be able to get this off my mind for the rest of the night if I didn't ask while I had the chance.

"Why did you ask me earlier if Eli and I were dating?"

He fell silent. I fiddled with the rim of my cup as I waited. He never took his eyes off the party. I wondered if he had forgotten I had asked a question.

"I just wondered. I didn't like him when he dated Bailey, actually."

"Why?" I asked.

He turned to face me.

"It was clear he wasn't into her. It seemed like she was just someone to bide his time with. I thought he was a player out to break her heart."

He couldn't have been led more astray. I watched Eli standing outside, chatting with Ren. Eli was as loyal as they came.

"*But,*" he said more loudly than before, "from the little bit I've seen him interact with you, I'm second-guessing my opinion. He seems like he may be different with you. Maybe he was waiting for you all along. But what do I know?"

I nodded.

His feelings made sense. He had been looking out for his daughter. I couldn't fault him for that. It put me at peace with his attitude toward Eli.

"I almost feel like I owe him an apology. I was pretty cold to him."

"I'm sure he doesn't even remember," I said. "And I'm sure if he did, he isn't holding a grudge."

The room fell silent.

"Well, I'm going to get back out there."

"Have fun!"

He smiled as I walked out. I felt so much better, like I could breathe again. It was time I really joined the party. I stepped out the door and spotted Ren and Eli still standing by the pool. I set my drink down. *This would be good.* I grinned. Nobody paid any attention to little old me. I jogged toward Ren and Eli on my tiptoes. They were never the wiser until I gave them both a good push and they fell into the pool, clothes and all. The entire party erupted in laughter.

"Abby!" Eli yelled.

I backed away from the pool, giggling.

"Oh no, you don't. You're going in!" Eli said.

He looked at Ren. They both lunged out of the pool and sprinted toward me. I shrieked and tried to run, but they blocked my escape. Each of them grabbed an arm and a leg, and in I went. They shed their shirts and landed in the pool next to me in seconds. This encouraged the few who hadn't ventured into the pool yet to join us all in the water. Breanne and Alexis swam over to us.

"She totally got you!" Breanne beamed at Eli and Ren.

Ren looked at me. "Yeah, and I don't think we've gotten her back well enough yet. What do you think Eli?"

Eli grinned. Ren jumped up and dunked my head under the water. I popped back up in a flash, laughing.

Eventually, we divided into two teams—boys vs. girls—and played bottom dwellers. This was all new to me, and finding the tiny poker chips at the bottom of the pool proved harder than I imagined. In the end, the boys beat the girls in both games. Then we played a few rounds of volleyball. Bailey and Ren were nominated as team captains. I ended up on Bailey's with Alexis, Austen, a kid who introduced himself as Jeremy, Ryan, and a girl I didn't know. Eli was on Ren's team with Zach, Breanne, Mason, and another girl I didn't know. A few just watched the game. I was excited to play against Ren and Eli. It gave the game more of a competitive edge. How nice it would be to beat them, though I knew the chances were slim. Bailey and I weren't cut out for a team, but maybe the others would carry us. I wondered if anyone on my team was any good. *One could only hope.*

Bailey served the ball. It sailed high over the net but was quickly smacked back over, right to me. I hit it, but it failed to make it over and landed back in the water next to me. *Shoot.* Not the start to the game I had hoped for. I smacked the water.

We didn't play by the "real" rules for volleyball, so we got away with a lot. By the end of the first game, we had our teammates' strengths figured out, but we still lost by a mile. The second game went much better, and we won by two points.

Once the second game ended, the pool cleared out so I took the opportunity to stretch my legs and swam a few laps. Before long, I noticed a body next to me. I stopped and waited to see who surfaced. I expected it to be Eli, and when Austen's head emerged, I was surprised.

"What are you doing?" I laughed, splashing him.

"Swimming!" He chuckled. "I love swimming laps."

"I didn't know that."

"It's a great workout. Coach has us swim a lot. Helps with our balance, too."

"Wouldn't have guessed. How's training going? Don't you guys practice like all summer?" I asked.

"Just a few of us get together to work out. Right before school starts, the whole team will be back at it."

"At least you get a little break."

"Yeah, it's nice to be able to sleep in."

Bailey came up next to us, splashing. "Let's play chicken!"

I splashed her back. "No!"

"Oh, come on!" She grabbed Ryan and pulled him over. "We're going to play chicken. Lift me up!"

Ryan seemed like he was game for it and lifted her onto his shoulders.

I hesitated, looking for Eli. He wasn't in the pool and seemed to be engrossed in conversation with Mason.

"Here," Austen grabbed my arm, stabilizing me, and went underwater. He hoisted me out of the water on his shoulders. I shrieked as I fought to keep my balance. Once I steadied myself, I looked at Bailey. She had her game face on, and I couldn't help but laugh at her. She looked so funny with her fake ferocity.

"All right, let's do this," I said.

Austen plunged forward toward Ryan and Bailey. Once we were close enough, I grabbed hold of Bailey's arms while not allowing her to grab mine. We wrestled back and forth. A few times, Austen and Ryan lost their balance and stumbled, making Bailey and I wobble about, but they recovered without falling. Alexis and Zach saw the commotion and joined in. I had a grip on Alexis's shoulder and a firm hold on Bailey's arm. Eventually, Alexis knocked Bailey and Ryan over, leaving just her and me to battle it out. I saw Eli out of the corner of my eye, watching. I couldn't figure out his face. The next thing I knew, Eli was in the pool with Breanne on his shoulders. This threw me for a loop, and Alexis knocked me down.

"You did really good," Austen said.

But I was too engrossed in watching Eli and Breanne play against Alexis and Zach. I knew it was innocent, and I had just been doing the same thing, but I felt a hint of jealousy rising within me.

"Thanks," I mumbled.

I got out of the pool and grabbed my towel. I needed to get away from these strange feelings. It wasn't like me to feel jealous, and I wouldn't give in to it. I went inside to munch on the food.

A few people came through the kitchen and said goodbye as they left the party. They all knew my name, but I couldn't recall a single one of theirs. I really needed to keep up better with the people around me. I looked out the window, hoping that the chicken game had ended, but it looked like it had started over with a few more players. I sat down and popped grape after grape in my mouth until Ren came into the kitchen.

"Hey, what are you doing in here?" he asked.

"Hiding out."

He gave me a perplexed look.

"I started feeling jealous," I said, pointing outside to Breanne sitting on top of Eli's shoulders.

Ren's eyebrows rose.

"I know. It's stupid. I don't even know why. I've never felt like that before. So I came in here."

"I see."

He sat down next to me and gazed at me with sympathetic eyes.

"You don't have to look at me like that," I said.

"Like what?"

"You're looking at me like . . . like . . . I don't know. Like you have pity for me or something. It's not a big deal."

He snorted.

"What?" I asked.

"Nothing."

We sat in silence.

"You know he's only interested in you, right?"

"Yes, I know. I don't think he would cheat on me or anything crazy like that." I paused. "Just seeing her on his shoulders. I don't know. It just sparked something. It's not a big deal. It's irrational, I know that, but that doesn't make the feeling go away."

"Yeah."

He looked like he wanted to say more, but he didn't.

"Let's get back to the party," I said.

"You sure?"

"Yeah, let's go." I paused at the doorway. "And Ren, can we keep this between us? I'm hoping he doesn't know what these feelings mean. I don't want him to think I'm overprotective or sensitive or something."

He smiled. "Sure."

Gradually, the party dwindled down to just Eli, Ren, Ryan, Bailey, and me. We hung out on the steps of the pool, talking as the sun set on the horizon. I leaned back onto the pool deck and watched the sky darken.

"It's not as beautiful as you," Eli whispered.

I blushed and bumped my shoulder against his. He planted a gentle kiss on my forehead and turned his attention back to our friends. Ryan talked about the upcoming vacation he had planned with his family. Bailey's eyes met mine for a moment, a touch of sadness clouding them. I could tell she wasn't looking forward to his trip.

I listened as he talked about the flight museum he looked forward to seeing in Florida and their plan to go to the beaches. It made me think back to California and the trip I had taken with Eli to visit my dad. I thought of Casey. With him, things were still confusing and strained, to say the least.

"We went to California," Eli said.

"I love California," Ryan said.

I chimed in. "It's where I grew up. My dad still lives there."

"I think Bailey mentioned something about that," Ryan said.

"It was a pretty good trip." I looked at Eli. "Do you know he got a bunch of candles and created this amazingly romantic picnic on the beach?"

"Did he?" Ren asked. He grinned.

A silent conversation passed between Eli and Ren.

"It wasn't a big deal," Eli said, glaring at Ren.

I could tell Eli was uncomfortable.

"Not a big deal! Seriously dude?"

"Am I missing something?" I asked.

All our eyes were bounced between Ren and Eli. Ren looked at Eli. Eli sighed and nodded. "Fine."

"When Eli's dad asked Eli's mom to marry him, that's exactly what he did. A candlelit picnic on the beach."

I found myself winded. Eli wouldn't make eye contact with me at first, so I gripped his hand. Our eyes locked.

"Really?" I asked.

"Yeah."

Time stood still for us. Everyone else vanished. His mom had just died a few months earlier, and here he had done such an amazing thing for me.

"I should get going," Ren said, breaking the trance that occupied Eli and me.

I jumped up, feeling embarrassed that I had let the moment sweep me away. I could understand why he wanted to leave after I realized how awkward we had made the conversation.

"We should probably go too," I said to Eli to give him the hint I wanted to talk alone.

"Right," Eli agreed.

We followed Ren into the house after gathering all our things. I was surprised to find the entire kitchen had been cleaned spotless. Not a single dirty dish remained, as if the party had never happened.

"Oh, I was going to offer to help clean up," I said, turning to Bailey.

She shrugged. "My dad's a neat freak. He probably didn't even realize he was cleaning until it was already done."

For a moment, I felt bad that he had to clean up that big of a mess without help, but Bailey made it seem like it wasn't a big deal. She should know better than I if her dad was upset.

I gave her a quick squeeze and whispered, "Thank you." The party was exactly what I needed, and I hadn't even known it. Bailey had struck again with her intuition.

I laced my hand in Eli's as we walked to our cars. Pulling his fingers to my mouth, I kissed them.

"What was that for?" he asked.

"No reason. I'm just happy that I get to be with you."

"Someone's in a good mood," he said.

"You're right. I am."

CHAPTER SEVEN

A week flew by in a bat of an eye, and when Saturday morning came around bright and early, my mom whipped into my room like a tornado, clapping her hands in excitement. I groaned. She threw back my curtains, letting in the light from outside.

"Mooom, it's only six a.m.!"

"Rise and shine, honey. We've got a lot to do!"

And with that, she disappeared again. I closed my eyes, willing myself to wake up. Seconds later, she returned, popping her head through the door and startling me. "Oh! I've got donuts!"

Ugh! I'm up! I threw back the covers and sat up, rubbing the sleep out of my eyes. I grabbed my phone and sent a text to Eli.

Up and at it early today . . .

When I finished throwing on my clothes and putting up my hair, I checked my phone. A message waited from Eli.

Not as early as me.

What did he mean by that? I shrugged it off and sauntered downstairs, unwilling to let myself look happy. It wasn't hard. Happy was the last thing I felt about moving day.

"We have to go pick up the moving truck. Then we can meet you and Abby at George's apartment. I'll text Abby the address." my mom said.

"Sounds good," Eli said.

I was surprised to hear Eli had already arrived, but now his text made sense.

The front door closed, and then it was quiet again. I snuck in as silently as I could, jumped out near where I had heard Eli's voice, and yelled, "Boo!" but nobody was there. Suddenly, I was grabbed from behind. I squealed like a little girl and jumped sideways. I smacked Eli on the chest as he laughed hysterically at me.

"You're so mean!"

"Me? You started it!" He smirked.

"Yeah, yeah. So where are these donuts I was promised?"

"How do you know I didn't eat them all?"

"You better not have." I glared at him.

"You did take a long time to come down."

"I did not!"

"Okay, maybe I didn't eat them all . . . yet!"

With that, he raced into the kitchen. I bolted after him, right on his heels. I clutched at his shirt to slow him down, but it slipped out of my grasp. Lurching forward, I bent down and grabbed his jean pockets, spun him around, and ran into the kitchen ahead of him. I snatched the box off the counter and flipped open the lid. Grinning at Eli, I licked two of the remaining four donuts. "Mine."

"You think a little saliva is going stop me?"

He snatched one of the glazed donuts that glistened with spit and took a huge bite.

"Gross," I said.

"What? It's not like I haven't kissed that mouth. Been there, done that."

I stuck my tongue out at him and picked up my donut.

My phone buzzed in my pocket. I pulled it out and tapped the screen. An address popped up, and I handed the phone to Eli. Directions weren't my thing, and I was glad Eli took the lead on that.

"So how long will it take to get there?" I asked as he looked them over.

"About twenty minutes."

I finished my first donut and started my second when my phone chimed again.

"They've picked up the truck. They're on their way to the apartment," I said.

Eli shoved the last donut in his mouth and tried to talk. Crumbs of donut flew from his mouth.

I giggled. "I don't understand a word you're saying."

He smiled a large toothy smile, showing me all the mashed donut in his mouth.

"Eww!" I protested and pretended to cover my eyes.

He tapped me on the arm, stood up, and pointed at the door. Time to go. I shoved the rest of my half-eaten donut in my mouth and soon realized it had been a giant mistake. My jaw could barely move enough to chew. We headed out the door, my mouth still preoccupied even though Eli seemed to have downed his without a problem.

Ugh! Boys and their insane ability to put away food.

We were well on our way to George's apartment when I regained the use of my mouth as the last bits of donut slid down my throat.

"Oh my gosh, how did you do that?" I gasped.

"Do what?" he asked. He looked perplexed.

"Shove that whole donut in your mouth? I couldn't even chew it!"

He chuckled. "Never underestimate my ability to eat."

I rubbed my jaw. *Oww.*

As the twenty minutes ticked away, I realized we were headed in a familiar direction. I sat up straighter in my seat, watching where we went more closely. The last two turns told me all I needed to know. We were at the same apartment building that Casey lived in. Butterflies filled my stomach. Eli pulled into the familiar parking garage. I felt excitement about the possibility of seeing Casey, but then it was overshadowed by worry about how Eli and Casey would get along. Of course, the odds of running into him were slim unless we went to his door and knocked. I breathed a little easier.

Eli weaved his way through the parking garage until he found an open spot. I was stunned that, in this huge garage, the first open spot we came to just happened to be next to Casey's car. I kept my mouth shut, resisting the overwhelming desire to say something but not wanting to put Eli in a bad mood.

We got out, and Eli looked lost for a minute.

"It's this way," I said.

"How do you know?" he asked.

"I've been here," I answered without adding more, hoping he didn't question me further.

I took off in the direction of the elevator.

"When?" he asked. "I didn't think you knew where George lived."

"I've never been to George's," I said.

He stared at me. I should have known he wouldn't drop it, and trying to hide it just made me look suspicious now.

I sighed. "Casey lives in this building." I kept my eyes on the ground. I looked so guilty, as if I had done something wrong.

"Wow," he said.

"What?"

"Nothing."

I pressed the elevator button. I knew he was on edge because he didn't like Casey and me not saying something sooner just looked bad. We stepped into the elevator and glided up to the tenth floor. Eli stepped in front of me and pushed me against the wall. My back pressed against the buttons, but I was lost in the moment and didn't pull away to see which floors I had hit. He lifted my chin to meet his lips and kissed me hard. I could feel his frustration in the kiss, but I didn't care. It was hot. I reached up and put my hands in his hair, pulling him closer. Now this could be the best stress reliever ever. The elevator chimed. I looked at the number of the floor we were on without breaking the kiss. Seven. We stopped.

The doors swung open, and I yanked myself away from Eli as if I had been caught with my hand in the cookie jar. Heat rushed to my cheeks as my eyes locked with Casey's.

Of all the buttons that we could have pressed, it had to be Casey's floor.

"Ah. Hi," he said. "What are you doing here?" His confused face looked from me to Eli and back again.

"Oh. Uh. Hi. My mom's boyfriend lives in this building," I said. "Well, at least he did. He's moving in with us today."

"Wow, big step."

"Yeah."

Eli stood back and remained quiet.

"What floor is he on?" Casey asked.

"The tenth."

Casey nodded. When the silence became uncomfortable, Casey finally spoke.

"Well, I'll let you guys get to it. I'll catch the next one. I'm headed down."

"Okay."

"I'll see ya later, Abby. Bye Eli."

"Bye," I said.

Eli nodded to him, and Casey waved as the doors shut. The elevator jolted and whisked us up again, stopping at the ninth floor as well before finally landing on the tenth.

I could see the irritation in every part of Eli's stance. His held his arms across his chest and leaned against the wall, looking up and away from me.

"Come on, Eli. He's my friend. I wouldn't make you stop being friends with any of your friends."

"None of my friends would put me in harm's way!"

"The list of people who haven't put me in harm's way is getting a bit limited, isn't it? Technically even Bailey should be on that list. Unless that's not what this is about."

Eli opened his mouth to speak but shut it again as if he wasn't sure what to say.

The elevator doors opened to a brightly lit foyer with windows everywhere. I stepped out and spotted George's open door right away.

I turned back to Eli. "Can we forget about it for now? We'll talk about it later. You're my boyfriend, and I love you."

He hesitated. Then he leaned down and planted a quick kiss on my lips. "You're right. I'm sorry."

I smiled. "Thank you."

I could hear my mom's voice coming from the apartment. I grabbed Eli's hand and pulled him inside.

"Hello," I called as we crossed the threshold.

George's apartment was cozy but very bachelor-like. It was obvious a woman didn't live here. An overstuffed leather couch sat in front of a huge TV. On the whole, it seemed clean despite the numerous packing boxes that were strewn around, but I couldn't say I cared much for the décor. It was far too masculine for my taste, and it couldn't touch Casey's.

"Hey guys, we're going to start in the bedroom."

We followed my mom into the room filled with boxes, a mattress set, and two dressers.

"Where's all this stuff going to go?" I asked. "Our house is already pretty full."

"We're not going to worry about that for now. Most of it will go in the garage until we can figure out what we'll keep."

"Okay."

We each grabbed a box and headed to the elevator and down to the loading dock where the moving truck was parked.

After countless trips up and down, my mom and I took a break while the guys handled the big things. Slowly, the apartment emptied out, and we were ready to go back to the house.

Downstairs, George pulled Eli aside. "Would you mind going through a drive thru on your way back to the house? I would, but I don't think this thing will fit."

"Sure, any requests?"

"Maybe some burgers and fries. Just whatever is on the way. This should cover it."

George handed him $50 before he climbed into the moving truck and pulled away.

Eli threw his arm around my shoulder and led me back to his car. "So, honey-bun," Eli said. "Where should we get lunch? It's on George." He grinned, holding up the money.

"You pick!"

We picked up four cheeseburgers and four orders of fries and went straight to my house.

I didn't think I had ever seen anyone eat burgers as slowly as we did. I guessed none of us were in any hurry to get back to work.

When my burger was almost gone, I felt my muscles tightening, and I knew that getting going again would be much more difficult if I rested longer. I finished my food and stood up.

"Time to get back to work," I said.

Alone, I headed to the garage to get started. My mom's car had already been moved out, so I opened the truck and set to work, starting with the smallest boxes that went to my mom's room. *Their room.* I knew I had better get used to it now.

Before long, everyone else joined me. The guys took over, pulling out the big things while my mom and I stacked the smaller boxes.

Soon, the truck was empty.

"Eli, do you want to join me while I take the truck back?" George asked.

"Uh, sure." Eli looked confused. I probably did too.

He made his way over to me and whispered, "Is that okay?"

"Sure, go ahead," I said.

I wondered why George wanted Eli to go with him. It was strange.

Eli kissed my forehead and got in the passenger seat of the truck. It rumbled out of the driveway, and my mom and I finished organizing all the boxes that didn't belong upstairs.

"I think I underestimated how much stuff there was," Mom said as she stood back to look at the boxes stacked almost to the ceiling.

"Yeah, I think parking in the garage is out of the question for a while."

"Yeah," she sighed. "I think so."

By the end of the day, the truck had been returned and the pizza delivered. We all sank onto the couch with our feet up, stuffing our exhausted faces. Four pieces in, I tossed my plate on the couch next to me.

"I'm stuffed!" I groaned.

"Me too," Eli said, rubbing his bulging belly.

"Well, thank you guys for helping out today. We couldn't have done it without you," George said.

I walked Eli out that night, despite my protesting muscles that begged for a hot bath and rest. I held his hand as we strolled down to the sidewalk.

"So, why did George ask you to go with him to return the truck?"

A smile spread across his face. "He wanted to get some scoop on you."

"What?"

He chuckled. "He wanted to know more about you so that he could 'bond' with you. Also, he wanted to have the what-are-your-intentions-with-her talk."

I rolled my eyes. "What did you tell him?"

I found it unsettling.

"I told him you like California and that you miss it and your dad a lot. I told him you love food."

I grinned. "So far so good."

"I told him you dislike horror movies, but you love comedies. I said you're adventurous and like going to new, outdoorsy places."

"Is that it?" I asked.

"I think so."

"I see. So what *are* your intentions?" I asked, wrapping my sore arms around his back.

"Hmm." He kissed my cheek. "I think . . ." He kissed my nose. "I intend . . ." He kissed my chin. "To kiss you." He kissed me long and hard as we stood locked in each other's arms.

When I pulled away, I was breathless. "I think I like your intentions."

CHAPTER EIGHT

The following week, Bailey arrived on my doorstep, her duffel bag in hand, ready for our two-night sleepover. I looked forward to some girl time. Time to be problem-free. Everything outside the two of us would be ignored at all costs.

"So, what do you want to do?" I asked.

"Let's go out," she said.

"Out? Out where?"

"I don't know. Movies, dinner, pottery painting, anything."

"I've never been to a pottery-painting place. Let's do that," I said, intrigued by this new plan.

I grabbed my purse, told my mom we were leaving, and off we went. I was excited to try something new, especially since Bailey seemed so excited. I blasted the music as we drove, we sang and danced along without a care.

The smell of paint and ceramic permeated through the pottery store. The bright colors on the example pieces captured my attention at once. Everything was painted to perfection, and I wondered how mine would come out. I guessed not so well.

It didn't take long to pick out which pottery pieces we wanted to paint—matching, flower-shaped jewelry boxes. Then we sat down to make them beautiful.

"So, when did you last see Ryan?" I asked.

"Yesterday," Bailey said. "Just before he left."

I remained quiet, unsure of what I could say to make her feel better. The repetitive sweeping motion of the paintbrush on ceramic soothed me, and I could feel myself relaxing as lavender paint engulfed the box.

"I have an idea," I said.

"What?"

"No more mentioning Eli or Ryan the rest of the day."

She raised an eyebrow but then smiled again. "Agreed," she giggled.

"So, have you been able to hang out with anyone else from school since the party? Besides me of course." I winked at her.

"Oh yeah, I've gone shopping a few times with Alexis, and Breanne stopped by my work to see me a couple times as she was passing by."

"Oh, fun. I haven't seen anyone since the party at your house," I admitted.

"Really? You should come with Alexis and me next time we go shopping."

"That would be fun," I said.

Two hours later, we walked out relaxed and energized.

"I can't wait to pick it up," I said.

"I know! I love to see how they come out."

Back at my house, we made two boxes of macaroni and cheese and devoured every bit while we watched a new chick flick we had rented on the way home.

I felt more at ease than I had for a while. Eli came to mind, and I wondered what he was doing at that moment. I missed him even though I had seen him just the night before. Since we had agreed not to talk about the guys, I kept my mouth shut and went back to watching the movie.

Bailey disappeared and returned a few minutes later, looking confused.

"What's with all the boxes everywhere? Did I miss something? Are you moving?" she asked.

"Oh! I can't believe I didn't tell you! George moved in," I said in a hushed voice.

"Your mom's boyfriend?"

"Yep."

"Wow! How's that been?"

I thought about it. "Different. It hasn't been very long."

"I bet. Wow. I can't believe it. No wonder you're always so busy. You can't catch a break!"

"No kidding," I said.

Bailey turned her attention back to the movie, but I could tell she was still thinking about George. I was glad she thought the same way as me about the parental dating stuff. We got each other, and having someone to talk to about it made it so much easier. I wished I had been talking to her more leading up to the move.

Just before the movie ended, the front door opened, and I could hear my mom and George talking.

"Girls," Mom called.

"Yeah?" I said.

"Come here please."

We paused the movie and moved toward my mom.

"What's up?" I asked when we got to the kitchen.

"George suggested we bring you girls some dessert," she said with a smile, handing each of us frozen yogurt with sprinkles and cherries on it.

"Oh, thanks," I said to George.

"That was so nice! Thanks!" Bailey said, her exuberant personality coming out as clear as day.

"I thought maybe we could all sit outside and eat them together," Mom said.

"Sure," Bailey agreed.

I followed Bailey outside and sat beside her. Much to my relief, she took over the conversation. I sat in silence, eating my frozen yogurt. I felt bad that I was shutting down, but I hadn't yet figured out how to behave in this new dynamic I faced with George and my mom. It wasn't like it had been with my mom and dad. That was natural, organic. This would take time to get used to, and maybe it would feel normal at some point. Maybe. But for now, it felt forced.

"Well, Bailey do you want to go finish our movie?" I asked.

"Oh, yeah! I almost forgot. Thanks so much for the ice cream."

"Of course," George said.

Bailey waited until we were sitting in the living room before she gushed.

"Abby, I think he's great."

"Really?" I asked.

"Yeah, he seems like he's really trying. Don't you think?"

I eyed her and wondered if it was only the ice cream or their conversation that had won her over.

"He's nice," I said, reaching for the remote without answering her question.

George was still on my mind when we went to bed that night. I couldn't help but wonder if my compassionate friend was slipping away into the land of accepting George. I shut off the light and willed myself to think about something else. Disneyland. The beach. My dad. Anything. Soon I felt myself drifting to sleep. The last thing I remembered was that I needed to call my dad.

It was dark in my room, and I could hear Bailey's even breathing. A faint glow of street lights filtered through the blind flaps, casting a striped pattern on the ceiling. The bright red numbers on my clock told me it was well past two a.m. My eyes drifted closed again.

Something grasped my wrist. I pulled away, but it held on, trapping me in its clutch. I twisted and pulled, yet its grip became tighter.

"No."

I heard my name, far away as if I was underwater. I clawed at the thing that held my wrist. Something stroked my shoulder, and I flinched away from it.

"Abby," a voice called, less muffled.

More aware, I fought harder. Someone held me. I had to get away. Not again. *Please not again.*

"Let me go!" I shrieked.

"Abby. Stop. It's me." Bailey's voice broke through my sleep-induced fog.

I slapped her hand away one last time, sitting up and scrambling backward. I brought my knees to my chest. Bailey held her hands in the air. The terrified look on her face grounded me. I dropped my face into my hands and sighed.

"I'm sorry," I said. "I'm so sorry."

I couldn't look Bailey in the eye the rest of the day, despite her best efforts to move on. There wasn't anything she could do to make me feel better. I had flipped out on her for no reason. I was so embarrassed. Nothing like that had ever happened before, and I never wanted it to happen again.

I escaped to shower, giving myself time. I kept taking deep breaths, hoping to alleviate the stress I felt. When I made my way downstairs at lunchtime, Bailey sat with my mom eating a sandwich. She glanced at me as I walked in, but I turned away. I couldn't face her yet. I sat next to her to eat, and once we were done, I did the dishes that were in the sink. I was doing everything I could to avoid talking about it. I couldn't I admit how badly I had been struggling with everything.

As I placed the last dish in the dishwasher, Bailey turned to me. "Do you want me to leave?"

"No," I said.

"Well then, I think you need to get over what happened. Don't forget, I was right there with you the first time you were kidnapped."

Knowing my mom was sitting in the next room, I grabbed Bailey's arm and pulled her out to the porch. I gestured inside. "My mom."

She nodded. "I get it. I get what you're feeling, probably better than most people you know. I'd never hold something like that against you."

My eyes lifted. She was insightful. She could always look at a situation with a critical yet sympathetic eye. She was a one-of-a-kind friend.

"Thanks. I really don't know what happened."

She put up her hands to stop me. "Say no more."

I chuckled. "Okay."

"Do you have roller blades?"

I gave her a strange look but nodded.

"Let's go skating!" she said.

"Where?"

"There's a rink not far from here."

"Uh . . ." I shrugged. It beat staying home. "Okay."

The skating rink exceeded my expectations. Music blasted from the speakers, and we danced as we coasted around the rink. We even made a few new friends because of Bailey's outgoing nature. People seemed drawn to her, and I could see why. She was fun to hang out with. I had to sit down often throughout our two hours there. My side ached, and sweat rolled down my face.

"What a workout," I said as we walked out.

"Isn't it? I love skating! Such fun."

"It was. I'm craving some pizza now!"

"Oooh, me too!"

"Good. We're ordering some."

I called it in when I got to the car and hoped it wouldn't take long to arrive at home.

"We're back," I called to my mom when we walked in the door, our skates in tow.

"Hey girls! How was skating?"

"So fun," Bailey said.

Mom looked at me.

"It was a lot of fun. I think we'll go back."

Bailey nodded. "Got that right!"

"We ordered pizza on the way home. We're just going to stick around here the rest of the night. I'm wiped out," I said.

"That's good. George and I are headed out." She checked her phone. "He's out there waiting for me now. I'll see you girls later. Be good!"

"We will," Bailey and I said in unison. Then we broke out into giggles. I sat down on the bar stool and laid my head down. "Ahh, I'm exhausted."

"Me too," Bailey said, plopping down next to me.

The doorbell rang, and I jumped up first.

"Grab some plates and drinks. We can eat in my room," I called to Bailey before I opened the door.

"What's the total?" I asked as I swung the door open and fumbled with the wad of cash in my hands.

"Ah . . . hi." Casey stood in front of me, looking nervous. I hadn't seen him since Eli and I had run into him in the elevator at his apartment building. We hadn't had the chance to talk that day, and I had been so worried about how Eli would feel that I had forgotten about the problems between Casey and me.

"Hey," I said, shoving the money back into my pocket. I stepped out onto the porch and shut the door behind me.

"I wasn't sure you would answer if I called," he said, searching my eyes.

"I would have answered," I said without hesitation.

"Oh," he said, looking up at me right away, his eyes bright and hopeful. He shifted on his feet and shoved his hands in his pockets. "Um." He paused. "I want to go back to being friends and teammates instead of being at odds with each other. I know I did and said some strange things, but I hope you can forgive me. I want to put all this weirdness behind us. Can we do that?"

"I would like that."

A smile lit up his face.

"I'm so glad to hear you say that. Are you busy right now? We could go do something."

"Oh. I thought you were the pizza guy. My friend Bailey is spending the night."

"No worries," he said, backing away. "We can do something another time. I'll call you."

A car pulled up to the curb, and a man popped out, jogging up to the porch with a pizza box in his hand.

"I'll see you later," Casey said. "Enjoy your pizza."

"Hi. That will be $15.16," the pizza guy said.

I handed him the money plus tip, snatched the box, and headed inside. I leaned against the closed door, gripping the pizza box so tightly my knuckles turned white. I took a huge breath and sighed. That wasn't a conversation I had been prepared to have, but I felt relieved. Things had gone well, and I hoped that we really would go back to the way things were before. I had missed hanging out with him.

"That took a long time," Bailey said when I made my way into my room with the pizza. "I was about to come down to look for you. I thought maybe you ate without me." She stuck her tongue out at me.

"Yeah. I was talking to Casey, actually," I said without making eye contact. I knew my face would give away just how flustered I felt after seeing him.

"Really? And you didn't invite him in? I want to meet this mysterious Casey!"

"Sorry, it was just a quick conversation. Next time," I said, but she pouted anyway.

"Fine."

I flipped open the pizza box, and the smell of hot, fresh pizza wafted into the room.

Bailey didn't bring up Casey the rest of the night, but he filled a good portion of my thoughts. When she asked about the details of my trip to California, I made sure to tell her just about everything, including every detail she hadn't heard at the party of the romantic night Eli had planned. The conversation left me feeling warm and fuzzy. I missed Eli. I made sure to skim over Casey's little stalking mishap, which I still didn't understand. I had decided not to dwell on it and hope for the best when he asked if we could move past it all. Casey was part of my team, and he hadn't let me down yet. I hoped I wasn't making a huge mistake.

CHAPTER NINE

The next evening, Eli arrived minutes after Bailey left, engulfing me in his arms and squeezing. "I missed you so much the last couple days," he said. "I vote no more girls' sleepovers. I missed you too much!" He chuckled. I watched his Adam's apple bob up and down and listened to the rumble of his chest.

"Oh, you survived!"

"By the skin of my teeth!" he said, holding his chest as if I had wounded him.

He could always put a smile on my face the minute he walked in the room. I laughed as I pulled out of our embrace. I couldn't wait to spend the evening cuddled up on the couch with him. He held out the horror movie he had picked out on his way over, and I shot him a disgusted look.

"Really?"

"What?" he said, grinning. "I heard it was good."

Horror movies were the last thing I would ever choose to watch, and he knew it.

I turned, crossed my arms, and walked toward the living room without answering.

"We don't have to watch it," he said.

"It's fine. I know you really want to watch it. But if I have nightmares, I'm calling you in the middle of the night."

I started chuckling until I realized he wasn't laughing. I turned around and saw the hurt look on his face.

"You can call me in the middle of the night if you have nightmares even if you didn't watch a horror movie." His seriousness grounded me.

"I know," I said.

"Good."

We stared at each other, locked in a moment of passionate

understanding. The horrible situations we had been through were not forgotten. I looked away to find the remote when I started to feel awkward about it. I flipped on the movie and walked to the doorway.

"I'll go make some popcorn," I said before I escaped to the kitchen.

What was that? Sometimes moments with Eli were so intense that it left me feeling overwhelmed and breathless. In those moments, so much passed between us: understanding, love, and serenity. I still didn't know how to act when things got that intense.

The soothing, rhythmic sound of popping popcorn filled the kitchen. I closed my eyes, listening to it and taking in the smell of butter filling the air. *Deep breaths in and out.*

"Hey honey," Mom said as she came into the kitchen in an elegant red dress. "George and I are going out tonight. Do you have plans?"

"Eli's in the living room," I said. "We're going to watch a movie."

"Oh, that sounds relaxing. Do you need anything before I go?"

I shook my head. George walked in behind her, still fastening his watch.

"All right. I'll see you later. Bye honey."

"Bye Abby," George said as he brushed past me.

I let their goodbyes hang in the air. Our conversations had been few and far between since George moved in.

"Hey, the movie's starting. You coming?" Eli asked, poking his head around the corner.

Then I noticed the popping had stopped. "Uh, I'll be right there." I grabbed a bowl and poured the popcorn.

I took a deep breath before returning to the living room and nestling in the crook of Eli's arm.

I ended up getting more into the movie than any other horror film I had seen. The things the characters were dealing with—stalkers, kidnapping, and murder—resembled our lives. For once, I could sympathize with them. Maybe I liked horror movies after all.

The next morning, I practically jumped out of my skin when my phone rang, waking me from a dead, dreamless sleep. Clumsily, I snatched it off the nightstand and almost dropped it.

"He-lloo," I said, my voice creaky from sleep.

Casey's smoky voice filled my ear. "Are you still sleeping?"

"I was," I grumbled, rubbing my eyes.

"What? The sun is up. The day has begun! Rise and shine, cupcake."

"You have far too much energy in the morning," I mumbled.

His husky chuckle made me smile even in my sleepy fog. I sat up and rubbed my eyes.

"You aren't working today, are you?"

"Not until the dinner shift at four," I said.

"Get up and get ready. I'll be there in twenty minutes. We've got plans."

"We do?"

Then I heard a click and knew he had hung up and had no intention of explaining. I looked at the phone and growled. *Eight a.m. Really?*

I threw back the covers and hoisted myself out of bed. He hadn't left me much time to get ready. A shower was out. I got dressed and threw my hair into a ponytail before putting on my makeup and strolling down the stairs.

George's voice was discernible from the next room when I entered the kitchen. I grabbed a granola bar and headed into the dining room where I knew my mom would be.

"Morning honey," she said as I walked in.

"Morning. Uh, Casey is coming to get me. We have plans, so I'll be back later."

"All right."

I headed into the living room to wait for him, but before I made it there, the doorbell rang.

"Hey stranger," Casey said when I opened the door.

"Hey."

"Ready?"

"Where exactly am I going?"

"You'll see." He smirked.

He enjoyed this secret far too much, and at my expense, no less.

I crossed my arms. "Will I now?"

When we got to his car, I was surprised to see Brad, Luke, and Ferdinand inside.

"Hey guys!"

"There she is!" they said in unison.

"You can sit here," Luke said, sliding to the middle of the back seat and patting the seat he had just vacated. The corners of my mouth rose, and I threw myself down next to him. My team. I had missed them.

I buckled in next to Luke, brushing his side as I did.

"Hey! Don't go getting fresh with me," Luke said.

Three heads whipped in our direction. My face grew hot. I threw my hands in the air.

"I'm innocent. I swear," I said.

"I'm just playing!" Luke threw an arm around me. He grabbed my cheek like a crazy aunt. "So serious."

Everyone smiled as they realized that, once again, Luke had gotten them.

I nudged Luke with my shoulder. "Brat."

"So, did Casey tell you what we're doing?" Ferdinand asked.

"No!" Casey jumped in before anyone could speak. "I didn't."

"Okay then," Ferdinand said. "My lips are sealed."

"You guys are mean."

"Nope. Surprises aren't mean," Luke said.

"Secrets are."

Luke leaned over and whispered in my ear, "Good thing it's not a secret then."

I stuck my tongue out at him.

"I'm beginning to think you have a problem with your tongue. Always sticking it out at me," Luke said. "Do we need to take you somewhere to have it looked at?"

I crossed my arms and stared out the window, not daring to stick it out again. I recognized some of the scenery that surrounded us, but after a few minutes, it became foreign to me. I watched my surroundings pass by and looked at street names, hoping to figure out where we were going.

After about thirty minutes in the car, we rolled to a stop next to a large sign that said, "Paintball." It was spray painted and splattered with an array of colors.

Paintball? Nerves settled in my stomach like I was suddenly careening downhill too fast. *Doesn't paintball hurt?* I cringed. All the guys jumped from the car, eager to go. Their pumped-up enthusiasm could not be ignored.

I stood back, unsure, while the guys fiddled with the paintball guns.

Luke stepped in front of me and bent to look into my eyes. His hands clamped down on my shoulders. "Are you ready for this?" he asked.

I couldn't help but chuckle at his goofy seriousness. Paintball must mean a lot to him.

I nodded even though I wasn't so sure. He handed me a gun filled with pink paintballs.

"We got pink just for you."

"Thanks," I said, glancing at the neon pink balls.

"Safety is here," he said, pointing. "Trigger. If you get shot, you have to leave the field. Don't get shot. Hurts like hell. All right? We're your team. Anyone else isn't, got it?"

"I think so."

They were just going to throw me in and expect me not to get shot. *Great.* This wasn't going to go well.

"Here," said Ferdinand. His tanned hand pulled at my chin, turning my head toward him. His other hand came toward my face, his fingers black. Carefully, he swiped his finger across each of my cheeks just under my eyes. Then he grabbed a container from his pocket and dipped his fingers in the pot of black goo.

"Do this," he said, holding both his arms out in front of him.

I looked at him, a little unsure, but obliged. Grabbing my hand, he slid his goo-covered fingers down one of my arms and then the other. When both arms were streaked with black war paint, he stepped back to admire his handiwork.

"You look great!" he said.

I looked down at my arms, curling my lip. "You have a strange idea of what great looks like."

He laughed. "Trust me."

"Okay," I said, shrugging.

This was their scene, not mine, and they would know better than I what was good or bad, but I felt like I had rolled in the mud.

Once they finished readying the guns, they pulled masks from each of their backpacks. Casey walked over to me, holding two.

"I have an extra, so this one is for you."

He handed it to me. Just as I was about to try to put it on, Brad came over.

"Here, I'll help," he said. He stepped behind me and put the mask over my face. "Can you see?" he asked, peeking around me.

I giggled as he adjusted it so one side wasn't blocking my sight. The mask covered my entire face and head. I wondered what the point of the war paint on my face was. It would be covered by the mask anyway. Brad strapped the mask on tight, and I could already feel the humidity on my face. This would get hot very fast.

"Let's go," Luke said. He hopped from one foot to the other like a kid who had eaten too much sugar.

We filed onto the paintball field. I took in its obstacles, everything from wood shelters and bridges to blow-up barricades. One thing remained the same: camo paint engulfed everything in a rainbow of color.

Two other groups entered with us and scattered. I found it hard to tell if they were all guys or if other girls were mixed in among the black clothing, camo paint, and face masks. I jogged to keep up with my team as they wound their way through the course. The maze looked complicated, and I knew I wouldn't be able to find my way out after the tenth turn we made. I looked back and couldn't see where we had come in anymore. The guys seemed to know the place well. I wondered how often they came.

Luke halted in front of a small enclosure. He looked around and darted inside. Each of us followed suit. The darkness made it hard to see where we were going, but I couldn't deny that it covered us perfectly from all of our enemies outside. Brad took charge as he always did. Pointing to Casey and Ferdinand, he gestured for them to go back the way we had come. Then they were gone. I watched, waiting for orders. Brad pointed to Luke and gestured toward the other door. Then he pointed back at himself and then at me. I was confused, but I didn't get the chance to ask questions. Luke dove from the enclosure and ran, shooting off paintballs as he sprinted for the next cover. When he reached safety, he peeked around and motioned for us to follow. Brad pushed me out into the open. My feet froze, my eyes searching for an enemy. Brad shoved me forward, pushing me toward cover.

"Move!" he shouted, his mask muffling his voice.

When we were safe, Brad grabbed my shoulders and turned me around.

"You have to be fast!" he said in a muted voice. "You can't stop!"

I nodded.

My hands shook. I didn't want to get hit with one of those mean little balls. Brad turned his back to me and pointed to Luke, who moved forward. I took a deep breath and followed, crouching down the way he did and imagining I looked like a duck waddling forward with my butt sticking out. Brad stood up behind me and shot off a few paintballs to cover Luke so he could make the dash to the next blockade. I took off after him, hoping I was doing the right thing. I was one step behind him when yellow paint spattered everywhere. I didn't feel anything, but I looked down at myself expecting to find paint all over me. *Only small splatters.* My eyes shifted to Luke, who held his arms in the air to surrender as he walked away. Yellow paint covered his shoulder. *Crap! Now what?*

I took off running as fast as I could, firing paintballs wildly in the direction I thought the attack had come from. I made it to the next cover without being hit, and that in itself felt like a huge feat. After all, Luke, a seasoned paintballer, had already been pegged.

Moments later, Brad caught up and pointed in a direction I didn't want to go. The obstacles were spaced too far apart and were only big enough to hide one person. He took off in front of me before I could object. I sucked in a deep breath and peeked around the corner. An orange paintball whizzed by my head, missing me by only centimeters. I squealed, jumping back. I took a couple deep breaths and lifted my gun.

I can do this. I stood tall and started jogging, shooting at everything that moved. I made it across the straightaway after firing more shots than I could count and leaned against the next barrier.

"Abby! You shot me!" Casey's voice ripped through the field.

Oops!

I leaned around the corner. Casey stood with his mask pulled up so I could hear him, pink paint across his chest. He held up his hands in defeat and walked away, shaking his head.

Dang it.

I found Brad behind a smaller barrier. It didn't give us much cover, but I would take what I could get.

"As far as I've seen, there are three left, maybe more. Ferdinand is over there," he said, pointing to where we were headed. I could see his large body as he peered around a cylinder.

A flash to the right caught my eye, and I fired, pink flew through the air. The next thing I knew, another set of hands were in the air in surrender. *Yes! I did it!*

Behind me, blue and green paintballs launched into the air. Brad and someone I didn't know raised their hands. It was just me and Ferdinand and whoever had escaped our paintballs so far. After making sure the coast was clear, I made my way to Ferdinand. The thought of being alone didn't sit well with me. The mask took away a good portion of my peripheral vision. As soon as I reached Ferdinand, someone jumped out at me from the side.

"Hands up," they shouted.

I lifted the gun to aim when a paintball pelted my chest. Pain ripped through my chest as the impact knocked the air from my lungs. I wanted to scream, but I bit my lip and held back. Ferdinand fired three shots, pelting the shooter in the chest, shoulder, and stomach.

Coughing, I forced my arms up.

Without warning, a paintball hit Ferdinand from behind, startling us both.

"Hey dude! One shot!" said the guy Ferdinand had shot three times.

"Sorry dude! Trigger locked up," Ferdinand said. "Let's go."

He put his arms up, and we walked out as losers.

A safe distance from our competition, I looked up at Ferdinand. "Your gun didn't really lock up, did it?" I asked.

He grinned, and a twinkle shone in his eyes. "What do you think?"

I looked away to hide my smile as we walked off the field. I looped my arm in his and leaned my head on his shoulder. I would never forget it. Solid, sweet Ferdinand.

All the guys had their masks pushed up to the tops of their heads by the time we approached. Paint splattered each of them.

"Aww man, I hoped you two could pull it off," Luke said when he saw us.

I shrugged, holding up my arms. "Sorry."

"Naw man, she was awesome. We were ambushed," Ferdinand said, throwing his arm around me. "She caught on quick, that's for sure."

I beamed at his compliment.

"Another round?" Luke asked, jumping up, gun ready.

"I'm in," said Brad.

"Me too," said Ferdinand.

"I'll sit out this round. That was . . . intense," I said.

"Go ahead," Casey said to the guys. "I'll wait here." He slid off his mask.

"Suit yourself," Luke said.

The three of them walked back to the field, leaving Casey and me alone.

"You didn't have to stay back with me," I said.

"You shot me!" His voice bespoke the utmost offense. I couldn't help but laugh.

"I'm sorry," I managed through my laughter.

"No, you aren't," he said, fighting the grin that spread across his face. "Didn't anyone ever teach you how to shoot a gun?"

I shook my head, still smiling.

"Were you closing your eyes while you were shooting?" he asked.

I nodded, biting my lip.

He shook his head as he tried to bite back a smile. "What are we gonna do with you?"

CHAPTER TEN

It had been less than two weeks since George had moved in, but I hadn't mustered the courage to call my dad. My mom hadn't told him, so it was left on my shoulders by default. One of the many wonderful "perks" of being a child of divorce.

The longer I waited, the harder it became. I could never keep things like this from my dad. I sighed. *Time to dive in.*

I picked up my phone and called him. It rang. And rang again. I switched ears as I listened. Part of me hoped he wouldn't answer, but alas, on the third ring his masculine voice filled my ear.

"Hi Dad," I said.

"Hey stranger."

"I know I haven't called much lately," I said.

"I knew once you got a car I wouldn't hear from you as much but goodness. Your calls have been nonexistent."

"Yeah. There's been a lot going on around here," I said.

"I bet."

"And maybe I've been avoiding it a little."

"Why?" he asked, more alert and no longer playful.

I hesitated.

"Abby?" He was using his stern, down-to-business voice. No more beating around the bush.

"George moved in," I said. I braced for his concern, worry, and hurt. He remained silent for a moment.

"When did that happen?" he asked.

His even voice gave nothing away, but I knew he was hurting. Who wouldn't be?

"A couple weeks ago," I said.

"I see. How do you feel about it?"

"I don't know. I guess I was mad at first."

"And now?" he asked.

"I'm not mad, but I wouldn't say I'm happy."

"Is he nice to you?"

He was in protective mode, and I felt bad he wasn't here to see that everything was fine.

"Yes, he's nice. It's just weird. A new dynamic. It's not like things used to be. I think I'm just going to have to get used to it."

"How's your mother?"

"She's happy. Really happy."

"Good," he said. "You know, you don't have to avoid me just because you have news you think I won't like."

"I know."

"Good. So what's new with you?"

"I went paintballing today," I said, smiling to myself.

"What? Somebody gave you a gun? Whose idea was that?" He chuckled.

"My friend Casey's, I guess. Ironically, I shot him on accident."

My dad erupted in laughter. "I guess he learned his lesson."

"Yeah." I giggled.

"Did Eli go?" he asked.

"No."

"Smart guy."

"Hey!"

I could hear the rumble of his laugh through the phone. "I'm just kidding."

"I know."

"How's the car?" he asked.

"Amazing, of course."

"Of course."

"I should get ready for work."

"Okay but don't be a stranger, got it?"

"I won't," I said, grinning.

"I love you, honey. If you have any problems, you let me know, okay?"

"Of course," I said.

"Bye."

"Bye," I mumbled.

*　　*　　*　　*

After working an exhausting, eight-hour shift, paranoia was the last thing I needed, but it reared its ugly head as I watched the dark vehicle behind me. I squinted my eyes as I tried to discern if it was the same SUV I had been suspicious of before, the one that had passed my house when I pulled into the driveway.

Briefly, I thought of the anonymous notes. *Is this the same person?*

I took a different route home and hoped they would turn off at some point. I headed toward Eli's house. Then I slowed my speed. Maybe if I went slow enough, they would go around me. Most people did.

I debated going back to work. Eli was still there. After a moment, I decided against it. I didn't want to bring danger there. I wondered if I should call Casey. He was the only other person I could call with something like this. Sure, Ferdinand, Luke, and Brad were options, but I didn't want to involve them if this turned out to be nothing. They would think I was crazy. Casey wouldn't. Well, maybe he would, but he would understand a bit more than the others. Maybe.

I held off and went fifteen under the speed limit. *I could get pulled over for going this slow. That might be a good thing right about now.* Cars zoomed past me as if I were standing still. Each driver sent me a disgruntled look of annoyance. Still, the black SUV stayed behind me. I came upon the street that turned into Eli's neighborhood, held my breath, and coasted around the corner. The SUV sailed around the corner behind me. My fear spiked, sending my heart thumping in my chest. I paid more attention to my rearview mirror than the road in front of me. When I made the second of the three turns to get to Eli's house, it still followed. I slowed to a stop as a kid ran out in front of me to retrieve a runaway skateboard. I watched the person behind me the entire time I was stopped, holding my breath as I anticipated the worst—someone getting out of that car. When I looked forward, the kids— who were actually more like my age—were staring at me like I was nuts for not continuing on my way. My cheeks heated.

I stepped on the gas pedal a little more firmly than necessary, and my convertible shot forward. I sped up at the next turn and zipped around the corner. Without looking back at the SUV, I pulled into Eli's driveway, praying Vince was home in case things went badly. I really hadn't thought this through. I took a deep breath and looked for the SUV.

There it sat, two doors down. I tried to breathe. The doors of the SUV hadn't opened. I watched it like a hawk. *Were they trying to kidnap me? Did they know Eli was at work? Were they counting on me being alone?* It killed me that I didn't know what they wanted.

I still hadn't spoken to Vince since he apologized. This might be the worst place I could have gone. He might not even talk to me, let alone help me after I ignored him when he apologized. That is if he was even home. If I left again, they would follow. I was sure of it. *But is that all they would do?*

Grabbing my purse, I palmed my phone and pulled up Casey's number on the screen. Then I jumped out of my car, ran to the front door, and pounded incessantly. I prayed it would open fast. It only took a moment for Vince to open the door, looking alert and worried. I threw myself into the safety of his arms.

"Whoa, Abby. What's going on?" He demanded and he didn't let go.

"Someone's following me!"

"Who?" he asked, pushing me aside to look down the street.

"I don't know. That black SUV," I said, pointing in the direction of the spot it had parked. "I swear it followed me before, too."

"What SUV?" he asked, confusion evident on his face.

"What do you mean? It's right . . ." I looked outside, and it had vanished. Not a trace of it remained. "It was there. It really was. I don't know where it went. You believe me, don't you?"

"Yes," he said. "Come in. You're shaking like a leaf."

"Thanks."

I walked into the entryway and was hit with a rush of familiarity. Yet, the house seemed bizarrely foreign too. It had been months since I had set foot there. The day Eli's mother was killed.

"Sit," Vince said once we entered the kitchen. He handed me a glass of water. Then he waited, giving me a chance to get my bearings.

"Sorry to come here and dump this on you. We haven't even been talking."

"That's not your fault," he said. "Like I said before, I'm sorry for how I behaved. But let's not talk about that right now. Tell me what you can about what happened."

I let out a deep breath. "I'd just left work when I noticed it behind me. It seemed to be following close, closer than other cars would. I even drove extra slow to get them to go around me, but it didn't work. I thought it might be following me after the notes and what happened before, so I came here. I don't know why. I knew Eli was working, but I guess I hoped I was being paranoid. Then they parked two houses down when I pulled into the driveway here. I thought I might hyperventilate."

"And this happened before?" he asked.

His calm demeanor made me want to scream, yet somehow it grounded me. *How was he not freaking out, too?*

"Uh, yeah. About a week ago, I left work and noticed it behind me when I turned into my neighborhood. I didn't think anything of it when it kept going after I pulled into my driveway. I figured it was a coincidence. But I swear it had to be the same car that was behind me today."

"Does Eli know?" he asked.

I looked into my glass and swished the water around in circles. "No."

"You should have told him," Vince said. He didn't look happy.

"I know, but I honestly did think it was in my head the first time. I never even thought about it again afterward."

"Never discount anything you feel. It's that intuition that's going to keep you on your toes and safe. Most of the time, a hunch is right," he said. "What notes are you talking about?"

"I've gotten some notes. One came in my mailbox. It said, 'See how easy it is.' Someone put the other in my locked car when I was at work. It said, 'For me to get to you.' Eli didn't tell you?"

"No," he said. A strange look crossed Vince's face, and I wondered what it meant.

"He was looking into them, and he said I shouldn't worry but after today? I can't help but worry they're connected."

"I don't blame you."

"There was something else. I'm not sure it was even real. I was so tired, I think I must have imagined it."

"Imagined what?"

"There was a dark car, maybe an SUV. I could have sworn the driver was wearing a ski mask. He waved at me as he drove by my work one day when I stayed late to hang out with my co-workers."

Vince's jaw tightened, making the muscles in his face bulge.

"It didn't seem like it could be real," I added, hoping to ease some of his concern.

"I don't think you imagined it."

I glanced down at my hands, hoping he was wrong. Then it dawned on me that Eli hadn't called, despite my unstable emotions. *Work wouldn't stop him from calling, would it?*

"Eli hasn't called," I blurted out. My heart began to pound with worry. *Did something happen to him?*

"Was he supposed to?" Vince asked. He stared at me with a bewildered expression.

"No . . ."

"Well, what's the problem?"

"He always calls when I get . . . scared . . . or anxious." I blushed.

"Oh, the bond. I forget how in sync you guys are. Hmm. That's strange. Maybe he couldn't pull away from work."

"Maybe."

There was just something strange about it. I didn't think Eli would let anything stand in the way of calling me.

Moments later, the front door burst open, and Eli rushed into the kitchen.

"Abby? What happened?" he asked.

"What are you doing here? You're supposed to be working." I stood.

"Don't worry about it. What happened?" he demanded.

"Eli, relax," Vince said. "Everything is fine. Abby was followed. She did good and didn't go home. They parked two houses down, but by the time I looked, they were gone."

"You were followed?" he asked, turning his attention back to me. This time he was a bit calmer.

I nodded. "This was the second time."

"What?" he asked. "This happened before, and you didn't tell me?"

"I thought I was being overly suspicious."

"I want to know about everything, even the things you think are nothing. I can't make sure you're safe if I don't know what's going on."

"I know."

He walked over and slid his arms around me, pulling me to my feet and into his body. "I'm glad nothing happened," he whispered. "I'm glad you came to my dad. I don't know what I would have done if something happened to you again. I know coming here couldn't have been easy."

"About that. Can you give us a few minutes?" I murmured so Vince didn't hear.

Eli pulled back to look at me and nodded. He left the room, giving us time to talk. Vince shot me a confused look.

I looked at Vince and smiled impishly. "I asked him to give us a minute. " I explained. "I've been thinking about what you said when you came by my house."

He nodded.

"I understand why you blamed me."

"Which is why?" he asked.

"Well, you needed someone to blame. I was the easy target until the real murderer could be held accountable. Sometimes that's how things work whether we want them to or not. I can't fault you guys for it. Besides, I stirred the pot with Pete."

Vince chuckled.

"Anyway, what I'm trying to say is, I accept your apology, and I hope we can go back to the way things used to be."

"I'm happy to hear that." He lifted his arms, holding them out to me. "New beginning hug?"

He embraced me when I threw my arms around him, but I quickly let go again. I smoothed my clothes.

"I should go talk to Eli," I said.

"Yeah. Tell him to let me know what the plan is when you're done."

The plan? I nodded and hid my confusion as I left the room. Surely being followed wasn't such a big deal that we needed to formulate a plan. It's not like they had done anything. *But would they have if Vince hadn't been home? What could we even do?* It wasn't like we could confront them. They were long gone.

I found Eli in his room. He had changed and looked really good in a pair of pale blue basketball shorts and a white ribbed tank. His shoulders bulged around the straps, and the white contrasted with his tan skin.

"Hey," I said.

"Get things squared away?"

"Yep."

"Good." He wasted no time getting back to business. "What kind of car followed you?"

"I don't know."

"Well." He thought for a bit. "What do you remember about it?"

"It was a black SUV. Tinted windows."

"That isn't very much to go on," he said.

I shrugged. "I know nothing about cars."

"I know." He sighed. Placing his elbows on his knees and his chin in his palms, he rubbed his temples.

"There's one more thing. I didn't think it was important until your dad seemed to think it was."

"What?"

"That night I stayed late after work, while we were all talking, I glanced out the window and saw someone drive by in a black ski mask. They waved at me."

"Abby, you're just telling me *now*?"

"I thought I'd imagined it or something because I was so tired," I said.

"Let's get you home while I think about what I need to do."

Eli seemed frustrated, not just with the situation, but with me as well. I felt bad that I hadn't told him about everything sooner.

"Okay."

He grabbed his keys off the dresser and headed for the door.

"I'll follow you home," he said as he walked to his own car.

CHAPTER ELEVEN

The sun warmed my skin. Beads of sweat rolled down my temples. I brushed them away. The perfect weather to lounge. I wanted to spread my arms at my sides and soak it up. But we weren't here for pleasure, though I couldn't recall what led us here. All I felt was uncertainty. Something wasn't right. I could sense it deep in my bones.

We passed tree after tree, and I brushed my hand against the leaves, wishing I wasn't here. Wishing I could swing up into one of the trees and hide. Wishing I could make all of this go away.

Eli crept along in front of me. Small plumes of dust rose around his feet with each step. My fear of what we were walking into might be enough to send me spiraling into a panic attack. How could he continue on?

Something moved to my left. My senses came alive, and my eyes darted about, but there was nothing there. I turned my attention back to Eli, making sure to stay close to him. My heart pounded in my chest. I tried to keep my eyes watching back and forth. I didn't feel like we were alone.

Ren stepped out of the trees to my right. I hadn't seen him coming despite my ever-searching gaze. His pace already matched Eli's. He acknowledged me with the smallest nod before turning his attention to the path ahead.

My attempts to stop them were useless. They ignored me as if I hadn't uttered a word. As I walked slowly behind them, a sparkle stood out in the distance. Closer and closer we came with each step until it became apparent the sparkle I had seen was the light reflecting off railroad tracks.

Someone stepped into view ahead of us, near the tracks, their face blurred. They broke into a run. Another person appeared directly in front of Ren. It seemed to happen all at once. Ren's lifeless body fell to the ground, and the other attacker's fist collided with Eli's face. I stepped back, trying to watch our assailants while putting distance between myself and the fight. Gravel crunched under my feet, catching Ren's attacker's attention. My breathing hitched as he made his way toward me. Blood rushed through my body at an unnatural pace. I couldn't hear anything. Before I realized what was happening, he stood in front of me. He lifted his arm, and all went black. . .

Hands gripped my shoulders.

"Abby! Abby, wake up," a deep voice said.

My eyes shot open, and I jolted upright, almost colliding with George's face. The bright light from my ceiling fan blinded me in my sleepy stupor. I rubbed the sleep from my eyes, giving myself a moment to figure out what was going on before trying to look at him again.

"Are you all right?" he asked.

"Yeah, I'm fine," I said, wiping the sweat from my forehead. "Why wouldn't I be?"

"You were screaming in your sleep."

"Oh," I said, playing dumb. I remembered my dream clearly. It unnerved me in ways nobody would understand.

"Can I get you anything? I could go wake your mom . . . ."

"No!" I snapped, cutting him off. "I mean, no. I'm fine, really. Just a bad dream. Happens to everyone."

He eyed me skeptically but stood anyway and retreated to the doorway.

Why did he come in here? I wanted to tell him I wasn't his problem, that he didn't have to pretend to care. After all, he wasn't my dad. He wasn't even my stepdad. But I couldn't bring myself to. Since my dad lived hours away, it felt nice to have George looking in on me, even if we hadn't developed a real relationship. Heck, part of that was on me, and I wasn't afraid to admit it. Everything had moved too fast. I wasn't there yet. Maybe I would get there someday. Maybe.

"Let me know if you change your mind."

Quietly, he switched off the light and shut the door. I fell back on my pillow with a sigh.

"Ah," I moaned. "Why me?" I blew out a deep breath and rolled over to go back to sleep.

I tossed and turned for a long time, worrying I might have my nightmare again. What if George came in with my mom in tow? George was a night owl. I knew this after countless nights of hearing the TV on downstairs when I got up to use the bathroom at two a.m. You wouldn't know it because he seemed to get up right around the same time as my mom every morning, looking as chipper as if he had slept all night. I always wondered if he fell asleep while watching TV and stumbled off to bed sometime in the night. If not, I was sure he fell asleep at work in the middle of the day. If my nightmares continued with such ferocity as they had tonight, his late-night ways wouldn't bode well for me. I wanted to keep them hidden from my mom. Surely he would tell her about my screaming tomorrow.

When I showed my face the next morning, my mom was pouring herself a glass of orange juice.

"Good morning," I said.

I waited, expecting her to question me about the nightmare.

"Morning honey. Want some eggs?"

My forehead furrowed. *She wasn't going to ask?*

"Sure," I said, trying to hide my confusion.

"Morning guys," George said as he walked into the room, still tightening his tie. He slid his arm around my mom, pulled her toward him, and kissed her forehead. "I've got to go. I have to be at the office early."

"Okay." She stood on her tiptoes and gave him a quick kiss before he walked away.

"See ya later, Abby," he said. He patted my shoulder on his way out. Not once did he hint at anything amiss. It was as if my freak out had never happened.

"Here," Mom said, handing me a plate.

I sat at the counter while she finished cooking for herself. I waited for her to say something—anything—but when she didn't, I couldn't stand the silence anymore.

"So, how did you sleep?" I asked.

Really? Did I just say that?

"Like the dead!" She laughed. "I think I hit the snooze button three times!"

"Wow," I said. "That's so not like you."

"I know! It's been that way since George moved in. I have to make sure I set my alarm now every day. I guess it's comforting to have him here."

This surprised and saddened me. For as long as I could remember, my mom's internal clock woke her every day before any alarm. It meant that my dad never brought her the same peace as George. In that moment, my opinion of George shifted. I was grateful for him now in a way I hadn't been before.

That evening, I worked the lunch and afternoon shift. Casey walked through the front door just as the dinner rush began and seated himself at one of my tables.

"Oh my gosh, what are you doing here?" I asked when I made my way over to him.

"Getting dinner. The guys will be here soon," he said.

"Oh, I get it! You guys wanted to make me your servant, huh?" I teased.

"You got me."

"When will the others be here?" I asked.

I glanced toward the door as it opened, wondering if it was my team, but an older couple walked in. Before my eyes made their way back to Casey, I spotted Eli clearing a table across the restaurant. His scowling eyes were locked on Casey. I groaned inwardly. *Here we go.*

"I'm early," Casey said.

"Want a drink while you wait?" I asked.

"Iced tea?"

"Be right back."

I wished Eli wasn't working. Even with his back turned, I could see that he was tense now. He would be mad that Casey and the others were here. Though, I didn't think he was as vengeful toward the others as he was toward Casey. I suspected part of it was jealousy, though I would never truly know. But I had hoped he would at least have been courteous.

I grabbed Casey's iced tea and a refill for another table and headed back into the dining room, but I stopped just before rounding the corner. Eli leaned on Casey's table, his face close to Casey's talking in a hushed voice. *What did he think he was doing?*

Casey's face looked tense, bordering on anger, but his mouth didn't move. I waited, watching to see what would happen. Then, like nothing was wrong, Eli picked up his bucket of dirty dishes and headed for the kitchen. I acted like I hadn't seen a thing and started walking again, smiling at Eli as I passed. A fake smile. *Would he notice?* He brushed right past me.

I set the extra drink at the correct table and headed toward Casey. My eyes bored into his as I walked tried to read his face. I set his tea down, leaned toward him, and whispered, "What was that about?"

Casey recovered himself and smiled, hiding that anything was wrong before. He shook his head and shrugged. "What do you mean?"

"Casey, I saw Eli over here. What did he say?"

"Nothing."

"Casey." I pursed my lips.

"Really. He didn't say anything. He just wiped down the table."

He was lying. *Why? What was he trying to do?*

I didn't get the chance to ask him because the guys walked in and rushed over, interrupting our conversation.

"Hey Abby," they all said, greeting me at the same time.

I giggled. "Hey guys."

"Wait, you work here?" Luke teased.

"Ha ha, very funny," I said, pushing his shoulder. "What do you guys want to drink?"

"Hmm. Can you list all the drinks you have to offer us?" Luke said as if he was asking an innocent question.

I shot him a dirty look.

"What?" he asked.

"You're mean," Ferdinand said, grinning.

"No I'm not. How am I supposed to pick something if I don't know what they have?"

"It's on the menu," Casey pointed out.

"Just bring us each an iced tea," Brad said, taking charge and ending the banter between us.

"You have iced tea?" Luke asked as if he were shocked.

I smirked. "Yes."

"Well, why didn't you say that? Yes, please. I'd like an iced tea."

"Okay." I walked into the kitchen to get the three glasses of tea. I was still grinning at their antics when I bumped into Eli. "Oops, sorry!"

"What's so funny?" he asked.

"Oh, nothing. The guys were just teasing me."

"Oh," he said, looking irritated. "Did you know they were coming?"

"Nope. Do you want to meet the others?" I asked, hoping he would say yes. Maybe if he liked the others, he would get along better with Casey.

"No, that's okay." He went back to the sink to do the dishes.

I couldn't help but feel like he wasn't trying very hard to be friends with them.

I grabbed their tea and headed back out, feeling annoyed.

"What do you guys want to eat?" I asked.

"Hey, what's wrong?" Casey asked, noticing my change in mood. He hooked my arm to get me to look at him.

"Nothing," I said. I tried to smile, but I was sure it looked forced. I pulled my arm away and tucked my hand into my pocket.

He cocked his head to the side. "We didn't upset you with our teasing, did we?"

"No, of course not!" I said. "Really, I'm fine."

Casey locked eyes with me for a moment but didn't press it. I looked at the other guys to take their orders.

"Bring us two large all-meat pizzas," Brad said.

"You got it."

I walked away without another glance in Casey's direction. I couldn't handle his intense concern.

After putting in the guys' order, I took a few minutes to go into the bathroom and pull myself together. I dabbed a wet paper towel on my eyes, cooling the warmth around them, and took a few deep breaths.

"Okay, Abby. Time to get out there and get over it," I said to myself. "They aren't going to get along, and that's all there is to it!"

Accepting that my two worlds would never combine was a hard pill to swallow, but I felt like a weight had been lifted off my chest. As if that shred of hope I had been clinging to was pulling me down and making me walk on eggshells around them. I guessed I had hoped that they would eventually click if they had time to get used to each other. Other than Casey's weird warning in California, he had shown no ill will toward Eli. I just wished Eli wasn't so stubborn.

When I stepped out of the bathroom, I checked on all my tables before making my way back to the guys to refill their teas. Brad, Luke, and Ferdinand were in a boisterous conversation as I filled their drinks. Casey, on the other hand, sat subdued. I tried to ignore it. As much as I wanted to, I couldn't fix everything. I had to remember that.

When I slipped two steaming, all-meat pizzas in front of the guys, their eyes went wide. All their hands shot forward to grab a slice.

"I'll leave you guys to it then."

I heard a few grunts as I walked away and smiled to myself.

As the night went on, Eli seemed to be avoiding me more and more. When I was in the dining room, he would go into the kitchen, but when I returned to the kitchen, he suddenly needed to clear tables. Despite his attitude about Casey, I decided to have a little fun with him and intentionally followed him around until he stopped in the kitchen and whipped around to face me.

"Is there any reason you're following me around?" he asked, exasperated.

A smirk spread across my face.

"You were doing it on purpose?"

I nodded, my smile growing.

"You little brat!" He grinned at me.

I couldn't stop myself from laughing. If nothing else, it broke the tension. He pulled me out of the kitchen and into the hallway, yet still out of view of the customers. Gripping my shirt at my hips, he pressed me against his body. I froze as anticipation tingled in my stomach. He swept his nose across mine, his hot breath on my face. He leaned in closer, grazing his teeth across my bottom lip and sucking it into his mouth. My heart rate picked up, and my breathing quickened. Then he released me causing me to stumble and then he was gone. I smiled to myself as my breathing returned to normal. I brushed my fingers across my swollen lip.

With a giggle, I straightened my clothes and ran a hand through my hair to smooth it out before venturing into the dining room. The guys were just getting ready to head out. Each gave me a quick hug before leaving.

When the time came, I clocked out and slumped into a booth to eat. It had been a long day, and I was looking forward to having dinner with Eli and going home to relax.

Minutes later, Eli slid into the booth next to me. His mouth was already full of pizza. He threw his arm around my shoulders and pulled me closer. I rested my head on his shoulder, relaxing into him. My feet throbbed in my ugly black sneakers. I couldn't wait to yank them off. They yearned to be unrestricted.

"I wish you didn't have to go back to work," I said.

"Me too. I'd love to go home with you, snuggle up on the couch, and watch a movie."

"That sounds heavenly," I said, closing my eyes and imagining sinking into the overstuffed couch that took up most of my living room.

Our boss came over when we had almost polished off all our food. "Eli, is your break almost over? "We need some tables cleared."

Eli shoved the last bit of his pizza in his mouth and jumped up. "Gotta go, babe." He kissed me on my forehead before grabbing his pizza pan and heading off to the kitchen.

I took that as my cue to leave, but before I did, I grabbed a napkin and wrote out a message for Eli to find when he cleared my mess away.

Thanks for cleaning up after me. Can't wait to see you tomorrow!
Love,
Abby xoxo

I loved leaving notes for people to find. I smiled to myself as I scurried out the door before he returned and caught me leaving it. I jumped in my car, still grinning like an idiot.

When I pulled out of the lot and glanced in my rearview mirror, a knot settled in the pit of my stomach. A black SUV fell in line behind me. My arms trembled as I gripped the steering wheel. *Was it happening again?*

I studied the SUV in my rearview mirror. In the dark, it was difficult to tell, but to me it looked different than the other SUV that had followed me. The front was shaped differently, and it was giving me more space. Still, it made me nervous, so I watched it closely as I drove. When it trailed me on the first turn into my neighborhood, I second-guessed where I was headed. *But it didn't look like the same car.* I squinted my eyes. *Was I just being paranoid this time?* Trust my gut. That's what Vince told me. But what was my gut telling me?

I turned again and held my breath, waiting and hoping that the headlights didn't shadow me. Seconds later, they flooded my rearview with light. Goosebumps rose on my arms as I pulled into my driveway. I gripped the steering wheel and squeezed my eyes shut.

"Please keep driving. Please keep driving," I whispered.

I opened my eyes one at a time, fearing the worst. I turned to look around, and when I didn't see headlights anywhere, I let out a huge breath in relief. Grabbing my bag, I opened my door and hopped out. I was almost to the door when I heard footsteps behind me and stopped dead in my tracks. My heart slammed against my chest. *Someone was behind me.*

"Abby?" Casey's voice made me jump.

I whirled around to face him. "You scared the living daylights out of me!" I shrieked, smacking him on the chest. "What the heck are you doing, sneaking up on me like that?"

"I didn't think I . . ." he said, trailing off. "Didn't you see me behind you?"

"What?"

"I waited for you to get off. I wanted to talk to you. Alone. You got in your car so fast, I couldn't get to you before you were already leaving."

I looked around him and saw the black SUV parked in front of my house.

"That's not your car," I said in confusion.

"Oh. Right. Mine's in the shop. That's a rental."

"Have you been following me around?" I asked.

"What?" He stared at me, worry and confusion tugging at his face.

"Someone's been following me. They drive a black SUV," I said, gesturing toward his rental car.

His face twisted. He looked at the SUV and back at me.

I sighed. "I'm sorry. I knew you weren't. I just don't know what's what anymore."

I rubbed my face. I felt ready to cry. Fear and adrenaline were pushing me over the edge. My body couldn't seem to handle it anymore. Not surprising, after all the things I have had to deal with lately. I suppose it caught up with you. A person could only handle so much.

"Whoa, hold on!" Casey stepped forward and pulled my hands away from my face. "Someone's been following you?"

"Yeah, and sending notes and looking at me with creepy ski masks. It's fine. Eli's handling it," I said, trying to brush it off. "I just thought they were following me again when your SUV was behind me. But then I thought it had kept going and I was being paranoid. That's the only reason I got out of the car. So it scared me when you came up behind me, that's all."

"I'm so sorry." He pulled me into a tight hug before he released me again.

"It's fine, really. I'm the one who should be sorry. I'm becoming an emotional, suspicious train wreck."

"Hey, I'm surprised you're getting on so well. Most people would fall to pieces after what you've been through."

"Thanks."

He was sweet to say so, but I didn't feel like it. I felt like I was falling apart. My freak-outs happened too often. First on Bailey, now on Casey. Who would be next?

"So, what did you want to talk to me about?" I asked, changing the subject. Compliments made me uncomfortable.

"Come on," he said. "Let's go sit on the curb."

I followed his lead and sat on the curb next to him. It made me think back to all the times I used to sit on the curb just to be outside.

"What was wrong earlier at the restaurant? Was it the guys?" he asked.

"Oh, don't worry about that. It wasn't anything you or the guys did."

"But you seemed so happy, and when you came back, it was like the spark in you had disappeared." He paused, turning to look up into the sky. "I could see you were trying to put on a brave face after that, but I knew it wasn't real. You weren't happy."

"It was nothing," I said, keeping my eyes on a crack in the pavement while I used a stick to dig out the dirt and muck in between.

"It was something."

I stayed silent.

"Come on, you can tell me anything."

I dropped the stick, looked up, and sighed.

"I used to hope that if you and Eli spent enough time around each other, you guys might wind up being friends. But tonight it became clear that won't ever happen."

"Why?" he asked.

I turned to look at him. "Oh please, you don't like him at all."

"That doesn't mean I wouldn't try to get along."

"I know. And you have been trying. I can see that." I looked away. "Except that time in California."

His eyes flickered a moment, darkening at the mention of California, and then cleared.

"So, why won't it happen?" he asked.

"Because Eli is too stubborn. I tried to get him to come meet the guys. He was completely uninterested." I blew out a breath.

"I see." He remained quiet for a long time. "We shouldn't have come," he said.

"No. I'm glad you guys did. I liked having you there. I don't want you to stay away because of Eli. He doesn't dictate my friends. He just doesn't want to be friends with all of them."

It seemed simple when I laid it all out there like that.

"I don't want to make things difficult for you," he said.

"You aren't. I promise. I just shouldn't have had such high expectations."

"Wanting your boyfriend and friends to get along isn't a high expectation. It's normal."

"Yeah, well it doesn't matter. I just had to accept it today, and it shook me up a little. I'm fine."

He put his arm around my shoulders in a friendly way and squeezed. "I'm glad. I just wish things didn't have to be so complicated."

"Me too."

I jumped when I felt a vibration against my leg. Casey fumbled to pull his phone out of his pocket. He put it to his ear and stood up, moving away from me.

I couldn't hear what he was saying, and I don't know why, but I really wanted to. I watched him talk, the light from the phone illuminating his face. I tried unsuccessfully to read his lips.

Finally, he shoved his phone back into his pocket and ran his hand through his hair. I could see his frustration. He exhaled and strode over to me.

"I've got to go," he said. "I wish I didn't have to, but I do."

"Oh, that's okay." I stood and gave him a quick hug. "I'll see you later."

"Bye."

He got into the horrible SUV and drove away before I went inside.

I hated how skittish I had been at the sight of a black SUV. I felt foolish for getting so bent out of shape about it. I needed to ask Eli what he planned to do. He had assured me he was on top of it. The time had come to put a stop to it.

CHAPTER TWELVE

The doorbell rang the next evening as I headed down from my room to wait for Eli to arrive.

"Hey," I said, throwing myself into his arms. "I missed you."

"Missed you too," he said, lifting me up and stepping through the door. "It's hot out there."

"Sounds like a good reason to spend our day off inside watching movies and eating ice cream." I grinned.

He nuzzled my ear and whispered, "Sounds like a plan, as long as I get to kiss that sweet mouth a few times."

I blushed. "I think that can be arranged."

He set me down, and we went into the living room. I popped in the first movie while Eli made himself comfortable by sprawling out on the entire couch.

"Hey, save some room for me!"

"There's room." He pointed at the floor in front of him. "Right there."

"Oh yeah?"

He nodded, a wicked smile filling his face.

I launched myself on top of him. He flipped onto his back, catching me just before I landed. His fingers dug into my side, making me squirm as he tickled me. Squealing, I tried to attack back but failed miserably. I wiggled back and forth as I struggled to get away. With one last jerk, I flung myself to the floor with a thud. Eli erupted in laughter.

"Oww," I whined.

"I'm so glad you found your spot," he teased.

I glared at him while I rubbed my throbbing hip. "That hurt!"

"Serves ya right for trying to take me on!" He grinned, holding up his flexed bicep.

I ignored him, scooted myself up against the couch, and crossed my arms across my chest.

"Oh, come on," he said. "I was kidding."

I ignored him.

"You're not really mad are you?"

I fought a smile but didn't budge.

His feet dropped to the floor, one on each side of me. He gripped my legs under the knees and lifted me onto the couch as if I weighed nothing. We fell back against the couch, and I was halfway in his lap.

"Better?" he asked.

I looked at him, staring into his bright blue eyes that seemed to search for something in mine.

I popped my finger into my mouth, and his head cocked to one side as he tried to figure out what I was doing. I never sucked on my fingers.

As quickly as I could, I threw my arm toward his head and shoved my wet finger in his ear. Then, as if nothing had happened, I pulled it back and dropped it in my lap.

"Now it is," I said, grinning.

He pushed me off his lap onto the couch next to him. "Eww Abby! Gross."

He made a face as he tried to wipe it out with his hand and shirt, but I was still proud of myself. I had gotten him back my way, and it had taken him by surprise.

I settled into the couch, enjoying my victory. Out of the corner of my eye, I could see a small pout on his face, and I smiled. We were even in my book.

When he decided he wasn't mad about his ear, he put his arm around me, and I leaned against him finding comfort in his strong arms.

It didn't get much better than sitting around with Eli doing nothing.

Halfway through the movie, George wandered in, soda in hand. He settled into the chair, his eyes locked on the TV screen.

"Mind if I watch with you guys?" he asked.

"Uh, no not at all." I stumbled over the words.

George smiled when we made eye contact for a split second. Despite his smile, all I could see when I looked at him was the worry and concern that had spread across his face when he woke me from my nightmare. I still felt so embarrassed.

I turned my attention back to the movie, but I was restless now and couldn't focus. Eli squeezed my hand, and I turned to look at him.

He mouthed, "You okay?"

I nodded.

"I'm going to get a drink," I whispered.

He nodded and released my hand. I slipped off the couch and tried not to block the movie as I left the room. When I reached the kitchen, I rushed to the counter, gripped the edge, and closed my eyes. I took a few deep breaths and tried to clear my mind. The sound of bare feet padding on the tile stole my attention. I tried to hide my dour expression and turned to the fridge without looking to see who had joined me. I hid inside the fridge like I was looking for something.

"Want something?" I asked.

"I don't have to watch the movie with you guys if I make you uncomfortable," George said, leaving the words hanging.

"No," I said much too quickly. "It's fine. I'm just getting a drink." I pulled a water bottle from the fridge and turned to leave the kitchen. I fled like someone had lit a fire under my feet.

Throwing myself down on the couch next to Eli, I sighed and tried to pay attention to the movie.

"What was that about?" Eli asked.

I turned to look into his eyes and considered what I should tell him. The concern grew on his face the longer I debated. I grabbed the remote and paused the movie.

"Come on," I said.

I pulled him by the hand out to the back patio where I hoped we wouldn't be heard.

"I had my nightmare again. I guess I screamed a few times because George woke me up."

"What did you say to him?" he asked, suddenly alert.

"Nothing. I pretended like it was nothing. We never talked about it again. In fact, we haven't even been around each other for more than five minutes since then, so I guess my anxiety got the better of me."

"Why?" he asked.

"I don't want him to ask me about it. I'm so afraid he will."

"He hasn't yet, so he probably won't."

"But what if he does? I have no idea what to tell him. I don't want my mom to know either. I thought for sure he'd tell her, but he hasn't so far."

"Relax. What's the worst that can happen if he does?"

I glared at Eli. "You obviously don't know my mom," I said. "I'll end up in some shrink's office talking about my feelings. I can just imagine it. 'Yes, I have nightmares and they come true.' I would be institutionalized before I could blink!"

"I wouldn't let that happen," he said.

"Oh yeah? What would you do?"

"I don't know, but I'd figure something out. I do have a lot of connections, you know," he boasted. "Stop stressing about it. Okay?"

"Fine. I'll try."

"Good. Besides, even if he asked you, you don't have to be honest," he said.

I made a face but couldn't disagree. "True."

I would try to let it go, but it wouldn't fix how embarrassed I felt. I didn't want George's pity, like I was just some little girl with terrible nightmares.

"While we're out here, I wanted to ask you if there's any progress on stopping the person whose following me."

"I'm working on it," he said.

"Working on it? How? It doesn't look like anything's happening."

Eli stood up and stepped behind me. He rested his hands on my shoulders.

"Relax," he said.

His fingers massaged the bumps and bulges in my shoulders and neck. I closed my eyes, letting his sweet gesture melt away my tension.

Then I sat forward again, pulling away from his touch. I turned my body sideways and craned my neck around to look at him.

"How can I relax? Someone is out there following me, and I don't know why."

A hint of a smile crept up on his face, and I felt my blood boil. Was he laughing at me right now?

"What's so funny?" I asked, glaring at him.

"Nothing," he said, his smile getting bigger. "You're just cute when you're all revved up."

He slipped his hands onto my shoulders and pulled me back against the seat. At first I stayed stiff and didn't let him, but eventually, I gave in. I took a deep breath as he began to rub my neck again.

"I just need to know what's going on," I said.

"I'm not sure yet. I'm still looking into it."

So much for getting reassurance. I sighed.

"It'll be fine. You'll see," he said. He slid his hand down my arm and grasped my hand. "Let's go finish our movie."

I stood and let him drag me inside. George was nowhere in sight when we entered the living room. The movie remained paused in the same place we had left it. I felt bad for abandoning the living room. I was sure George had taken it as a sign we didn't want to watch the movie with him. He had done nothing wrong. This was all because of my irrational worry. *Maybe I'm more like my mom than I thought.*

We spent the rest of the evening lounging like couch potatoes. When it was time for Eli to go, I was sad to see our time end and even more worried about going to sleep. My irrational fear of the nightmare needed to end.

I tossed and turned that night, thinking about George. At one point I grew tired of lying in bed and went to the kitchen for a snack.

I froze at the bottom of the staircase when I heard the soft murmur of the TV. *George.* He was still up. I should have known. I contemplated going back upstairs—I even turned around and went halfway back up—but in the end, I went downstairs anyway.

I grabbed my snack and a glass of milk and sat down in the darkened kitchen. I could hear the voices on the TV over the sound of my chewing. I glanced at the clock. Two-thirty a.m. The voices stopped just as I was wondering when George went to bed.

I paused a moment, listening. Waiting for a single sound. There was nothing. Suddenly, George stumbled into the kitchen in a pair of flannel pajama pants and a black shirt. He pulled his shirt up, exposing his abs as he scratched his belly. I remained motionless, unsure what to say or do. He opened the fridge, grabbed the orange juice, and strolled to the cabinet to get a glass. I could hear the juice sloshing into the glass. He took a quick drink before turning around. As he turned, holding the jug, he made eye contact with me and jumped. He dropped the jug, and juice sprayed all over the kitchen.

He flipped on the light, blinding us both.

"Abby! You scared me!"

"Sorry." I clambered up to help him clean up the mess.

"What are you doing up?" he asked.

"Couldn't sleep."

"I see."

I gathered all the sopping rags and threw them in the laundry room while George wiped everything down with a wet towel. He stood as I came back into the kitchen and tossed the towel in the sink. "Good as new."

I went back to my snack and was surprised when George came and sat next to me.

"Does this have anything to do with your nightmare the other night?" he asked.

I stared down at my snack. I didn't know what to say.

"I assume that's why you were screaming in your sleep," he said.

"Um . . . I guess."

I didn't want to reveal that I was having recurrent nightmares—which I would be plagued with for the rest of my life—but I found I couldn't lie to him. I felt compelled to tell him the truth. *Why?*

"So, what's the dream about?" he asked.

"Uh . . . I don't really want to talk about it," I said, fighting the urge to tell him. *Why did I even want to tell him?*

"Got it. I understand." He stood. "Let me know if you need anything."

He started to leave the room.

"Actually," I said.

He turned to face me. "Yeah?"

"I wanted to thank you for not telling my mom. She worries too much."

He smiled. "No problem. But if this continues, you should tell her."

I nodded. *Not a chance.*

He left the kitchen and disappeared upstairs, leaving me by myself.

All of the sudden, being downstairs alone frightened me. I threw out the rest of my snack and jogged upstairs. My adrenaline kicked in as an irrational part of me worried a boogeyman was waiting in the dark to jump out and grab me.

CHAPTER THIRTEEN

Buzzing broke the silence as I sat engrossed in a book. I snatched my phone off the desk without looking at it.

"Hello?" I said.

"Hey, did Bailey call you?" Eli asked.

"No?" I said. "Why?"

"Oh, you're still home, right?"

"Yes, why? What's going on?"

"Oh, nothing to worry about. At least I don't think so." He seemed to consider this. "Bailey wanted me to meet her at your house. She said she has a surprise for us."

"Oh really? She didn't even call to see if I was home."

"She asked me if you were," he confessed. "It's okay that I told her yes, isn't it?"

"Of course. It's just weird she wouldn't call me first."

"I thought so too, but she seemed really excited. I'll be there in a few minutes."

"Okay!" I hung up the phone and wondered what the surprise could be. Maybe she got a car. That would certainly be something she would want to show us so dramatically. I jogged down the stairs two at a time, hoping to catch a glimpse of Bailey when she arrived. Eli showed up first.

I opened the door before he reached it.

"Hey," he said.

"Hey!" I hugged him as he came in and shut the door. "Do you know when she'll be here?" I asked.

He shook his head. "She said she would text me."

"Oh."

I couldn't sit down, even though Eli did. I stood by the window, peeking out at the street every so often.

"Would you come over here and sit down?" he asked. "You're making me anxious, and I don't even think it's a big deal."

I grinned. "Fine."

He leaned back, put his arm around me, and closed his eyes.

"I could really use a nap."

"Oooh, me too." My eyelids fluttered as I leaned into him. His spiced cologne relaxed me.

"This is nice," he whispered.

"Mmm . . ."

I never heard his phone, but he shifted on the couch, jostling me from my comfy place to pull it from his pocket. He glanced at it.

"She's here."

"I get to see her surprise first!" I squealed and ran to the door, leaving Eli in my dust.

Eli was only a few steps behind me when I froze at the bottom of the steps. I gasped. There it sat. In broad daylight. Darkened windows, all black. The SUV. My breathing grew erratic. I tapped Eli's arm over and over as he thumbed through his phone absently. My voice wouldn't come when I tried to say his name. Bailey was nowhere in sight.

"Eli," I whispered.

"Hold on."

"Eli!" I said, louder this time.

"Just a sec."

"Eli, look!"

"What?" he huffed, glancing up.

I pointed at the SUV, and it sparked a reaction from him I hadn't expected. He took off running. The SUV roared to life and took off, driving away from my house without giving us a glimpse of who was inside. Eli's direction changed in a split second. He raced to his car as I stood still, hesitant to make the wrong move. Would he want me to come with him or stay behind?

"Come on!" Eli said.

"Oh!"

I jumped into gear, jogging over to his car and hopping into the passenger seat. Eli wasted no time, throwing the car into gear before I even shut my door. It slammed shut from the momentum of the car. I gave Eli a sideways glance, and the focus on his face was intimidating. It gave me chills.

He sped through the neighborhood, turning this way and that, every so often catching glimpses of the SUV just before it disappeared from sight again.

I gripped my seatbelt at my neck and held the side of the seat with my other hand. "You're going a bit fast," I said.

"If I don't go this fast we're going to lose them!"

Stress lines pitted his face as he concentrated on the road ahead. Just looking at them made my face hurt. He weaved between two cars, which were probably driving the speed limit, as if they were standing still.

His nerves wreaked havoc on my already withering hope. There was no question now that the SUV had been following me. Part of me wished I had said nothing. We wouldn't be here now if I had just kept my mouth shut. The last thing we needed was another confrontation, but I knew that eventually something would have happened anyway. My stalkers were trying to make a point. I just wished I knew what they wanted.

"We won't catch him if we get pulled over either," I said under my breath.

"Abby relax. We're not getting pulled over, and we've almost caught him. Look." He pointed to the lane next to ours. The SUV was boxed in three cars ahead of us. It was just what we needed to close the gap.

I crossed my arms and leaned back, sucking in a deep breath. I hated this. Moments ticked by. We were only two cars back now. One. Then, as if in the blink of an eye, we pulled in behind them.

I had to give Eli credit—his driving skills proved quite incredible, even if they terrified me.

Eli's face looked tense. His lips tightened with each passing moment. His whole body was rigid with tension. I hated seeing him on edge—and worse, I hated feeling as on edge as he looked.

The SUV took us close to the edge of town, and when they pulled into a parking lot, I sat up tall, watching. This journey was coming to an end. Then I realized we had arrived at a park. Surely no one would come to a park if they were up to something. I relaxed against the seat. Maybe we were blowing this out of proportion. Or maybe the park was a good place to go for cover. It seemed to have an element of innocence that might throw anyone off.

We parked a long distance away from the suspicious SUV and waited. The driver didn't emerge for a good five minutes, as if he was waiting for something or someone. When the door finally popped open, I jumped. The man shut his door, looking around, no doubt searching for us. He seemed satisfied that we had not followed him into the park before he ventured away from his car. He wore a hat, which shielded his face and made it impossible to see him clearly.

"Let's go," Eli whispered.

Apprehensive and unsure, I hesitated several seconds before I followed. My heart raced. No good could come from this, but what else could I do?

The park was swarming with people, and that helped settle my fears somewhat. Surely the presence of so many people would prevent a violent confrontation. But I couldn't dismiss the gnawing suspicion in my gut that something wasn't right.

The squeals of children and the calls of their parents to children who had ventured too far or high on the jungle gym filled the air. I watched a cute little towheaded boy run by us, away from his mother. For a moment, I smiled, remembering the times I had spent with my parents at the park. But now wasn't the time to reminisce, and I shook away the thought. I needed my head in the game.

Eli's hand on my arm snapped me back to reality. He pulled me forward. In the distance, I could see trees in neat lines, evenly spaced apart. My body shuddered. My feet stilled, rooted in place. My breath caught in my chest, and my dream came crashing down on me. Flashes of the attack and surroundings just before took over. Trees. Shimmering sunlight through the trees. *This was it. This was my nightmare.*

"No," I whispered.

"What?" Eli asked.

"No," I said under my breath. My head shook from side to side.

Eli's hands gripped my arms, his fingertips digging into my flesh. "What is it?"

"My dream. The trees . . ." I pointed, hoping he would understand what I was saying.

"I'm right here. Come on, we're losing him." He pulled me along, despite the warnings blaring in my head.

"Eli, no. We can't."

"We have to," he said, pulling me forward.

My feet felt heavy and didn't want to budge, but on we went. As we entered the tree line, I felt a sense of déjà vu taking over. My legs wobbled beneath me. Eli released my hand, oblivious to my unsteady feet as he crept forward. The mystery person had long since vanished into the trees. This was a trap. I knew what we were walking into, but I couldn't do anything to stop it. Eli wouldn't listen. He wouldn't turn back. I wanted to warn Ren, knowing from my dream that he would show up at any moment. But it was too late for that now. My dream was coming true. There was nothing I could do. I closed my eyes and took a deep breath. I needed every ounce of courage I could muster. I needed to be ready to fight. But when the time came, would I fight? Would I be able to pull myself together? That was the whole point of knowing what would take place—in theory, it gave me the upper hand. So far it hadn't proved useful. But I had to try.

I marched on, following Eli. I tried to recall all the little details of the dream. The air around me felt thick with heat when I took another deep breath. I dripped with sweat. With each step, a plume of dust puffed into the air in a dirty haze. I could feel the granules of dirt sticking to me. With the back of my hand, I brushed away the sweat that dripped from my forehead, feeling the grit against my skin.

"Eli, this isn't good," I whispered.

He ignored me.

"Eli, we need to leave."

He waved behind himself at me in a shooing motion and continued on. The trees surrounded us now sprawled out above our heads, letting the sunlight trickle in between the leaves and illuminating the ground in an array of patterns.

Ren stepped into view. He nodded at me. My desperation settled in deeper. I waved frantically for him to go back, but just as Eli had, he waved me off. He stepped next to Eli and marched forward like they knew what they were doing. They couldn't possibly know. *How could they?* They didn't see what I saw. If they had, we wouldn't be here, would we? *Would it even make a difference?*

I panted, trying not to hyperventilate. Tears stung my eyes. I could see the glimmer of metal ahead, and I knew what was coming. The moment I had feared for so long was here. The curiosity I felt about the identity of the attackers was overshadowed by a sense of helplessness. But I had to remember—Eli knew about my dream. I had described it to him the best I could, so he had some idea of what we were walking into. I could only hope he had shared it with Ren. I hated to think Ren might be walking in blind, loyally protecting us as he always did.

I stopped just short of the tree line and braced myself, staring at the spot where I knew one of our assailants would materialize. I clutched my chest in anticipation.

A black shirt came into view. Without hesitation, my eyes flew to his face. Horror washed over me. It was like the wind had been knocked out of me.

"No," I whispered.

Casey's eyes met mine for just a split second. His eyes held something just before he lunged at Eli. *Was worry? Fear? Remorse?*

When the second attacker came into view, I wasn't surprised to see the man who had stepped out of the SUV. I couldn't help but feel like I had seen him in the past. Before I could warn Ren, the man's fist connected with his jaw. Ren fell to the ground in a heap. My heart launched into overdrive. I stepped back. Gravel crunched under my feet. The man's head twisted toward me. I tried to run, but my feet wouldn't respond. I stood frozen as I watched him approach me. His face scrunched into a snarl.

"Please," I begged. "Please . . ."
His fist swung forward.

*   *   *   *

Jolting. Bumping. Clanking. I was being jostled about. My lip throbbed. My head ached. *Where am I?* I squinted, opening my eyes. It was dark, but sunlight poured in through a large opening. The steady rhythm continued to bounce me around. It could only be one thing. A train. *How did I get on a train?*

I sat up despite my body's protest. My head swam as a dizzy spell overcame me. I squeezed my eyes shut, coaxing the lightheadedness to subside.

I heard a shuffling sound and opened my eyes. A metal rod swung at my face.

*   *   *   *

When I woke again, the sounds around me hadn't changed. The train seemed to have gained speed. The bumps were louder. The jostling continued, more forcefully. My stomach lurched.

"Let her go," a man shouted.

Casey?

"Wha . . . How did you get here?"

Eli? What was going on?

"Do you think you're the only one who can jump on a train?" Casey spat.

"Casey?" I mumbled.

The blood in my mouth garbled my voice. I tried to open my eyes, but only one would open. Instinctively, my hand reached for my eye. I winced when my fingertips brushed it. It was swollen shut and hurt something awful. Then I remembered the metal pole. *Who hit me? Was there someone else here?* None of this made sense. *What was going on?*

The two of them stood face to face, fists clenched at their sides.

"You shouldn't be here!" Eli growled.

"Eli?" The hoarseness of my voice made me croak, but no one paid attention to me.

"None of us should be here. What are you doing? Why would you do this to her? You can't possibly think you'll get away with this."

"Watch me!" Eli shouted.

Casey snapped and rushed forward, crashing into Eli.

"Stop," I tried to shout, but nothing came out. My words were stuck in my throat.

Eli and Casey toppled back into the metal wall of the cargo car, shaking the whole thing. They scrambled away from each other as they made their way to their feet. The rocking car made it difficult for both of them to gain an advantage. I watched them bob back and forth, stumbling.

"Don't," Eli warned. Casey moved forward, ignoring Eli, who smirked. "Stupid move."

Casey dropped to his knees, holding his head.

"Ahh!" He grunted in agony.

"I warned you," Eli snarled.

"Stop," Casey wailed, holding his head to the floor. "Stop! Please stop!"

"Eli?" My voice gained volume, snapping Eli's attention to me.

"Well, well, well, she wakes," he said, his voice full of venom.

"What's going on?" I asked. My voice broke so many times I wasn't sure he understood me. I sat upright, praying I would stay that way, holding my throbbing head in my hands.

"Oh, you'd like to know what's going on?" he asked.

Out of the corner of my eye, I saw that Casey had recovered. I still didn't know who the enemy was. No one else was here. Clearly, it was one of them. I just couldn't wrap my head around what was going on. These were two of the most trustworthy people in my life, yet one of them was hurting me. *Why?*

"Well, let's see," Eli said. "Today is the day you die."

"What?" Nausea overtook me. My head spun.

"Oh, don't start with me."

"Why are you doing this?" I asked, panic taking over.

"Are you honestly that stupid? You don't have a clue, do you?"

I stared at him.

"You got my mother killed. If it weren't for you, she would still be here. You'll pay for that."

"What? I thought you didn't think that anymore. I thought you loved me."

He laughed. "Oh please. Any feelings I had for you died the day my mother did. I'm surprised you bought my little act. I certainly wasn't very good at it. And your neediness all the time. Gag. It made me sick." He kicked my foot. "Get up."

"I-I-I don't think I can," I stammered.

Eli turned to Casey, who was pulling himself to a standing position.

"I wouldn't try anything," Eli said.

He bent down, grabbing me under the arms and hoisting me up. He twisted my arm behind my back. I whimpered as pain sliced through my shoulder.

"Oh, I'm sorry. Does this hurt?" he asked, twisting harder. Pain ripped through my whole arm until I felt a snap. "Oops, I think I broke it."

I yelped as he continued to put pressure on it.

"Please," I begged. "Please, stop."

Tears stung my eyes. He pushed me forward, but Casey stepped into our path.

"Move," Eli said through gritted teeth.

Casey raised his hands in front of his body. Seconds before we collided with him, he yelled, "Abby, duck!"

As quickly as my body would allow, I ducked out of the way. My reflexes were off, and I wasn't quick enough. Eli threw me sideways, and I landed on my stomach at the opening of the train car. My stomach lurched, and I fought to keep myself from vomiting. My head hung out of the doorway. My fingers grazed the edge of the car, watching the tracks below me race by in a blur. The train was really moving. It made me dizzy. I pushed myself away from the opening and sat back on my heels. Then I toppled over from the momentum. The dizzy spell wouldn't let up.

What had Casey done? Eli had been thrown into the wall, and he wasn't moving.

Casey scurried over to me. "Are you okay?"

"No, I'm not," I said, tears streaming down my face.

Nothing about this was okay. I was fighting for my life against my boyfriend, who I had thought loved me. My head spun, haze obscured my vision, and my arm throbbed. I was sure it was broken. *How on earth could I be okay?*

Movement behind Casey caught my attention. Casey dropped to his knees. His face contorted in pain. I wanted to reach out and soothe his pain, but I couldn't. There was nothing I could do. Or was there?

I took a deep breath and willed my head to stop spinning. Gathering myself in a squatting position, I wobbled back and forth, hiding behind Casey's large frame. When Eli got closer, I leaped out from behind Casey and kicked Eli right where it counted. He dropped to the floor, clutching his groin and swearing. I stumbled unsteadily and fell to my knees. Pain sliced through my arm, and I pulled it against myself. I took a deep breath, closing my eyes and breathing through the pain. Eli was still on the ground, so I took the opportunity to crawl with one hand back to Casey, not trusting my legs to work properly beneath me. Casey recovered more quickly this time, but I noticed blood dripping from his ears.

"Thanks," he grunted.

Just as Casey recovered the last of his bearings, Eli grabbed me from behind. I flailed, but it was no use. One hard shove, and I was in free fall. Time seemed to stand still as I plummeted helplessly through the air, past the doorway, and off the train. The gravel below me looked harsh and unforgiving. I shrieked and waved my good arm, as if by some miracle I could slow myself down. Then, just before I hit the ground, a gust of wind lifted me. It felt as if arms were wrapped around me, catching me from my fall and seeming to soften my landing. I slid across the gravel, scraping my unhurt arm and hip. I lay there, holding my broken arm and staring at the sun. The earth felt like it was spinning. I shuddered. I wasn't dead. That was something.

CHAPTER FOURTEEN

Tears filled my eyes. I ignored the tingle, letting the tears slip down my swollen cheeks. I shook from head to toe as fear and adrenaline took hold of me. I had no idea where I was, and I doubted I could trust my legs to carry me far. I licked my lips, feeling the sting of a cut and tasting the familiar metallic zing of blood. I lay staring up at the sky, contemplating where I had gone wrong. What had I done to end up like this?

Moments later, I heard Casey's voice not far from me. I turned toward him trying to see where his voice came from. My head spun, clouding my vision. I closed my eyes and willed it to stop.

"Abby?" Casey's shouts came in panicked bursts, some louder than others. "Abby?"

"Over here," I howled as loud as my dry throat would allow. "I'm here! Casey."

Gravel sprayed across my body as he skidded to a stop next to me.

"Oh my god." His voice came out just above a whisper. "I never thought he'd do it. Are you okay? Can you move?"

I tried to take stock of my injuries. My head throbbed, my arm ached, my eye wouldn't open, and I wasn't sure I could stand on my legs. My boyfriend—*ex-boyfriend*—had just thrown me off a speeding train. Despite the pain, I couldn't help but feel like I should be more injured after my fall. *How was that even possible?* I thought of the gust of wind I had felt just before I landed but shook it off.

I nodded to Casey. "I'm okay," I said. Carefully, he brushed a tear from my cheek. I turned away and tried to collect myself.

"No, you aren't."

He took hold of my chin, turning my head to face him. His lips crushed down on mine so forcefully it took me by surprise. After a moment, I kissed him back without reserve, taking in the comfort he offered. He pulled away and looked me in the eyes. This time, he lowered himself slowly, giving me plenty of time to turn away, but I didn't. Instead, I held his gaze, inviting him to continue. His lips met mine. Then again. He deepened the kiss as I reciprocated. His tongue swept across my lips, and I parted them, letting him explore. He cradled my face. Then he pulled away and rested his cheek on mine, his breathing came in breathy puffs.

"I'm sorry," he whispered. "I shouldn't have done that."

Before I could respond, he stood and pulled his cell phone from his pocket. He hit a few buttons and held the phone to his ear. He paced back and forth next to me. A wave of dizziness hit me, and I closed my eyes.

"We're off." He paused. "The jerk threw her off. Yeah. She's banged up, but I think she's okay."

I sighed.

His jaw clenched, and he seemed frustrated. "Just GPS my phone, and text me how long it will take you to get here. Bye."

He tossed his phone on the ground next to me and sat down, placing my head in his lap. Gently, he coaxed my hair away from my face without touching any of my injuries. I would hate to see what I looked like right now. I cringed just thinking about it.

"What did he do to you?" Casey whispered to himself. Sadness was etched on his face.

His phone buzzed in the gravel. He glanced at the screen before he stood, brushing the dirt from his hands. Moments later, he shoved the phone back in his pocket.

"There's a road that way." He pointed to his right. "They'll pick us up there."

I didn't have to ask whom. Of course our team would be there to pick us up. But how did they know we would need to be picked up when Casey called? He hadn't explained it in so many words.

The next thing I knew, Casey bent down, sliding one arm under my neck and the other under my knees. He lifted me up and walked toward the road.

"Whoa, you don't have to carry me," I protested, almost immediately regretting it when my head began to reel.

"Hush, I'm carrying you."

I didn't argue again. Chances are I wouldn't have gotten far on my own anyway. Instead, I nestled my head into his shoulder. He walked slowly on the uneven ground.

"Your gift. What does it do?" I asked.

"What?"

"Your gift. I felt it, but I'm not sure what it was."

"You're asking about that now? We have to get you to the hospital."

"We're going. Tell me," I said.

"You need to rest."

"Please?"

"You're insane." His green eyes focused on the path ahead. "We're almost there. I think I can see the black pavement."

"You didn't answer me," I said.

"You're relentless." He sighed. "Fine. My gift is air manipulation."

"Air manipulation."

"Yeah, I can pretty much make it do what I want. Throw someone back, push someone forward, cushion your fall . . ." He trailed off as if he were embarrassed.

"You broke my fall," I said, realizing that the gust of wind I had felt was Casey protecting me like he had wrapped his arms around me himself.

He gritted his teeth, nodding, but wouldn't make eye contact with me.

Letting my capable eye close, I breathed him in. I don't know if it was the adrenaline or the fear, but I was overcome with a deep sense of exhaustion. I felt myself slipping away. The movement of his steady gait lulled me, rocking me to sleep.

"Thank you," I whispered.

"Of course. I'd do anything for you."

I couldn't be certain if I dreamed his words or if they were real. The next thing I knew, he was shifting me around as he laid me down in the back seat of the car.

Voices surrounded me.

"Oh my god. Are you sure she's okay?"

"I can't even look at her."

"That bastard."

Someone's hand thumped against the roof of the car, causing me to jump. I opened my eye. Casey looked down at me, his worried expression twisting my stomach.

"Shh," Casey said amid the sea of voices around me.

This wasn't Casey's car. I knew that just by looking at the seats. I had been in his car countless times. His car even smelled like him, but this one didn't. Not even a little bit. I lifted myself up to see who was driving. Brad stood beside the driver's seat. My head swam. I groaned.

Casey leaned toward me. "Just relax. We'll get you there. Don't worry. Lay back and rest."

Brad jumped behind the wheel, and all the doors closed, but nobody else got in. *Where did everyone go?*

The car moved forward and gained speed.

"Where's Casey?" I mumbled.

"Don't worry. He'll meet us at the hospital. He had something to do first."

I wondered what could pull him away at that moment when all I wanted was him to be at my side. He had to know that.

It felt like we drove for a long time, longer than I expected, and when we got to the hospital, Brad said we had to wait a few more minutes before going in.

"Casey's running late," Brad said.

I didn't understand why we had to wait for Casey. My headache didn't help. I lay back against the seat and closed my uninjured eye.

When the car door opened a short time later, I was relieved to see Casey. Blood trickled down his face from a cut on his forehead. He held his right arm close to his body.

"What happened?" I shot up, forgetting how badly I was injured.

Realizing what I had done before even I did, Casey rushed forward and braced me when the dizziness threatened to overtake me.

I groaned, holding my head.

"Come on. I got you a wheelchair."

Brad came around the car, and between the two of them they helped me into the wheelchair. Brad squatted in front of me.

"You and Casey were in a car accident. The tire blew and he lost control. He hit a tree. Okay?" he whispered.

I nodded. Our cover. This was our story. I hadn't even thought about what we would tell people. Obviously, the truth was out. The events of today would be brushed off as nothing more than a bad car accident. It disheartened me, but I was relieved they had thought of something. The truth seemed unbearable. To have to tell people, including my parents, that my ex-boyfriend had betrayed me and done the unthinkable. Nobody would ever understand the position I was in with the Protectors, even if they believed me. It wouldn't be surprising if they thought I was crazy or hit my head too hard or something. It helped some that the Protectors would hold Eli accountable.

The minute they pushed me through the doors, I was swept away by a nurse. Casey was taken in another direction. I wished he had come with me. I hated the thought of facing my injuries alone.

First, the nurse took me for a CT scan. They made me change into an ugly, open-backed gown, which was easier said than done. Honestly, the nurse did most of the work. Then I had to hold still, which was easier than I expected. After all, moving hurt. I stayed as still as a statue while my mind flooded with questions.

I hoped that Brad or one of the others had at least called my mom.

She would be worried sick, and I would bet my dad would be on the next flight out. Maybe it was a good thing I was alone for the tests. They would probably be the last alone time I had for a while. I doubted my mom would let me out of her sight after my . . . uh . . . car accident.

Thirty minutes later, they had me in another room with my arm held away from my body. I winced each time they made me reposition it. Pain radiated through my arm. I yelped when the nurse lifted it from the table and placed it back into my lap.

"I'll take you to your room now," she said as she wheeled me away from the x-ray room.

I exhaled in relief. I couldn't wait to lay down in a bed. The dizziness subsided some, and I was able to stand and climb into the bed with little help. The nurse draped a heated blanket over my legs, and it felt like heaven. My body relaxed into the bed. My arm even seemed to throb less.

"Can I get you anything else?" She rested her hands on the footboard.

"Some water?" I asked.

"You got it. Be right back."

She returned moments later with a small foam cup and a little pitcher filled with ice water. She set them both on the wheeled table and positioned them within reach of my good arm.

"Here's some pain medicine too," she said, placing a small cup on the rolling cart.

"Thank you."

"We have to wait a few more minutes for the results of your tests, but the doctor will be in with them shortly. Press this button if you need anything, okay?" She pointed to a small button with a plus sign on it. I nodded, and she left the room.

Lying back against the pillow, I let the icy water slip down into all the cracked and dry places in my throat, soothing the parched ache. Then I tossed the pills in my mouth and swallowed them with one gulp of water.

My eyes hurt—one, I assumed, from being struck and the other from trying to stay open. I relented and let them both rest.

CHAPTER FIFTEEN

I didn't know how much time had passed when I woke to a soft brushing on my hand. I blinked back the exhaustion from my eyes and was relieved that my hurt eye opened a tiny slit. The shock of the bright light stung, causing it to water. My mom sat at the side of my hospital bed.

Tears streaked her face. Her nose and eyes were rosy, and I wondered how long she had been sitting there.

"Oh baby, are you okay?" she asked. Her voice trembled. She reached out to caress my cheek. Her fingers barely missed the swollen mound that had engulfed my eye.

"I'm fine, Mom," I croaked.

Quickly, I took a drink to expel the hoarseness.

"Has the doctor come in yet?" I asked.

"Nope, I haven't," a masculine voice said from the doorway. A man with a bright white smile stepped into the room carrying an array of x-ray films. "Hi. I'm Dr. Warren."

I watched him closely as he walked in. He appeared to be my mom's age. He studied the films, never the wiser to my intense scrutiny of his every move. In one swift maneuver, he slipped the films into the lighted board on the wall and flicked it on. Each of the images illuminated for us to see. He pointed to the images of my head.

"These show a mild concussion, though I don't think you have anything to worry about. However, if you show a change for the worse, let us know right away. As for the arm?" He moved to the next image and pointed. Even from where I sat on the bed, I could see where it was broken. "The ulna bone is broken. We'll need to set it and cast it. The cast will stay on for about four weeks. If at the end of that time it hasn't healed properly, you may need surgery to correct it. Any questions?" he asked, looking at both of us.

I shook my head and glanced at my mom.

"When can she come home?" she asked without skipping a beat.

"We're going to keep an eye on her overnight just to be on the safe side, but I'm confident she'll be able to head home tomorrow."

"Okay," she said, exhaling.

"I'll take you to get that arm fixed. Are you ready?" he asked.

"Do you want me to go with you?" Mom asked.

I shook my head. "I'll be all right. Why don't you call Dad?" I suggested, hoping to get some space from her panic.

"Good idea. If you change your mind, send someone to get me. I'll be right here."

"Thanks, Mom."

I knew I wouldn't change my mind. Just staring into her anxious face sent my nerves on a wild roller coaster. I had enough anxiety for the day.

I turned to the doctor, nodding, and off we went.

"So, a car accident, huh?" he asked.

"Yeah."

"Were you the passenger?"

"Yeah."

"Looks like you got lucky."

"I did."

I thought back to the deranged look on Eli's face just before he threw me off the train. A shiver ran down my body, and a lump lodged in my throat.

"Are you okay?" the doctor asked.

"Huh?"

I realized he had stopped. He looked at me with a concerned expression. *Never a good thing when a doctor looks at you like that.*

"Oh, yeah. I'm fine."

My cheeks warmed. I had to pull myself together. I couldn't keep checking out like that if I didn't want people to worry about me. Especially while on concussion watch. He seemed hesitant to believe me but pushed me along again anyway.

He wheeled me into a room not unlike the one I had the x-ray taken in. I could see an x-ray table to the side. A cheery looking man smiled at us as we entered.

"Welcome to my laboratory!" He chuckled as if he were an evil villain.

Dr. Warren leaned over and whispered in my ear. "Trust me, you're in good hands. I promise." He handed the man my films. "Broken arm, Jeremy."

"I'll have her fixed up in no time," he said, grinning at Dr. Warren.

Dr. Warren turned and shot me one last wave before he left me alone with Jeremy. I gave Jeremy a long look while his back was turned so he could examine my x-rays. His maroon scrubs fit him loosely, despite how overweight he was.

He turned to look at me as he leaned back on the counter. I felt myself squirm under his close appraisal. With my countless injuries and the made-up story, I didn't like being put in the spotlight.

"So, what happened to you?" he asked.

"Car accident."

"Ouch! What did you hit?"

"My friend hit a tree. I was the passenger. He blew a tire."

Jeremy nodded. "Happens a lot. So should we get that arm taken care of?"

I nodded but regretted it when my head spun.

"First, I'll give you a shot to numb your arm. That way it won't hurt when I set it. You shouldn't feel a thing past the needle poke."

I hated needles and just thinking of getting a shot sent my stomach flopping. I closed my eyes and gritted my teeth when he held my arm up. It hurt like heck, but it was over quickly, and soon the pain in my arm subsided.

Next, Jeremy handed me a board of colors. "Pick one," he said.

I looked it over, and only one stood out. I pointed to it.

"Good choice."

Before my arm completely numbed, he wrapped it. The white, gauzy material was wet and warm. What I could feel felt good. I relaxed into the wheelchair. The hard part was over, I told myself.

It took another thirty minutes to finish up. Once the cast was on and my arm set, he took another x-ray to be sure it was positioned properly. I hoped so because I just wanted to go lie down. I breathed a sigh of relief when he gave me a double thumbs up.

By the time we finished and a nurse wheeled me back to my room, I could tell the sun had set.

My mom's face had returned to its normal color, and her worry seemed to dissipate the minute the nurse brought me into the room.

"Purple, huh?" She smirked.

I glanced down at the purple cast around my arm. "Yep."

"Well, all right then."

The nurse took my vitals again and left us alone.

"Okay kiddo, I'm going to get us dinner from wherever you want. Name the place."

"Mmm! How about a good burger? I don't care where from."

"You've got it. I'll be back in a little bit. Need anything else?" she asked in the doorway.

I almost shook my head but changed my mind. "A chocolate shake. A big one." A chocolate sugar rush was exactly what I needed to help me through this . . . well, whatever this was.

Mom grinned and walked out the door.

Leaning against the pillow, I sighed. I saw a package of wet wipes on the rolling table and used them to clean up my face. The wipes came off a burnt red color around my mouth, where my cut was. *Geez, couldn't someone have told me I was still covered in blood?*

Now that I was alone, questions ran through my mind. Eli had turned on me. How had I not seen the signs? Casey had known all along. He had tried to warn me, but I had ignored him. I was even mad at him for it. And yet, he still came back and saved me. How had he known? I needed to talk to him. *Where was he?*

"Abby?" a male voice startled me from the doorway.

My head whipped up. Ren stood there, looking sheepish. His lip was swollen but clean, and a bruise had formed on his cheekbone. Fear swept through my body. Ren had been there. I had forgotten he had been there. Ren was like family to Eli. He had to have been in on it. I sat up straighter, scooting away from the door and bringing my casted arm against my body.

Ren raised his hands in the air in surrender. "Abby, I'm not going to hurt you. I don't blame you for thinking that, though." His gaze dropped to the floor, defeated.

"What are you doing here?" I demanded.

"I wanted you to know I had nothing to do with what Eli did. I had no idea what he had planned."

"Why were you there?"

"That's a good question. One I don't have the answer to. Only Eli knows why he wanted me there to see it and to be ambushed with you."

I turned away to look out the window, feeling the familiar sting of oncoming tears. He made his way into the room and faced me in front of the window.

"I would never hurt you. He had us all fooled," he whispered. "You may not believe me, and that's okay. But I had to come see how you were."

"I'm fine. No thanks to you," I spat. Tears stung my eyes.

"You're right," he said.

I sniffled, trying to stifle the emotions flooding me.

"What the hell was that, anyway? Why was he trying to—" My throat hitched. I cleared it and began again. "Why was he trying to . . . kill me?"

He shook his head. He didn't have an answer. I might never know what had come over Eli, but I knew one thing for certain: I never wanted to see Eli again.

Ren looked me in the eyes. I could see they were clouded with worry and fear.

"Does Vince know?" I asked.

He nodded. "He took off to find him."

"Abby?"

I turned toward the familiar voice, relief filling me. There were stitches in Casey's head, and a sling held his arm close to his body.

"Hey," I said, smiling. "I was beginning to wonder if you went home."

"And leave you here? Not a chance."

Ren met him on his way in. He gripped Casey's shoulder. "Thank you for saving her when I couldn't."

Casey nodded.

"Bye Abby. Please remember, if you need anything I'm here for you, always."

He walked out of the room and didn't look back. Sadness washed over me. Eli hadn't just tried to kill me. He had torn up what was left of his family. Ren and Vince would never be the same. It wasn't the way Protectors behaved, and it wasn't the way Eli had been raised. Vince was a good man and an amazing Protector, and Ren was too. It was why they had been friends for so long. My heart ached for them. They had lost both Elizabeth and Eli.

Casey scooped up my hand in his.

"I thought I was going to lose you today," he said.

"You came for me."

"Of course I did."

"But how did you know?" I asked.

He looked down at our intertwined hands. "I didn't. Not until it was already happening."

This confused me even more. "If you didn't know, why were you there?"

His eyes focused on mine. "Eli was our assignment."

"What?" I asked. This was not what I had expected.

"After Elizabeth died, Edward got word that Eli started running with a nasty crowd that's been on our radar for years. These people . . . they're bad. At first, he thought Eli was just trying to find Elizabeth's killer, but when it continued after Ian . . . was taken care of, Edward knew there was more to it. So he put us on the case. We've been tracking him everywhere. Up until today, we didn't know quite what he had planned, but we had our suspicions. For starters, the man he had following you."

"Eli sent the stalker?" I asked.

He nodded.

It all made sense now. Eli never called the day I showed up at his house because he already knew what was going on. He must have rushed home when he got worried his dad might get too involved.

"Why didn't you tell me?" I asked, wanting to be mad that he had kept this from me.

"We couldn't. Edward didn't want you to know. He said it might compromise the investigation."

"You tried to warn me, though," I said, remembering that day on the beach. I had been furious with him.

"I got in a lot of trouble for that."

"And I was so horrible to you." I felt ashamed. "I'm sorry."

"You didn't know." He shrugged. "I just wish I would have known everything sooner. You wouldn't be here in this condition. I don't know how we missed it. We should have figured out who he was after."

"He put on a good act."

He nodded. "Unfortunately so."

I hadn't known, but I still shouldn't have been so rude. I felt terrible.

"I'm so glad you're here," I said.

His presence soothed me. I knew with no uncertainty that he would do everything he could to keep me safe. He already had. Of course, it didn't hurt that he was also delicious eye candy.

"I wouldn't be anywhere else," he said.

"Did the others go home?" I asked.

"Ah, no. They dropped me off and went back to get my car," he said.

"Your car?"

"Yeah. It was sort of . . . wrapped around a tree."

"What?" I shrieked.

"Shh! It had to be believable," he whispered.

"But it's your car!"

"I'll get it fixed, or if it's too bad, I'll get a new one. It's not a big deal."

I thought about how long I had saved up to get my car, and I knew if anything happened to it I would be heartbroken.

"I'm sorry."

It was my fault that his car was now in need of repairs that would cost who-knows-how-much.

"Don't be." He smiled, lifting my chin up.

A thought struck me. I couldn't remember the last time I had my phone.

"Do you know where my phone is?" I asked.

Casey reached into his pocket and slipped out my little pink phone. "I'm sorry it's cracked. Eli threw it out before he got on the train."

I picked it up and inspected the damage. It was cracked, but it still worked.

I had a few missed calls from my mom, but nothing other than that. I thought of Bailey and wondered what had happened to her. Eli told me she had a surprise for us. Maybe that was fake, too.

"All right. A chocolate shake, cheeseburger, and fries coming right up," my mom said, bursting into the room.

Casey dropped his hand back to his side and turned to face her like he had been caught.

"I know you didn't mention fries," she said, looking up from the bag and catching sight of Casey. She set the food down and looked him over. "I take it you were the driver," she said, her voice bordering on contentious. I reached for his hand again.

"Yeah. I'm so sorry, Mrs. Martin. My tire blew. I lost control and hit a tree."

She looked him over again. Then her eyes fell to his hand in mine. He pulled away, but I grabbed tighter.

"Well, it's just good that you're both okay."

I sighed, letting the breath I had been holding escape. I hoped everything would be fine between them, and I couldn't be more relieved she wasn't being harsher.

My mom handed me the chocolate shake and pushed the table cart so it hovered over my legs. She laid out my burger and fries in front of me.

"Want some?" I asked Casey.

He hesitated.

"Go ahead. It's more than I can eat," I said, nudging my fries toward him.

He snatched a handful and crammed them into his mouth.

I giggled. "Hungry?"

"Guess so," he said. "Didn't feel it until I smelled your food." He stood up and shoved his hands in his pockets. "I'm going to go down to the cafeteria to get something to eat. I'll be back in a bit, okay?"

"M'kay," I mumbled through the food in my mouth.

My mom watched him as he shuffled out of the room and wasted no time once he was out of earshot. "So, Casey huh?"

"Yep," I said. I grinned at her when she waited for me to explain.

"That's it? That's all I get?"

"What do you want?"

She clutched her chest dramatically. "I'm insulted! I saw you two holding hands. Now dish!"

My mouth went dry. The memory of Eli on the train came flooding back. I tried my best to push it away and keep it at bay, but it was no use. When I thought of him, fear threatened to overwhelm me. Tears brimmed in my eyes, but I refused to let them fall. I flashed back to the look on his face—the sheer hatred on his features. Swallowing hard, I grabbed the milkshake and shoved the straw into my mouth.

"Eli and I broke up," I said.

"Oh honey, I'm sorry."

I shrugged, trying to look nonchalant. I glanced away as emotion swept over me. The familiar sting in my eyes.

"That explains the milkshake," she said.

Despite my unstable emotions, I couldn't help the grin that spread across my face.

"Yeah, I guess."

"Can't say I didn't see it coming."

I rolled my eyes. She had thought just because I hung out with Casey, I was drifting away from Eli. Maybe there had been truth to that.

We let the silence settle over us while we finished eating. When she crinkled up her garbage, she said, "Do you want me to stay with you tonight?"

"No, I'll be fine. Go home and sleep. George will miss you." I grinned. "Where is he, anyway?"

"Oh, he rushed here as soon as he got my message. You were out getting your cast. I told him everything was fine and sent him back to work. He's got a lot going on there right now. I didn't figure he needed to be here."

I was grateful she hadn't had him stay.

Casey returned, looking much better than when he first came in. The color had returned to his face, and some of his grimace had disappeared.

"Well, I'm going to take off then," she said when he entered. "Do you need anything before I go?"

I shook my head. "Thanks."

She leaned over me, placing her hand on the top of my head. She kissed my forehead like she used to when I was little and clicked her tongue as she looked at my face.

"You should put some ice on your eye. I'll tell the nurse to bring you some on my way out," she said. "See ya later, Casey."

She gazed at him a little longer than I would have expected, and I wondered what she was thinking. She had seemed to accept the accident, yet she still acted reserved toward him. I guess I couldn't blame her, but I hated that she would never know him for the true hero he was.

When she left, I turned to Casey. He made himself comfortable in the chair next to my bed. We were alone, and my thoughts drifted back to his kiss. I had refused to acknowledge our growing closeness because of Eli. It wasn't until his lips touched mine in that intense moment that I realized how strongly I felt for him and how badly I wanted to kiss him again.

I had never craved a kiss so much, not even from Eli, and that intrigued me. Maybe it was just the leftover adrenaline seeking release.

While Casey stared at the doorway, I studied him, letting my eyes get to know every dimple and scar on his face, looking at him like I would a boyfriend. He fidgeted back and forth, his back pressing into one side of the chair and then the other. I grinned as I watched him. He looked at each side of the chair, pulled the release lever, and the footrest sprang free. He leaned back, his feet lifted in the air. He fidgeted again, then stilled and closed his eyes. Then he sat upright, dropping the footrest back down.

"Yep, I can work with that," he said with a grin.

"What?" I asked in amusement.

"The chair," he said as if I should have already guessed. Then he looked confused. "You didn't think I was going to leave, did you?"

I shrugged.

He leaned forward, resting his elbows on the bed. "I'm not leaving your side."

The serious look on his face was both endearing and a little worrisome. I had briefly wondered if Eli might return. Casey seemed concerned that it was a real possibility, but I hoped he was gone for good. I laid my head on my pillow and stared off at nothing.

"What will the elders do?" I asked.

Casey looked away. "I don't know." He reached over me to lift my cast off the bed. "How long do you have to wear this thing?" He set it back down and stared at it with total disgust, like leeches were latched to my arm.

"Six to eight weeks," I said, frowning. "But I can still go swimming. They gave me one that can get wet."

"Really? That's awesome. We'll have to test it out. I bet it sinks."

I laughed. "I hope not!"

He chuckled.

I was in mid-laugh when I heard Bailey's timid voice. "Abby?"

My head shot up. "Bailey? What are you doing here?"

"Ren called me." Her eyes were red, and she entered the room as if she wasn't sure if she should. Nothing about this seemed like Bailey.

"What's wrong?" I asked.

"You tell me! You're the one in the hospital. I've been so worried all night! I came straight here when I got off work."

"Ren got you worked up for nothing. I'm fine." I lifted my casted arm. "This is the only lasting problem."

"What happened?" she asked.

"Eli went psycho. He had some guy following me around to scare me. Then he acted like we were going to investigate it, but it was all a ploy to get me alone. He attacked me and dragged me onto a train. Luckily Casey was there and intervened. Eli still managed to throw me off the train though."

Her eyes widened. "He threw you off a train?"

"Shh. Yes. Everyone else thinks we were in a car accident," I said, motioning to Casey.

"So this is the Casey I've heard so much about," she said. She reached out to shake his hand.

I giggled to myself. *Leave it to Bailey to make me smile in such a terrible situation.*

"It appears I owe you some thanks for saving my best friend here."

"I would do it again in a heartbeat," he said, looking at me.

I blushed.

"Thank you for coming, Bailey. It means a lot that you're here."

"Of course I'd be here." She reached over and grabbed my cast, lifting it up and inspecting it. "I can't believe he did this."

"Me either." Tears threatened my eyelashes, and I blinked them back.

We'd both dated Eli. Neither of us would have expected it out of him. It hurt.

"I'm just glad you're okay."

"Me too," Casey agreed.

"Oh, Bailey what was your surprise?" I asked.

"My what?" she asked, looking bewildered.

"Your surprise. Right before everything went down, Eli called me and told me you had a surprise for us and were meeting us at my house."

Her forehead crinkled, and her head cocked to the side. "I haven't talked to Eli in weeks."

Of course. Then everything clicked into place. There was never a surprise. It was all an act, part of the whole plan. The text he got was from the guy who had been following me.

"It was all part of his plan," I whispered. "Ugh! I'm not wasting another minute talking about that scum!"

Bailey pulled out her phone. "It's almost 10:30. I've got to get home. I have to open tomorrow."

She leaned down to hug me, raised her eyebrows, and mouthed, "He's hot." I grinned and hugged her.

"Call or text me if you need anything. Got it?" she asked, looking at me pointedly.

"I will. Thanks, Bailey."

She hurried out of the room, leaving Casey and me alone again. I looked down at my fingers.

"So, about that kiss," I said. I had planned to be more subtle about broaching the subject, but my anticipation got the better of me.

"Abby, wait."

"No, I—"

"Don't worry about it. I let my emotions take over, and I shouldn't have," he said, cutting me off. "I just want you to get better. I don't want to complicate things for you more than they already are. Just forget it happened."

I crossed my arms, pouting. "Well, that's too bad. I've been dying for another one." I couldn't believe I had said it out loud even if it was how I felt. I chalked it up to my bold new persona, or maybe it was just the intense desire to kiss him again. Either way, it was out, and there was no taking it back. Not that I would want to.

My stomach flopped.

In one swift move, Casey stood just enough to lean over and press his lips to mine. I could feel my cut pulling as I drew him in closer. His hands slid into my hair on both sides of my head. He held me there, kissing me tenderly. There was so much emotion behind it—desire, hope, and relief.

Moments later, someone cleared their throat from the doorway. Casey stumbled back and fell into the chair again. I grinned, blushing that we had been caught.

"Ah, sorry to interrupt. I have to get her vitals," the nurse said.

She pulled her cart into the room and slid the blood pressure cuff onto my arm. Then she handed me an ice pack. "For your eye," she said.

A few minutes later after asking me about my pain, checking my blood pressure, looking at my eyes, and taking my temperature, she left.

"Well, that was awkward," Casey said after she left the room again.

"Ah, yeah." I giggled.

He scooted his chair closer to the bed and rested his hand on the bed next to mine. It was an invitation. He wasn't going to push me. He would give me control of how far I took things. I appreciated his thoughtfulness, but I decided right then that my love for Eli had ended the moment he threw me off a moving train. As much as I had tried to ignore it, there had been a barrier between us ever since he had come back to me after his mother died. I was more than ready to pursue whatever Casey and I had. I wouldn't wait another minute. I reached over and put my hand on top of his. He tried to hide it, but a grin touched the corners of his mouth. I relaxed, closing my eyes and pretending not to see it. Eventually, I drifted off to sleep.

CHAPTER SIXTEEN

Casey spent the night at my bedside in the recliner. I knew it couldn't be comfortable. His presence was the only reason I slept at all between nurse visits. Without him, I wouldn't have been able to shake the nagging fear that Eli or one of his helpers would come back to finish what they started. My mom would not approve of Casey staying the night, but I didn't care. Sometimes moms didn't know best.

After a nurse woke me for one of my vital checks in the middle of the night, I watched Casey sleep for a while. He looked so tranquil. I hoped with all my heart that our troubles were over, at least for now if not for good. I drifted back to sleep just as I noticed a sliver of light on the horizon.

I awoke to brightness in the room and Casey gone. I worried for a split second before he waltzed back into the room, carrying coffee in one hand and a donut in the other.

"Good morning, sleepyhead. I snuck these from the nurses' station!" He grinned. "Eat quick before they bring your boring breakfast."

I took massive bites of the chocolate iced donut, earning me a raised eyebrow from Casey.

"Hungry?"

I cocked my head to the side and shot him a *what-do-you-think* look.

Once I got a good look at my actual breakfast, I was relieved that Casey had slipped me the donut. Since I was still a little hungry, I awkwardly, one hand hindered by the cast, picked at the most appealing things on the plate.

Just as I finished my breakfast. Edward stepped through the door surprising not just me but Casey as well. Casey jumped to his feet and bounded to the foot of my bed. I was confused by Casey's defensiveness. He acted as if Edward was there to attack me.

"What are *you* doing here?" Casey blocked Edward from coming any closer.

"Is that any way to greet your superior? " he chastised Casey. "It's fine that you're upset. Comes with the territory, but I will not tolerate insubordination. " Edward's cockiness was evident. "Now if I could have a few minutes alone with Abby, we have some things to discuss." Edward's tone was a force that could not be reckoned with. Casey knew that, but he faltered as he stood his ground, torn between loyalty to his superior and loyalty to me.

"Casey, it's fine," I said.

He hesitated, worry etched on every inch of his face. Then he stormed out of the room, slamming the door behind him.

Now that I knew some of the things Edward had been doing behind my back, I wanted answers. Particularly about why he felt the need to use me as bait without telling me. If he couldn't be honest with me about something like the investigation into Eli, why was I on the team?

"How are you feeling?" he asked.

"Like you care," I spat.

"I see. Casey told you."

I didn't answer. I tried to let my anger fizzle out so I didn't stumble over my words.

"Why didn't you tell me something was going on?" I asked.

"I couldn't risk you knowing and compromising the investigation."

"You don't trust me?"

"It wasn't that." He sighed. "Knowing would have changed your behavior. You would have been skeptical of Eli. You wouldn't have trusted him. It would have undermined everything we were working to learn. I'm sorry if you disagree with the method I used, and I'm sorry you were hurt, but we got the information we needed. Let me remind you, you are safe."

I glanced down at my arm. *He called this safe?*

"Do you always put your team in jeopardy to get information?"

"That isn't fair. This wasn't a normal situation. Being on any team of Protectors is dangerous. That's why we're immortal. Do Protectors get hurt? All the time, but we heal exceptionally fast. I'm in new territory with you. We have never accepted someone who isn't one of our own, someone who isn't immortal."

"So, why me? If it's so out of the ordinary, how do I even fit in?"

"Well, that's what I'm trying to figure out. Bear with me. Please."

I remained silent.

"I do have one question for you."

"What?"

"The note when you took your driver's test. Who did Eli say it was from?"

"Wait, what?" *How did he even know about that?* My head spun.

"The note the testing instructor gave you. What did Eli tell you about it?"

"Nothing. I figured it was from someone connected to Pete, like all the others."

"Is that what he said?"

"No, I guess I just assumed."

"Didn't you notice it was different than the others?"

"Why? What is this about?"

"The note was from me."

"But why?

Edward lifted his arms and gestured around us. "This. This is why. I had hoped it would scare him back into line. Obviously, it didn't work."

The expensive paper and neat handwriting came to mind.

Tell Eli to watch his step. We're watching. Always watching.

It all made sense now and fit what Edward was saying. How else would he have known about it?

I had almost forgotten about the notes, but I was glad to have closure on that one. And maybe Edward wasn't so bad after all. *Maybe.*

The rest had to have been from Eli's helper or maybe even Eli himself.

"Get better, Abby. I'll be in touch."

Edward stood and walked out the door without giving me time to ask more questions. I sighed. *Where do I stand?* I didn't fit in anywhere. I wasn't a Protector. I wasn't immortal. And I absolutely wasn't normal, so what was I? *Where do I fit in?*

Casey came back into the room the second Edward departed.

"You okay?" he asked.

"I'm fine."

Though I couldn't be certain how true that was. I needed time to figure it all out. Time to fully understand.

Casey stared down at me with concerned green eyes. I reached out and brushed his hand to reassure him. He bent down, kissing me softly on the lips, just once. Just enough to show me he was there for me.

My mom and George came an hour later to take me home. She pursed her lips when she saw Casey. George's eyes were focused on me, and he didn't even take in the look my mom gave Casey. Casey hadn't changed his clothes, and I knew she wondered if he had stayed the night. She wouldn't be happy when she found out. It was worth it, though. Just having him there comforted me. I worried I wouldn't sleep at home without him. If my nightmares were bad before, what would they be like now that my boyfriend had thrown me off a train and tried to kill me? My mom would never understand how I felt, and I vowed never to tell her.

She handed me clean clothes from home. I couldn't wait to get out of the stiff hospital gown.

"How ya holding up?" George asked.

"Fine," I said. "Ready to go home."

"Sorry I wasn't here yesterday. Your mom said you didn't need me here, and work was crazy," he said. He seemed genuinely disappointed. Whether that was out of concern for me or for doing the right thing, I didn't know, but I was touched just the same.

"We'll step out while you get dressed unless you need help," she said.

"No, I'll be fine. Thanks, Mom."

"I'll go get the car," George said to my mom as they walked out together. Casey squeezed my hand and followed, shutting the door behind him.

Getting out of bed on my own proved more challenging than I thought it would. When Casey had helped me stand the night before, I didn't think he had done very much, but he must have done most of the work. Once I was on my feet, I was fine though. *Something to be thankful for.* I slipped into my cotton pants and pulled the hospital gown off. The buttons on the gown's shoulder made it a lot easier to get my cast out of the sleeve. On the other hand, my baggy t-shirt was a struggle. By the time I threaded my cast through the armhole, I was sure I had stretched it out.

"OK, I'm done," I called.

I sat down in the chair while I waited for them to come in. Casey entered first, pushing a wheelchair. I narrowed my eyes at him.

"What? Nurse's orders!" he said.

"That's right," the nurse said as she came in behind him. "Hospital policy."

"Fine."

Casey slipped my flip-flops onto my feet and held out his hand to help me up.

"Your chariot awaits," he said with an exaggerated bow.

I giggled at his display. "You're such a dork."

"The biggest." He grinned. His eyes met mine, bringing me back to the day we worked out together in his apartment. The awkward tension between us had been overwhelming, but he had eased it with his silliness.

I settled myself in the wheelchair, and the nurse came over to talk to my mom.

"She needs to take it easy for the next week. I'd recommend no work for at least that long, maybe longer. That will depend on how she's feeling." She turned to look at me. "Make sure you're going to your doctor's appointments for check-ups on your arm. Questions?"

I shook my head.

Work. I hadn't even thought about work. It would be some time before I could carry a pizza, let alone a tray of drinks. It didn't help that I didn't want to go back. Knowing I had worked there alongside Eli was too much to handle after everything that had happened. Everything had been a lie. I needed a new start. I would miss all my co-workers but first things first—getting better.

"I think we've got it. Thank you so much," Mom said. "Let's get you home, Abby."

Casey stepped behind me and rolled me toward the door.

When George arrived at the curb, Casey helped me into the car while my mom grabbed my belongings.

"Call me later?" he whispered.

I nodded.

He kissed my cheek before he waved goodbye. I hated to leave him behind, but I knew my mom was not up for letting him come over, not until she could see I got rest first. If only she knew how much better I would rest with him there.

CHAPTER SEVENTEEN

I sat bolt upright in a cold sweat, woken by a nightmare. I could still feel the wind whipping past me as I fell from the moving train. The same nightmare had plagued me since the incident. I knew he was still out there. Fear of him coming back was present more than I wanted to admit, and I lived a little on edge. *What if he came back one day to finish what he started?* I suspected Casey felt the same way. Maybe that was why he had been so present.

Seven weeks had passed in the blink of an eye. A week ago, my doctor said I was fully healed. They removed my cast, leaving my arm pale where the sun hadn't touched it. Casey recovered weeks earlier as far as my mom knew. She had been perplexed by just how fast. If she knew that he had thoroughly healed within a day of the incident, she would have freaked. Since then it had been a running joke between Casey and me—he was a superhero with the power to heal immensely faster than a mere human like myself. In all honesty, our joke wasn't far from reality.

Casey and I had been practically inseparable since the "accident," much to my mom's chagrin. For weeks, she asked almost daily where Eli was and why he wasn't coming by, even though I told her repeatedly that we weren't friends anymore and never would be. She finally stopped about a month after he attacked me, much to my relief.

Life had been fairly normal for a change. George and my mom seemed happy together. I felt grateful for that, but his continual presence was hard to get used to, even though it had been months. I had learned long ago that he was used to living alone. I couldn't count the times I had fallen into the toilet when he forgot to put the seat down. It wasn't all bad, of course. I daresay he grew on me in some ways, though I would never admit that to anyone.

Casey and the rest of the team hadn't received any assignments from the elders. They had given us all three months off to recover and regroup. Part of me wondered if their mission was actually to protect me during their "time off," but I didn't know for sure.

Casey often complained about how watchful Edward was, though I hadn't seen it. I still had no idea where I stood with the group, and I hadn't been invited to any of the meetings. Edward said it was because I still needed time to heal, but I suspected it was because he didn't want to see me until he had answers. At the moment, I was content not to see him.

School began two weeks earlier. I both loved and hated being back in the halls. On the one hand, I worried about juggling homework and work again. But at the same time, it was great to be with all my friends and feel normal. I wished Casey could be at school with me, but he was older and had already graduated. Seeing Bailey daily was nice, though. I missed her zest for life. After my accident, I sealed myself off for a couple weeks out of fear. Casey tried coaxing me to go out more and to call Bailey back, but I didn't. Her texts went unanswered until the day she showed up at my door to yell at me for ignoring her.

She made me go with her to dinner that night, and it felt good to hang out. Really good.

From then on I made a point of getting out of the house every day at least once, even if it was just for a walk around my neighborhood. I wasn't feeling quite so vulnerable.

A couple weeks later, I found a new job as a barista after taking a month off to recover. The coffeehouse next door to my old job hired me on the spot. It was perfect—I got a fresh start, yet I could still see my old co-workers when they came in for their caffeine fix.

I glanced at the clock. *May as well get up.* I pulled myself out of bed and dressed. The next day was Sunday—time for back-to-school shopping with my mom. Yeah, it was a bit out of the norm going after school started, but she had said that's when all the good deals are. Besides, shopping for clothes with a cast is no fun!

I was excited, yet I found myself unexpectedly nervous. Our relationship had changed a lot in the past year. Our once-close bond seemed to have dissolved in the face of work, friends, George, and Casey, but I hoped that would change starting with retail therapy tomorrow. The hidden problems that surrounded Eli and I had disappeared the moment he had, leaving me a lot less on edge and more myself again. I felt stronger. Maybe that came with growing older, or maybe it came from tragedy. I would never know. I no longer felt the need to stay one step ahead of those around me all the time, and that was a huge relief.

The doorbell rang, snapping me from my daydream. I could hear George's deep voice as I descended the stairs. "Hey Casey. Did you and Abby have plans?"

"Ah . . ." Casey said.

"Yes, we do," I said, strutting into the room.

George turned to face me. "There she is. Does your mom know where you're going?" he asked.

Stepdad mode. I rolled my eyes. "Yes."

Casey stood with his hands in his pockets, watching our exchange with a grin on his face.

"All right then. Have a good time. And drive careful—it looks like we're in for a monsoon."

I grabbed Casey's hand and pulled him out the door, slamming it behind us.

"Wow, in a hurry?" He chuckled.

"Something like that."

I glanced up at the sky and knew George was right. A storm was headed straight for us. Clouds billowed in the dark eastern sky, and lightning flashed in bolts amid the menacing white and purple clouds.

Monsoons had been hitting sporadically since the middle of July. I loved monsoons. The beautiful buildup of clouds far in the distance swept in with a wall of dust and wind that could darken the sky. I was sad to see they had tapered off as the season came to an end.

We climbed into Casey's brand-new car, a gorgeous, pearl-white Audi. The first time I saw it, my mouth dropped open. He said he had been saving and brushed it off like it was nothing. Maybe it *was* nothing . . . to him. The modesty of his statement made me smile.

Casey drove to his apartment, but instead of heading into the building, we went for a walk by the lake. It was my favorite thing about his place. It felt like the closest thing in Arizona to the beach I missed so much.

He grabbed my hand as we walked. It felt nice to relax with him.

"So, how's school?" he asked.

I turned and glared at him. "Fine. How do you think it is?"

He grinned. "I think I'm glad to be done with school."

I landed a playful blow to his arm. Using my hand, he spun me into his body as if we were dancing. Before I knew what he was doing, he dipped me and brushed his nose across mine. I could feel the heat of his breath on my face. My breath hitched in my throat. Closing my eyes, I parted my lips in anticipation of his kiss, but instead he righted me, spun me out, and pulled me along again as if nothing had happened.

"Tease," I said under my breath.

Out of the corner of my eye I could see him smirk, but he didn't say a thing.

By the time we reached the lake, the wind had picked up and blew my hair into my face. Casey stopped and stared out into the water.

"Let's sit," he said.

He lifted me onto the brick wall behind us before pulling himself up next to me.

"I love watching the water," he said.

"It's beautiful."

I couldn't remember the last time I took the time to just enjoy nature, but this was spectacular. We watched the storm approach, the water reflecting the storm clouds and lightning.

"I think it's time I talked to Edward." I ignored Casey's look of surprise and continued to stare out at the lake as if I hadn't just spoiled our serenity.

"What do you think he's going to be able to tell you?" he asked, his demeanor calmer than I would have predicted. It seemed like he had been waiting for this, and I would be lying if I said I was surprised. He knew I wouldn't just leave things alone forever. And even though I hadn't had another precognitive dream, it was only a matter of time.

I shrugged. I didn't know what he could tell me, and I couldn't begin to guess how our conversation would go. "I want to get to the point where I can make a difference with my dreams. Change fate, you know. I've failed every time so far. Maybe he can help me."

He sighed. "I don't know."

A crack of thunder sent us ducking as if something were crashing down on us, and the rain started with ferocity, catching us off guard and giving us no chance to escape. Casey lifted me down from the wall, and I expected to make a run for it, but when I looked up at him, he started laughing. He raised his arms and held them out to his sides, his hands flat like he rested them on walls. Suddenly, I didn't feel the rain. I looked up and saw that Casey had formed a shield of air over us. Not a single drop penetrated the invisible wall, but the rain flowed all around us, as if we were in a bubble. I watched in amazement as the rain came in sheets around us.

"Oh my god, Casey!"

I gazed around us. Everyone else had disappeared the instant the rain started, running for cover no doubt. Casey's eyes were on me as I took in the full weight of his ability.

"This is amazing," I said. "You're amazing."

"Not as amazing as you," he whispered.

I reached out past the barrier, and the rain pummeled my hand, drenching it in seconds. I pulled it back, placing both of my arms around Casey's neck.

"Let it fall," I whispered against his lips.

All at once, the rain fell down on us, and his arms reached around me. He lifted me off the ground, pulling me closer to his lips as he deepened the kiss. I melted into him. This was bliss. The rain fell on our faces dripping from all of the angles of our faces. I shivered as the wind picked up, making its way into my rain-soaked clothes.

Thunder rocked the ground beneath us, and he set me back on my feet.

"We should get out of the rain."

A lightning bolt zipped across the sky, illuminating the threatening storm clouds.

"M'kay," I said. I was on cloud nine.

"Come on," he said. "I want to make you dinner."

A smile spread across my face, and I intertwined my fingers in his. We were drenched by the time we got to his apartment.

"I'm dripping on your floor," I said as he closed the door behind me. I glanced down at the puddle forming at my feet.

"Come on, I'll get you something else to wear."

"Wait! I don't want to track water all over your apartment."

He turned around and put his nose to mine. "It's tile. That's what they make towels for," he whispered. He kissed me before turning and heading toward his bedroom.

I followed him with an awkward cowboy walk as I tried not to let my cold, water-stretched clothes touch my skin, tensing each time I failed. I shivered as I stood in the doorway of his bedroom. He emerged from his closet, shirtless and wearing dry sweatpants, carrying a stack of clothes in his arms.

"Here," he said. "You can change in here. There are clean towels in the bathroom if you want to dry off. Just hang your wet things in there." He pointed to an open door on the other side of the room. "I'm going to go start dinner."

He put his arm on the small of my back as he brushed past me, and my wet shirt touched my skin just long enough to send a chill down my body. I looked down at the puddle I stood in. After sliding off my shoes, I carefully stood on one foot at a time to take off my wet socks, hoping to diminish the amount of water I got on his carpet.

His room smelled like spiced sandalwood, just like he did. I shut the door behind me and went straight to the bathroom. Just like the rest of the apartment, the bathroom didn't disappoint. The clear shower doors were spotless, and the marble walls sparkled. I set my shoes in the shower and hoped they didn't leave black marks. When I changed, Casey's clothes were huge on me, but they were warm and snuggly. I towel dried my hair and used the towel to mop the floor in front of his door before hanging it back up.

As I made my way to the kitchen, the smell of something glorious filled the whole apartment. My mouth watered.

"Mmm, something smells good," I said. "Is that onion and garlic?"

He nodded, smiling. "Hey, how do they fit?"

"Big!" I giggled. I lifted the shirt up a bit to expose the tightly synched waistband.

He looked up from the stove and smiled. "You look better in my clothes than I do, even if they are big."

I blushed. "So what are you making?"

He grinned and looked back at the stovetop. "You like risotto, right?"

"One of my favorites."

"You have a lot of those," he said.

"I do," I said, smiling. "Can't help it. I like food, *a lot*."

I went into the living room and headed straight for the window. The view was incredible. I watched the rain pound the ground below us. It felt like we were almost in the clouds, though I knew the lightning was higher than it looked.

"How do you not just sit in front of this window all day long?" I asked.

"Sometimes I wish I could," he said.

He came around the couch, carrying two glasses of ice water, which he set on the coffee table. He sat down in front of them.

"If you want to talk to Edward, I think you should," he said. He didn't make eye contact with me until he finished speaking.

"Really?"

I hadn't expected that. Once the rain began, our conversation had ended, and I expected it to stay that way. At least until I brought it up again.

"Yeah."

"I didn't think you would want me to," I said.

"I don't, but that doesn't mean you shouldn't."

"I'm confused."

"Just because I dislike Edward sometimes doesn't mean he can't answer questions I don't have the answers to. He has a lot of resources that I don't."

I nodded. He didn't agree, but he wouldn't object either. "Thanks."

He walked over, put his arm on the small of my back, and kissed my cheek before returning to the kitchen. Minutes passed. I could hear a clinking sound when he dished up our plates. I made my way over to the couch to wait, and moments later he handed me a plate with visible steam rising from it. It smelled heavenly. My mouth watered as I looked over the creamy risotto dotted with peas.

"Do you want something else to drink?" he asked. He gestured to the glasses of ice water.

"No. Water is good."

I lifted the fork, and the steam hit me in the face.

I dared to take my first bite without allowing it to cool. The heat bit into my tongue but only for a moment before it cooled and the flavor spread its creamy decadence across my mouth.

"Mmm! This is so good."

I ate a few more bites, and my stomach announced how pleased it was with a rumbling growl.

"I'm glad you like it," he said with a smile so big it revealed dimples I hadn't known he had.

"Do you cook a lot?" I asked.

"Yeah. I rarely eat out."

"But eating out is so *nice*," I said. "No cooking, no dishes."

He chuckled. "Yeah it is, but I don't mind cooking. Besides, I usually go alone, and that just isn't as fun."

"Oh, not even with the team?" I asked. I was confused by why he would go alone. I figured he would have to chase girls away. He was so attractive and smart. Something about him drew me in, and I couldn't imagine I was alone. Didn't he have other friends? Protectors?

"Well, I mean we hang out, but we do other stuff."

"Other stuff?"

"You know, like paintball, laser tag, video games. That kind of thing."

"Oh, so you guys never go out to eat together?"

"Not often. They go with their girlfriends. Sometimes they come here, or we go to one of the other guys' places," he said.

"They have *girlfriends?*" I practically dropped my fork at this. *How did I not know?*

"Off and on."

"Have any of them had girlfriends since I've known them?" I asked. I was curious now.

"Yeah, Brad and Ferdinand do. Luke dates a lot but hasn't had a girlfriend in a while."

It didn't surprise me that Luke didn't have a steady girlfriend. He seemed like the date-around kind of guy who just didn't commit. Everything about him screamed "ladies man."

For a group of guys, they seemed to know everything about me, yet I realized just how little I knew about them. I shouldn't be surprised. Protectors were secretive. They had to be—job safety and all—but from now on, I would ask a lot more questions.

I sat back against the cushions and continued to shovel the risotto into my mouth.

"So, what's your favorite food?" I asked.

He considered this for a moment. "I love all steak, of course, but filet mignon is my favorite."

I half-listened to him talk about food while my mind drifted back to Edward. Casey was so open and accepting. It was a breath of fresh air after Eli. I had a running list of all the things that had been wrong in our relationship that I had never realized were bad things. This was just another one to add. What he called *protectiveness* was actually just an excuse for him to stand in the way of something I wanted but he didn't. I know he would have been one hundred percent against me going to Edward. It made me that much more grateful for his absence.

"Abby?"

"Huh?"

"Are you okay?" Casey asked. He looked at me strangely.

"Yeah. Of course, why wouldn't I be?"

I shoved a bite of food in my mouth to hide my embarrassment.

"You zoned out there for a minute."

"Sorry." I blushed under his critical eye and looked down at my plate.

"Don't apologize." He lifted my chin so he could look in my eyes. "You are so beautiful."

My cheeks heated. I wanted to look away, but I didn't. I held his gaze. He leaned in, and I closed my eyes. Then I heard the sound of a fork sliding on glass. Then the fork landed in my lap, bringing bits of risotto with it. I jumped, startled, and my eyes popped open.

"I'm sorry," Casey said, furrowing his brow.

He rushed to set his plate on the table and seized the fork from my lap. Then he looked back at the rice on my borrowed pants as if he was deciding what to do next. The problem seemed to stump him. His eyes darted back and forth from my lap to his plate.

I erupted in giggles. Once they started, I found I couldn't stop them. A smile crept up on Casey's face as he looked at me, his cheeks tinted bright pink. The laughter overtook my body, and I threw my head back, giggling.

"Really, it's not that funny," he said.

His smile grew. I could tell he was fighting back his own laughter. This made me laugh even harder. I had to try hard not to double over into the risotto that still lay in my lap.

Casey shook his head and gathered bunches of rice into his hands while I tried to get a handle on my merriment. Finally, I managed to pull myself together as he stood to wash his hands. Small bits of food still clung to my pants, so I finished the job and headed into the kitchen.

"Sorry. I don't know why that was so funny." I smirked.

He looked at me with a huge smile on his face. "I love it when you laugh."

I don't know what it was about compliments that made me so

uncomfortable, but I immediately looked at the floor, blushing. I wanted to be brave and confident, but I went to putty when he said sweet things to me.

He wrapped his arms around the small of my back, hugging me tight. His hands were still wet, and I could feel the dampness seeping through the shirt. But everything disappeared the moment he kissed me. On impulse, I rose to my tiptoes to meet his lips. Casey's other hand made its way into my hair. He stepped forward without breaking the kiss, and my butt hit the counter. He lifted me up and set me on the counter so I was at the perfect height to continue exploring his kiss. My heart raced. His pushed his hands up the back of my shirt, pulling me closer. I arched my back, pressing my chest into his and I slid my hands up from his neck into his hair. I pulled back, my breathing heavy. When I looked into his eyes, all I saw was hunger, hunger for more. His hands moved further up my back, past my bra, and he held me close.

For the first time, I wondered about his experience. I never had to worry about it with Eli. He had always shown me he knew where to stop, and he could sense how I felt which gave him the advantage of never pushing me farther than I felt comfortable. Before that, no boyfriend had ever made me feel like it mattered. Our kisses had never gotten heated. To be honest, they had never gotten past the nervous awkwardness.

As we sat there with his hands caressing my back, I felt my nerves kicking in. I hated "the talk." In my mind, I figured Casey had more experience. After all, he was older, which made it that much harder to broach.

"Do you want to change?" he asked, pulling away to look at me.

I glanced back down at my clothes. Smudges of food dotted the pants.

"I probably should, but I hate to steal more of your clothes."

"Nonsense."

He pulled me down from the counter and turned toward the hallway, pushing me to his bedroom. He threw a new pair of pants and a t-shirt on the bed, gave me a quick wink, and left, shutting the door behind him.

I breathed a small sigh of relief at having avoided "the talk" for the moment. Or so I thought. After I changed and made my way back to the couch, he put his arm around me. I rested my head on his shoulder. He leaned down, kissing the top of my head.

"Abby?"

"Hmm?" I said. My eyes were closed as I relaxed against him, breathing in his scent and listening to the even rise and fall of his chest.

"Are you nervous when we kiss?" he asked.

"No," I said, my eyes popping open. "Why?"

Nerves settled in the pit of my stomach. *Here it was.*

"I just get the feeling you're worried when things get a bit . . . heated."

I sighed, sitting up and turning my body to face him.

"I'm not nervous about kissing you."

"Okay but you are nervous?"

I looked at my hands. "I've been nervous about this conversation. I don't even know why."

"Oh," he said. "You know I would never push you to do anything you weren't comfortable with, right?"

I nodded. "I trust you. The thing is, I haven't had many boyfriends. Eli was my first real one, and what a disaster that turned out to be," I said, rolling my eyes. "Anyway, what I'm trying to say is that I haven't gone farther than kissing."

"Oh," he said. "Is that all you were nervous about saying?"

I nodded. "And I'm not ready to go any farther . . . yet."

He smiled. "Me neither, but I should tell you I've gone a bit farther."

His eyes looked deep into mine as if he was asking if that was okay. It was what I had expected. "I don't need to know," I said.

"You sure?" he asked.

I nodded.

"Okay. I'm an open book if you ever want to talk about it," he said.

Without saying another word, I settled back against his shoulder. He grabbed a universal remote to turn on the TV and bring the fireplace to life in unison. "The talk" could have gone way worse, and I felt grateful to have it behind me. We were on the same page.

He turned on a movie and shut off the lights. The storm continued to rage outside, bursts of lightning brightening the room every so often. It didn't get much better than this.

I breathed a sigh of relief and relaxed deeper into the couch, letting my body mold into it. Now this was normal. As normal as a girl could get in the Protector world, anyway.

CHAPTER EIGHTEEN

It was dark. Pitch black. Where am I? I took a few steps forward, my arms out in front of me, testing the ground. Hard. Concrete.

A door opened behind me. Light engulfed the other half of the room, revealing nothing but empty space and a wall. A figure stood in the doorway looking in. I shrunk back until my back slammed against the wall . . .

With a thud, I hit the ground, breaking me from sleep. Another nightmare? But was it a nightmare? Nothing seemed to happen. Though it had felt like I didn't belong there, like perhaps I needed to hide. My mind raced with possibilities. I couldn't help but fear what I didn't know.

"Abby?" Casey said, his voice hoarse with sleep.

Casey? I willed my eyes to focus. I looked around. I was in his apartment, the fire still crackling, giving a little light in the dark room. How long had I been sleeping?

Panicked, I jumped up and raced to the kitchen. The microwave read 12:12 a.m.

"Oh crap! Casey! I'm late!"

I could hear him shuffling around before he met me in the kitchen, looking like a deer in the headlights.

"My mom is going to kill me," I whined.

"Come on," he said, grabbing my hand.

He snatched his keys from the entry table, and we rushed out the door. In the elevator, I huddled up against Casey, using his body for strength and comfort. The elevator seemed to take forever, at least twice as long as normal.

"Did you fall off the couch?" Casey asked, still rubbing the sleep from his eyes.

"Yeah," I said.

I chose not to reveal that I had another dream. I was confident this was another precognitive dream. It felt different in all the same ways. The others had also been vague at first and became more detailed each time. *Maybe I will get more insight before this one came true.* It had been a while since my last dream, and I had hoped they were a thing of the past. Now my optimism had been shot down. It wasn't over, and it never would be. Edward seemed to think it was a gift, something I would have for the rest of my life. He even expected me to develop more gifts. I thought that was nutty, but I would have never believed in this one either. I had to grasp the reality that nothing was out of the question anymore.

Casey sped toward my house. The goody-goody in me worried we might get pulled over, delaying my arrival further, but with amazing luck and zero traffic we made it in ten minutes. A new record.

At my house, I gave Casey a quick peck on the cheek and raced to the door, coasting in at 12:31 p.m. and hoping to be under the radar. I tiptoed through the entryway and headed toward the stairs when I heard what I had been hoping to avoid.

"Abby?" my mom's stern voice called.

I cringed. I glanced down at the boy clothes I wore and cringed again. That made it look worse than it was. Changing my course, I headed into the living room where I had expected her to be waiting. George sat next to her on the couch. *Great.*

"I'm sorry. We fell asleep watching a movie," I said.

I looked back and forth between them, waiting with bated breath. I used to be able to pinpoint exactly how my mom would act and what her go-to punishment would be, but this was new territory. I hadn't been in trouble since George moved in, and even though he wasn't officially my stepdad, he had kind of taken on that role. It was a gray area, and until now, it hadn't been a problem. As I waited for what seemed like forever for one of them to speak, I wondered if now would be.

"It won't happen again," I added.

Their silence killed me. I began to sweat. My heart drummed in my chest. Their eyes were fixed on me.

"OK," my mom said.

And that was it. She looked down at her book and returned to reading. George held my gaze for a second longer, winked, and picked up his book.

I backed out of the room. *What just happened?* Never had I gotten off so easy. They hadn't even noticed the clothes. I smiled to myself and bounded up the stairs.

Throwing myself on my bed, I pulled my phone out and typed a quick text to Casey. *No punishment! Can't believe it!*

Once I hit the pillow, I was out in minutes and didn't wake again until my bedroom door opened. I squinted, trying to see in the bright light.

"Mom?" I said.

"Time to get up! Get some breakfast so we can go shopping!" She hopped on the bed, bouncing it.

"Ugh!"

She pecked a kiss on my forehead, jumped off the bed, and left the room.

George was eating a bowl of cereal at the breakfast bar when I walked into the kitchen. I raised an eyebrow.

"Your mom said she wasn't cooking breakfast today. I was surprised too. Between you and me, I don't mind. I was beginning to miss my cereal anyway."

"Really?" I asked.

"Really. I was a bachelor, you know." He grinned, showing off his white teeth. "Cereal became dinner a lot."

"You're crazy. I hate cereal."

He laughed. "How can anyone hate cereal?"

"Easy. You just do." I nodded my head once to emphasize my point. I grabbed a granola bar out of the cabinet and held it up to show him. "See, no need to eat mushy cereal for breakfast."

"Your granola bar has nothing on my bowl of cereal."

I took a big bite, flaunting it, and headed toward the stairs when the phone rang. I grabbed it as the second ring sounded.

"Hello?" I said.

"Hi Abbs! Just the girl I called for!"

"Hey Dad!"

We had talked just about every day after my "accident." It was nice to catch up, but I would bet it was because of him being concerned about me. One weekend he flew down for the night just to see me. He said he missed me, but I figured it had more to do with being worried. After a little while, his calls spaced out again, but not far until he knew the cast had come off and my arm had healed.

"What have you been up to this week?" he asked.

"School, work, and hanging out with Casey. I'm going back-to-school shopping in a few minutes with Mom."

"Oh, the annual trip! I remember how much you always looked forward to that." He paused. "It's a little later than normal, isn't it?"

"Still do, and yeah, we didn't want to go with my cast," I said.

"Ah, that's right. Tell your mom I'll send her a check to help out with it."

"OK," I said.

"How's everything else?"

"Good," I said. "I came in past curfew last night." I don't know why I told him. Maybe it was because I felt like I had gotten off too easy with my mom. I cringed, knowing he wouldn't like it.

"Oh yeah?"

"Yeah. I was at Casey's, and we fell asleep watching a movie."

"What did your mom say?" he asked.

"Nothing. I'm surprised. No punishment. Nothing. She just said, 'Okay,' and went back to reading."

"Wow, that's something," he said. His voice held something I couldn't place. Was it curiosity? Or apprehension?

"It won't happen again."

"That's good to hear."

"Hey honey. Are you ready to go?" My mom came into view. "Oh, you're on the phone."

She mouthed, "Sorry."

"Hey Dad, Mom is ready to go."

"All right, have fun! I'll talk to you later."

"Love you," I said.

"I love you too, honey. Bye."

I hung up and turned toward Mom. "I'm ready."

The first two stores were a bust. Almost everything in my size was sold out, and what was left was terrible. The third store, however, had a lot that fit me, and it was running a huge sale. We ended up leaving with two full bags.

"Well, that was a good store," Mom said as we walked out.

"No kidding. I'm glad we went there."

"Lotions?"

"You read my mind."

As we walked into Bath and Body Works, the fruity and flowery scents submerged us. Some of them were so realistic they made my mouth water.

We separated as we browsed, smelling everything and picking up a few things that stuck with us. I even found some car air fresheners and got a couple. After I felt like I had seen everything, I wandered up to my mom at the register.

"All done?" she asked.

"Yep."

She held out her hands for me to give her my selections. She sniffed each one as she set them on the counter.

"Some of these may disappear," she said, grinning at me.

"Get your own!" I laughed.

She glanced at the credit card in her hand and then back at me.

"I am," she said with a wink.

I rolled my eyes. "I'm hungry."

"I've been craving pasta."

"That does sound good."

We went to a bakery cafe with numerous pasta dishes on the menu. My stomach rumbled as we walked in and basked in the delicious smells of cooking food. The second I dropped myself into the booth, I sighed. It felt great to sit down. We wanted to try so many things on the menu, so we split two entrees—our favorite, Alfredo, and baked ziti. Then we ordered Mozzarella sticks as an appetizer.

I sat back and sipped my cola as I people-watched around us.

"So, how are things going with Casey?" she asked.

"Really good." I smiled, thinking of him.

"You guys have sure hit it off."

"That we did."

"Have you heard from Eli lately?"

I tensed. I had thought she had finally stopped talking about him. I glared at her and wished for the hundredth time, I wished I could explain to her what had really happened. A fight didn't seem to register with her as enough to keep us apart.

"Can you stop bringing him up, please?" I asked a little more harshly than I would have liked. "I thought we'd gotten past this. We broke up. There's nothing more to say."

"You guys were best friends, though. Why can't you still be friends?" she asked. I was annoyed by how whiny she sounded.

"We don't want to be friends. It was a clean break. He's moved anyway." I threw the last part in, hoping it would convince her he was gone for good. For once, she seemed to accept that answer.

"Okay, okay. Consider this the last time I'll bring him up."

"Thank you!" I paused a moment. "What about you and George? Still think he's great with morning breath?" I said, teasing her. I hoped that the quick turnaround would help her forget about Eli once and for all.

She laughed, and I felt myself relaxing.

"I still love him with morning breath."

"Eww."

The waiter delivered our food. As we ate, our conversation became sparse again, but we had returned to our comfortable state where I didn't feel the need to try to fill the silence or sit staring off into space, wondering what to say. Despite her slip with Eli, I felt like we were connecting again.

We meandered to three more stores before calling it quits and ending our day with pedicures to complement our new sandals.

When we arrived home, we were surprised to find dinner waiting for us, cooked by none other than George.

"Wow George, I'm impressed. It smells really good," I said.

"Well, thank you, Abby," he said, taking a large bow.

It was the first time he had made a meal for us—or at least for me. I was even more astounded that it was really good. He hadn't seemed like the cooking type.

*　　*　　*　　*

The next day I got countless compliments on my new clothes. Bailey even asked where I had gotten them, and she only shopped at the store where she worked because she got such a huge discount. My good spirits carried me into work that afternoon, feeling as though the day couldn't have been going any better. I smiled to myself as I tied on my apron. *Nothing can ruin my mood.*

Edward

This meeting could not be put off any longer. Almost everything was in place. It was time. Her desire for answers would serve in my favor, I was certain.

Ambushing her in this way felt stalker-like. Watching her at work just felt disgraceful. She was cautious of me. I could see it in her eyes. Eli's little tirade was an unfortunate complication. And now that Casey had inserted himself into a large part of her life, I couldn't seem to get her alone. Perhaps she would forgive me for coming here, but regardless, I needed to talk to her alone. I couldn't take the chance that Casey would persuade her against me. If it wasn't already too late. Casey didn't trust me, though I couldn't fault his perseverance, his extensive training made him work tirelessly to investigate the truth. But this was one thing he would not get out of me. *One day he may see things my way, but until then, this is a secret she and I will share.*

As she made her way around the counter, I saw my opportunity to talk to her. She spotted me the moment I stepped foot in the door and instantly tensed. That was one thing I would have to remedy. Her emotions were far too easy to read. I needed her sharp and unreadable if this would ever work.

"Can we talk?" I asked.

I followed her eyes as she looked around. I could not stop my gaze from following hers. *What was she looking for?*

"Um . . . give me a sec," she said.

She walked behind the counter and into the back room.

I was nervous for the first time in a century, and a silly girl was the cause. I could not recall the last time the opposite sex made me jittery. It was not attraction to her—she was much too young for me. I just couldn't lose her. There was much to learn from her. Too much to gain from her.

I shoved my shaky hands into my pockets. She should not see me sweat.

"Where should we sit?" Abby's timid voice asked.

"Outside," I said without skipping a beat. My voice was self-assured, as usual. I would allow none of my nerves to show.

She led the way to a table outside. I found a simple delight in her clever ability to pick a secluded spot. Maybe training her would not be as difficult as I expected.

CHAPTER NINETEEN

Never had I expected Edward to show up to talk to me, let alone come to see me at work without giving me notice. I hadn't contacted him yet, despite my discussion with Casey a few days earlier. Even though Casey was on board, I had still been putting it off. I couldn't even say for certain why. My newest dream should make me rush to him. Instead, I found myself nervous and unsure.

I made sure to pick the most remote outside table for the impromptu meeting. If being around Protectors had taught me anything, it was that secrets were best kept quiet.

Once we sat down, I stared at him, waiting for him to get started. After all, there had to be a reason he was here.

"I'm sorry for showing up unannounced like this, but I wanted to have a chance to talk. Just you and me."

I nodded.

"I know you have been waiting for answers about your gift. Unfortunately, I have been unable to find any conclusive answers. I cannot locate anyone else like you."

Great.

"Originally, I had hoped to find another, someone who could mentor you, since clearly, this is new territory for us both."

"So then what?"

"My next idea is to pair you with one of us, someone also gifted in dream-sight."

I felt myself get excited and nervous all over again. If nothing else, I might learn how Protectors managed their talents.

"I'd like that," I said.

"I thought you might. There's one catch."

Here we go. "What?"

"I want to know what you learn about your gift. I must admit, I am curious to know if your talent is like ours or if it has its own distinctions."

I nodded. "Done."

This was a small favor in exchange for what he was doing for me. Putting another Protector at my disposal to teach and train me was a huge step forward.

"When do we start?" I asked.

"Three weeks."

I bit my lip.

"Lucian will be in touch."

Lucian. That was the name of the person who may just be what I have been hoping for.

"Got it."

"Good. Now, I must ask. How are you doing?"

How was I doing? Wasn't *that* a loaded question. I weighed the answers in my head but decided to go with the truth.

"Honestly, I've been better."

"I'm sorry to hear that. I want you to know we are doing everything in our power to bring Eli to justice. His deplorable actions are unlike our kind. Unfortunately, you have witnessed the worst of our kind, while seeing only a limited amount of the good. I assure you—the good far outweighs the bad."

I didn't know why he felt the need to say it, but it was something I had needed to hear. I had seen a lot of bad come from the world of the Protectors.

Edward stood. "I will be in touch."

With that, he strode away, gliding to a car parked two spaces down. I had never seen Edward's car before. I smiled as I looked it over. It screamed *Edward.* A sleek, silver Aston Martin in pristine condition, exactly the polished sophistication I would have expected from him. I watched it coast out of sight before I headed back to work.

As the afternoon faded into night, I got more excited until not a single nervous worry remained. After work, en route to my car, I saw a shadowy figure three cars away. I squinted. The light shifted, revealing half of the person's face. *Eli?* I gasped, stumbling over a parking divider and falling to my knees. *Ouch.* It couldn't be. I snatched up my keys from the ground and clambered to my feet, my eyes darting back to where he had stood, but no one was there.

My breathing was erratic, and my heart raced. I ran the rest of the way to my car and sped out of the parking lot. Grabbing my phone, I dialed Casey.

"Hey! How was work?" his masculine voice purred.

"I . . . think I saw . . . Eli," I managed to say despite my ragged breathing.

"What?"

"I think I saw Eli," I said again, a little more clearly this time.

"What do you mean you *think* you saw him?" I could hear shuffling on his end of the phone.

"In the parking lot at work. It was dark. I'm not sure it was him. Maybe I'm just seeing things."

"Why would you think that?"

"When I looked again, nobody was there."

"That doesn't mean anything. Where are you?" he asked.

"Almost home."

"I'm headed over. Do me a favor?" he asked.

"What?"

"Keep driving around the block until I get there."

After what I had been through with Eli, I wasn't taking any chances.

"Let me know when I can stop driving in circles," I said.

Three laps later, Casey awaited me. I made a break for his arms, my body still trembling in fear.

"You're fine," he whispered.

Then the dam broke. I sobbed, standing in the driveway, wrapped in the safety of his arms.

"Why does this have to keep happening?"

"I don't know," he said with sadness in his voice. "I've called the team. And Edward."

I pulled back momentarily to look at him and wipe the tears away. "What are they going to do?"

"Brad is on his way over. We'll be working in shifts around the clock, two of us at a time. You will never be unprotected until he is found."

"Casey . . . that's too much. What if he's never found?"

"We'll find him."

"What will we tell my mom?" I asked. I had to find some way this plan would fail. I hated the idea of them uprooting their whole lives just to protect me. Not that having them around didn't make me feel 100% better, and if it were just Casey, it might be a different story. I felt like I could ask more from him since he was my boyfriend. But the whole group? Too much.

"She won't know."

"Oh," I said.

"We'll park two houses down, and make rounds throughout the night. No one will even know we're here. It will be fine."

I wasn't getting out of this.

"I know," I said, resting my head on his chest.

"Let's go inside."

"I don't want to. My face is all puffy from crying." I pouted.

Casey cupped my face between his hands. "You look beautiful."

I rolled my eyes. "Fine. We'll go inside, but we're avoiding my mom. I'm not explaining all of this," I said, making a circle around my face in the air.

"Deal," he said, taking my hand and marching to the door.

My mom wasn't home. "She must have gone out for ice cream or something with George."

Then a knock sounded on the door.

"That would be Brad," Casey said.

I stalked behind him to the door, letting him answer it.

"Hey troublemaker," Brad said, peeking around Casey.

I waved in a rainbow shape as if I were ten all over again. I felt awkward that so much fuss was being made over me. I was acutely aware of how much danger I was in if Eli was nearby, waiting for the right time to strike.

"Thanks for coming," Casey said. He gave Brad a friendly slap on the back.

"Ah man, you know I wouldn't be anywhere else."

I led the way into the backyard. I didn't want to chance my mom and George walking in on our discussion. When I sat down, I brought my knees up to my chest and wrapped my arms around them. Brad sat across from me, with Casey at my side.

"So, when are Ferdinand and Luke taking over?" Casey asked.

"Three o'clock. Six-hour shifts." Brad said. "Edward's orders."

Casey's jaw tightened, but he nodded.

"Abby, can you tell me what you saw?" Brad asked.

I swallowed hard.

"When I left work, I wasn't paying attention. I was mostly looking at the ground. When I glanced up, I saw someone a few parking spaces away from my car. I looked more closely, and light shone on his face for only a split second, but it looked like Eli. Then I tripped over a parking divider and fell. I scrambled to my feet, worried he might do something, but when I looked around again, the person was gone. I looked all over the parking lot too, but I didn't see anyone around."

"You fell?" Casey asked.

"Yeah, I kind of forgot until now."

I lifted my right pant leg up to my scuffed knee. In the middle of my shin, a cut oozed half-dried blood.

"I'll go get a wet cloth. Where is your first aid stuff?" Casey asked.

"In the cabinet next to the fridge."

He breezed past me into the house. Brad stood up and pressed his fingers around the cut, steering clear of the blood.

"It doesn't look bad. Probably hurts though," he said before sitting back down.

When Casey returned, he gingerly rubbed away the blood. Even though he tried his best to be careful, it still stung like crazy. I grabbed his hand to stop him.

"Why don't you let me do that?" I said through gritted teeth.

He gave me a sheepish look and handed over the rag. I went to work cleaning and bandaging it up. Casey and Brad sat in silence, but I could feel their eyes on me.

"You know you guys can talk while I'm doing this," I said without looking up.

Brad jumped up. "I'm going to go to my car and fill in everyone on what happened."

Casey nodded. "I'll be out in a bit."

And then Brad was gone.

Now that we were alone, I remembered that I still hadn't told Casey that Edward had come to my work to see me. Maybe getting our minds off Eli will help us all feel a little less on edge.

"Edward came to see me today," I said.

"What?" His face looked puzzled. "Did he tell you Eli was back?"

"It had nothing do to with Eli," I said.

"Then why did he come by?"

"To talk about my gift."

"I know we talked about it a couple days ago, but I didn't know you had called him," he said, looking almost hurt.

"I didn't. He just showed up. I was as surprised as you are."

His forehead wrinkled. "Oh, that's not like him. He's all about making plans."

"That's what I thought too."

"What did he say?"

"He said he's been looking for someone else like me—human and gifted—but he didn't find anyone."

"I'm sorry," he said.

"Yeah, I was too, but he offered me something that might be just as good."

"What?"

"A mentor," I said.

"Really? Someone with the same gift?"

I nodded. "I mean, I know that since he'll be a Protector, things might not work the same way. Our gifts might not even be the exact same, but I'm hopeful he might be able to help me."

I let myself get excited again, despite the Eli situation. *In just three weeks, I might begin to get the answers I had been hoping for.*

"Who is the mentor going to be?" he asked.

"Edward said someone named Lucian? Do you know him?" I asked.

Casey's eyebrows raised. "I don't know him, but I know *of* him."

"Oh yeah?"

"From what I hear, he's pretty powerful. He's next in line to become one of the elders."

My mouth fell open. Someone that high in the ranks was coming to train me? That was unexpected. All my unsure nerves came flooding back.

*   *   *   *

It had been three days since my team began their round the clock shifts. So far nothing had happened other than the guys watching me do my homework and following me around like personal bodyguards at all hours of the day. Casey had been right too—my mom had noticed nothing out of the ordinary. The only times they couldn't see me at every moment were during school and at night. But we were still in close contact even then, talking on the phone and texting. Edward had even called a few times to check in.

The boys were all feeling on edge and tired. I couldn't blame them. At the moment they had no life and weren't getting much sleep. Casey hung out at my place lot more often now, which was nice, but it hardly counted because he was so tired all the time. One thing was certain—I couldn't wait for this to be over. Every so often I wished I had kept what I had seen to myself, but then reality hit me. I still had moments when my arm wasn't what it should be. Then my desire to catch Eli and bring him to justice kicked back in tenfold.   On Friday afternoon, I headed to work for the closing shift. Luke and Ferdinand were following behind me, close enough to see me but far enough back not to make it obvious.

I walked in, ignoring them, exactly as I had been instructed to do. They had said this might entice Eli to come out of hiding. Basically, I was bait again. At least this time I knew about it.

I took the trash out after dark, intending to draw out anyone lurking nearby. As I wheeled the large, overstuffed can outside, I watched the shadows, double- and triple-checking them to be sure nobody was hiding among them.

Further out in the parking lot, Ferdinand's large frame emerged from his car, his watchful gaze never leaving me. I diverted my eyes from him. I didn't dare wave or draw attention to him. If someone were watching, they would know something was in the works.

I took my time unloading the heavy bags into the large dumpster, giving Eli or his goons ample time to make a move. Then I strolled back inside. I was almost frustrated when I got back inside without incident.

I sighed. This was what Eli wanted—for me to live forever in fear. Frozen in a world where I never felt safe. That would be far worse than death.

I spent the rest of the night sulking, and when I clocked out for the night, I trudged to my car without even glancing at my surroundings. With a heavy sigh, I peeled out of the parking lot without checking to make sure my team could catch up. I assumed they were behind me. At home, I slammed my car door and marched into the house. I was so over this.

Ten minutes later, as I sat soaking in a hot bubble bath, my phone buzzed on the floor. I reached out, briefly wiping my hands on my towel before grabbing it. A text from Casey.

Is everything okay? The guys said you seemed upset.

I groaned. Another perk of people watching your every move—no privacy.

I'm fine.

My phone dinged.

Why do I get the feeling that's not true?

I realized this conversation would be easier if I called him, so I hit the call button and put the phone to my ear. He picked up on the second ring.

"Hey, what's going on?" he said.

"Nothing."

"Abby."

I sighed. "I'm starting to feel frustrated. Not that I mind the guys being around. But I feel like a burden just going about my day. I just wish if Eli were going to do something he would get it over with."

"I'm sorry," he said.

"I didn't want you to be sorry. You and the team . . . you're already doing everything you can for me."

He fell quiet.

"Look, I'm just having a girl moment. I'm fine. Okay? You don't have to fix this. I will just finish soaking in my nice hot bath and go to bed. I'll feel better in the morning."

"You're in the bath?"

After all I had said, that's what he wanted to comment on? *Guys.*

"Yes," I said, smirking.

My answer hung in the air, leaving silence in its wake.

"Was there anything else?" I asked.

He spoke, but it came out as a croak, so he cleared his throat and started again. "No, that's it."

"All right. I'll let you go," I said, continuing to smirk to myself. I found it amusing how frazzled he was.

"All right. I'll be there tonight around one o'clock. You'll be sleeping, but know that I'm there."

"Thanks."

"I love you," he said.

I smiled. "I love you too."

He hung up, and I set my phone back down on the floor. Closing my eyes, I relaxed back into my bath, welcoming the heat on my tired and sore muscles. After a while, I started to drift off, and the water had cooled, so I got out and went straight to bed.

Some time later I awoke, startled. It was dark. I scanned the room, searching for the cause of my sudden wakefulness. I jerked when I heard a loud rattling at my window.

My window? I'm on the second floor.

I jumped out of bed, my heart racing, and yanked the blinds cord. The blinds sprang upward, revealing an angry, familiar face pressed against the pane. I bit back a scream. *Eli.* I stumbled back, away from the window, and snatched my phone from the nightstand. I held it close to my chest, frozen in fear, not knowing what to do next. He continued fumbling with the window with one hand, trying to get it open.

Suddenly, his face was pulled out of sight. I dove for the window, desperate to see what had happened. All I could see was murky darkness.

I texted Casey. *Where are you?*

No response. I paced my room, debating what to do. *It's the middle of the night.*

I took two more steps before I made up my mind. Throwing on a short robe, I raced downstairs and toward the back door. I didn't dare turn on the lights. The last thing I wanted was to draw attention to myself. I squinted as I searched the darkness, but I saw nothing but shadows. I held my breath, waiting for something—anything—to stand out. A flash of movement caught my eye. Someone had flipped over the wall back into the front yard.

I darted to the front door and opened and closed it as quietly as possible. I tiptoed outside, stopping between each step as I crept off the porch, hoping I wasn't walking into something I shouldn't be. When I reached the edge of the driveway, I noticed the guys congregating next to Casey's car. I bolted straight for them, my bare feet silent on the warm ground.

"What happened?" I asked, winded.

Casey spun around, grinning from ear to ear. "We got him!"

He picked me up, spun me around, and hugged me close.

"What?"

"We got him! He tried to climb in your window. Did you hear him? Is that what woke you?"

"Yeah. Where is he?"

"In the car," Casey said, pointing.

"The elders' security detail will pick him up soon," Brad said. "Since I'm no longer needed, I'll catch you later."

"Thanks, Brad," I said.

He nodded before walking to his car and pulling away from my house.

"What happened? How did you get him?"

"Casey kicked butt, that's what happened," Luke said.

Casey rolled his eyes. "An hour ago, Eli drove by like he was checking out the place, so I called Brad and Ferdinand to come down just in case. A little while later, I saw him slinking up the road. It didn't take long for him to come up to your house and go for your backyard. He didn't see me, so I had the element of surprise. He had no idea I was even there. He only got to the window because I needed a moment to get over the fence without him spotting me."

"You should have seen it, Abby. Casey practically flew up the wall and grabbed Eli by his pant legs. Eli hit the ground so hard it knocked him out cold! Good thing too, with that gift of his."

"Did you get hurt?" I asked, my head whipping back toward Casey.

Casey held up his arm. It looked like it had just stopped bleeding. "Just a scrape. No big deal. All that matters is that he isn't a threat anymore."

I sighed. I felt so relieved. I gave each of them a hug, lingering in Casey's arms. "Thank you guys for watching out for me."

Ferdinand and Luke nodded in unison.

"What are friends for?" Ferdinand asked.

"You need to get back inside before your mom finds you out here," said Casey. "She'll hate me!"

"You're right," I said, making a face.

I gave him a quick kiss and bounded back into the house, slipping into my room.

As I sunk back into my pillow, a wave of relief washed over me. It was over. Finally over. A huge smile filled my face.

Over.

*   *   *   *

"They want me to what?" I shrieked.

"I'm not supposed to have told you, but I wanted to give you a heads up."

"How could they expect me to do that?"

"I don't know. If it were up to me, it wouldn't have even crossed my mind." His hand rubbed my back.

I rested my head in my hands. *How could I face him again?* Just the thought sickened me. What would he do when I walked in the room?

"Who will be there?" I asked.

Casey's face turned serious. "I'm not sure."

I could tell he knew more than he let on. I let it go. It wasn't important. The one person I never wanted to see again would be there. Nobody else mattered.

"When?" I asked.

"If I had to guess, tomorrow."

At least it would be over soon. I was grateful for that much.

"The elders will contact you today."

I looked up into Casey's eyes. The worry in them all but broke my heart. I wanted to assure him I would be fine, but I just didn't have it in me.

"Will you be there?"

He nodded. "I can't be near you, though. I'll be sitting with anyone else who shows up."

I leaned my head into him and stared off into nothing.

"Do you want to go for a walk?" he asked.

I scrunched my face. "It's too hot."

"Then let's go get ice cream."

"Oooh, now you're talkin'!"

Later that evening, after Casey had gone home, I got the call I had dreaded all day. My caller ID said, *Unknown*.

"Hello?" I answered.

"Abby?" an unfamiliar female voice said.

"Yes?" I had expected it to be Edward and was thrown off when it wasn't.

"My name is Theodora. You may remember me from our meeting?"

I recalled my meeting with the elders. Three faces came to mind: Edward, James, and Theodora. She had a stern face and pointed nose if I remembered correctly.

"Ah, yeah. Of course."

"Oh good," she said, seeming uninterested. "I am calling you because your presence is needed tomorrow at a hearing for Eli Jacobs."

"Oh?" I said, trying to sound like this was new information.

"We will need to hear your side of the story."

My side? Was there a question about what happened that day?

"Why is this necessary?" I asked before I could stop myself. I couldn't help but feel like it was rude of me to ask someone in her high position that kind of question.

"It's how our punishment system works. To determine proper punishment, we need all witnesses and victims to tell their stories and answer questions. The human system works similarly, I believe."

I pictured the courtrooms I had seen on TV and the one in which the judge granted my parents' divorce. I imagined myself in the chair next to the judge. Theodora had a point. Everyone deserved a fair trial. I wondered if the room would resemble a traditional courtroom or if it would be more like a conference room. Or something different entirely.

"Yes, it is."

"I believe Casey will also be going. Would it be all right to assume he will drive you there? Otherwise I can give you the address."

"Casey will drive me," I said without hesitation.

"Excellent. We will see you tomorrow."

When the phone went dead, without a goodbye I wasn't surprised. Theodora was all business.

Casey wanted me to call him the minute they called me. I wasted no time.

"Hey." He sounded a little breathless.

"What are you doing?" I asked, my curiosity getting the better of me.

"Working out," he said.

I should have known. He spent a good chunk of his free time working out. Often I joined him, sometimes just to watch. It wasn't a bad show if you know what I mean.

I pictured him in basketball shorts and a white tank top, his bulging shoulders flexing with each repetition.

I cleared my throat. "Theodora called."

"What did she say?"

"Basically what you told me they would. They want me to come tell my story."

"I see."

"I told them you would give me a ride there. I hope that's okay."

"Of course."

"Good. I didn't want to take on trying to find the place. The time Ren brought me to a meeting with the elders, I would have thought I was in the wrong place and left."

Casey's laughter filled the phone. "Yeah, they're good at covering their tracks. I had similar thoughts the first few times."

"I should go. I was going to call Bailey and see if she wanted to go to dinner," I said.

"What a good idea. Have fun!"

"I'll try," I said.

"Bye!"

I hadn't planned to ask Bailey to dinner. It had just crossed my mind moments before I blurted it out. She was the one person who could help me sort through my feelings.

Her phone rang and rang until her voicemail picked up. I hung up, feeling bummed she hadn't answered. I set my phone down next to me and looked out the window. The light in the sky had barely faded, leaving the brightest rays to flood my room as the sun sank into the west.

My phone burst to life, ringing on the bed next to me.

"Hello," I said without looking away from the window.

"Hey Abby! Sorry I didn't answer when you called. I went to get the mail," Bailey said.

"That's okay," I said, hopeful she might be free.

"What's up?" she asked.

"Are you doing anything right now?"

"Nope," she said. "I did have plans with Ryan, but he got called into work because someone got sick."

"Oh, that's great," I said, before realizing how I sounded. "I mean, not that he had to work or that his co-worker is sick. I just meant it was great that you were free."

She giggled. "I knew what you meant. Did you have something in mind?"

"I was thinking about grabbing some dinner."

"I'm starved!"

"Great. Do you want me to pick you up or just meet somewhere?" I asked.

"Let's meet somewhere."

"Name the place."

It took ten minutes to get there, and when I arrived, Bailey was already waiting by the door, a huge grin on her face. Her green eyes sparkled under the fluorescent sign as I approached. She reached out and gave me a big hug. Then we strode into the restaurant arm in arm.

It had been a long time since I had been to a salad buffet, but the minute Bailey suggested it my stomach rumbled. After piling our plates to the brim, we found a table and sat down.

"How have things been going in school?" she asked.

"Good. Did I tell you I'm taking two extra classes to get ahead?"

"Really? Are you planning to graduate early?"

"That's the plan. I'm already so close in credits that it's silly not to. I mean, if I didn't I'd only have three classes next year. I'd much rather graduate early and get on with my life. Maybe go to college." "Oooh, I'd love that. I wish I were that close. I failed my math class last year, so I have to retake geometry while taking algebra. It totally sucks. I had to give up one of my electives!"

"That does suck. I'm not good at math either. Otherwise, I'd help you. I barely squeak by," I said, making a face.

"How is everything else? Casey?"

"I want to say good. I really do. But it's not."

"Oh no! What'd he do?"

"Oh! Casey didn't do anything. Everything with him is good." I paused, looking up at her. "Eli came back."

"What?" she said, dropping her fork on her plate.

"That was basically my reaction, except I tripped and fell."

"Wait, what? Start at the beginning."

So I did. I started with the day I saw him as I left work and finished with when Casey had caught him. Then I paused, waiting for her to digest it.

"Wow. I wondered why you hadn't been very talkative the last couple days. I should have known crazy was hitting the fan and called you!"

"Yeah. That's not all. The elders want me to tell my story about the day Eli snapped. Tomorrow. In front of them and god-knows-who-else. And Eli will be watching."

"Oh gosh. Abby, I'm sorry. That's going to be really hard."

I nodded. "I haven't been able to even think about Eli without my chest tightening with anxiety. And they want me to talk about it in front of him."

"I can't even imagine." She pushed the food around her plate. "Can Casey go with you at least?"

"Yeah, Casey will be there. He has to tell his side of the story too."

"Well, at least you'll have someone there. Without that, it would be so much harder."

She didn't have to tell me. I didn't know what I would have done if he wasn't going to be there. Demand he be allowed? Maybe.

"How have you been feeling, anyway? We haven't really had much time to talk about everything since school started."

"I've been good. My arm is all healed up," I said, holding it up.

"Does it still hurt sometimes?" she asked, wincing. "I've heard injuries like that hurt for a long time, and sometimes they ache at times for the rest of your life."

"Well, it's sore sometimes, and my strength isn't back, but for the most part I think it will feel normal again."

"I hope so. I've never broken a bone."

"I don't recommend it."

Bailey's serious face filled with laughter.

"I'll take it off my bucket list!" she said, giggling.

After four more trips to the buffet—once for dessert—I felt stuffed. So stuffed that all I wanted to do was go home and crawl in bed. Bailey and I walked to the parking lot together and said goodbye there.

I was glad I had thought to go out with her. Even though she didn't have any pearly bits of wisdom to help the next day go better, but she had gotten my mind off of it. At any rate, I was sure I would sleep well after eating all that food.

CHAPTER TWENTY

Butterflies camped out in my stomach, and I didn't think they were going anywhere until after I left the elders' meeting. I rummaged through my closet for something to wear. *What did you wear to a trial among immortals?* I tossed another shirt across the room. I had already tried three outfits on, but nothing seemed to work.

Finally, I decided on a black skirt and a dressier t-shirt. I looked in the mirror and nodded to myself. This would be something I would wear to a human courtroom. I left my hair down so I would feel less exposed.

I went downstairs to eat breakfast with my mom and George. She took one look at me and was already curious.

"Wow, don't you look nice. What's this for?" she asked.

"Casey and I are going on a date, that's all."

I knew my clothes would stand out, and she would wonder why I had dressed up so I had my story ready. Casey picking me up supported it just the way I had hoped.

"Sounds special. What are you doing?" she asked.

"A party for one of his friends. It's at some hotel."

"Wow, that sounds really fun," she said.

I shrugged. "Should be."

I couldn't muster any more enthusiasm than that, and I hoped she wouldn't notice.

Casey arrived a short time later looking utterly heart-stopping in dress slacks and a white button-up shirt. His tie still hung limply at his neck. I grabbed hold of it as he stood on my doorstep and pulled him down to kiss me.

"I'm sorry, I couldn't resist," I said against his lips. "You're . . . just . . . so . . . hot," I said kissing him between each word.

"Mmm! Maybe I'll have to dress like this more often."

I nodded.

"Are you ready to go?" he asked.

I groaned. "Can we just ditch it?"

He grabbed my arm, pulling me along, "Come on. It'll be over quick, and I'll be right there."

I didn't pay attention while we drove, thinking over everything I would have to say. There had been gaps of time I hadn't been awake during the attack that I hoped Casey could fill in. We still hadn't discussed what happened while I was unconscious. I just wanted to put it behind me. Knowing that I would hear that part of the story for the first time in front of everyone made me feel unprepared.

"So, Edward wanted me to ask you not to speak about the dream you had that foreshadowed Eli's attack."

"Why?" I asked. My face scrunched in confusion.

"He thinks it will be better not to discuss it. He said to just tell it as it happened."

I shrugged. Edward would know better than I. "Fine."

That will at least cut down some of my talking time.

We parked in a parking garage and walked across the street to a tall commercial building. We rode the elevator to the top floor, and when the elevator doors opened to a room that looked like the lobby, I glanced at Casey wondering if we were in the right place. He stepped to the left and pressed a spot on the wall, and a number panel exposed itself. He entered a code. As if by magic, the wall opened to the left of the panel.

I knew not to be surprised by anything the Protectors did, but sometimes it still took my breath away. Especially as I walked into the mysterious room. In some ways, I could see that it resembled a traditional courtroom. Three chairs sat at the front—I assumed for the elders. I also noticed a few chairs toward the back facing the elders' seats. I didn't see a witness stand, nor were there tables for the plaintiff or defendant. Instead, one chair faced the front in the center of the room. I suspected that would be where I would sit while I spoke.

"We're early," Casey whispered.

I followed his lead as he sat in the first row of chairs behind the single chair. I noticed one other chair that had been pushed against the wall. It had to be for Eli.

A door opened to our left. Edward, Theodora, and James stepped in, dressed much like Casey and myself. Once they took their seats, a door next to the lone chair by the wall opened. In walked a large man, his presence alone was intimidating. He stepped to the side, giving way to Eli. Eli looked disheveled and unshaven. I had never seen him look so terrible. His cold blue eyes never left me, and the scowl on his face made me shiver. Casey's arm slid around me, rubbing my shoulder. I looked away. I wouldn't give him the satisfaction of my gaze. A second burly man stepped through the door behind Eli, just as Eli sat down. The guards kept him contained, and I was more than grateful to see they were so large. Eli was strong, but I doubted he could take on two men of their size.

Behind us, a few more people filtered in. Just before Edward stood to begin, Ren and Vince appeared at the other end of the row in which Casey and I sat. Their faces hung in sadness, pale and hollow. They nodded in our direction but made no move to approach. I gave them a half smile.

I turned my attention to Edward.

"Hello," he said. "Thank you all for being here today. Today we will hold Eli Jacobs accountable for his attack on Abby Martin and Casey Jefferies. Each side of the story will be told, including Eli's, and we will decide on Eli's punishment. If you are speaking today, it is imperative you speak the truth." Edward looked around as if he was trying to find someone.

"I think that does it. First, I would like to call Abby to come up," he said, motioning toward the chair in front of him. I stood and moved forward, turning back once to look at Casey.

As I sank into the chair, my breathing quickened, my mouth felt dry, and my heart raced. I held my hands together to keep them from shaking, and I looked up at Edward.

"You may begin," he said, sitting down and folding his hands on the table in front of him.

Casey

When Edward called her to the front, I held her just a moment and then released her. I fought the overwhelming urge to keep her next to me. To defy orders. At the apprehension on her face, I longed to whisk her away as fast as my feet could carry us. I wished I could send a breeze to cool and comfort her, but our gifts didn't work here. True to form, the elders long ago made sure such precautions were taken in this place where criminals were put on trial. Since their gifts were rendered useless, they were left with no ability to fight back. I knew it was the only way Eli was still held captive. His gift was strong. I knew all too well how strong. I glared at him as he stared Abby down. He didn't deserve to be in the room with her. He didn't deserve to gaze at her beauty.

I couldn't see her face now, but I could hear the tremble in her voice as she began to tell her story. At moments, she stumbled over the words. I hadn't heard her tell the story before. I never wanted to push her. She wanted to forget as much as I did. But selfishly, I found myself enthralled listening to her. So many questions had yet to be answered. *How had he blindsided her?* I had been racking my brain for months trying to understand how he had pulled it off.

I glanced at Edward as Abby spoke. His late-night phone call the night before had caught me off guard. *What would it matter if she spoke of her gift here, of all places?* I relayed the message, but I still wasn't sure it was the right move.

Edward had always been a good superior; I had always liked him until

Abby came along. His intentions had yet to become clear to me. He took such an intense interest in Abby and her gift. It unnerved me. I hoped she would be cautious around him. He was powerful, with many resources. It left me feeling vulnerable to his wishes. After all, I answered to him.

Why he felt the need to pull someone as high ranking as Lucian from his normal duties to help her lay beyond me. Nothing about it felt right. I hoped Lucian could help Abby, yet a sliver of me—my selfish side, if you will—wished he couldn't. Then Edward wouldn't be able to use her or her gift for whatever he had planned. But, for now, only time would tell.

Thank you for giving this series a spin.

If you enjoyed this book, consider leaving a review on Amazon, Goodreads, and/or the retailer of your choice to help other readers find this book.

Stay in touch with
C. M. Boers!
Find out about upcoming releases, giveaways, and chats!

Website: www.cmboers.com
Twitter: @CM_Boers
Facebook: https://www.facebook.com/boerscm
Instagram: CM_Boers

Keep reading for a sneak peek of

Retreat

Book four

CHAPTER ONE

My heart raced in the darkness. I felt cornered with no escape. I took a few steps. My footsteps echoed around me. The room sounded huge, yet still felt as if the walls were closing in on me. I held my arms out in front of me, testing the ground with my feet. Hard. Concrete.

I shook my head, trying to recall what led me here, but everything blurred in my mind.

This is wrong.

Disoriented . . .

Alone . . .

I need to get out. I shouldn't be here.

A door opened behind me. Light engulfed the other half of the room, revealing nothing but empty space and the furthest wall. I swiveled around on my heel to face the light. A figure stood in the doorway, looking in. I shrank away until my back slammed against a wall.

No.

Taking the only opportunity, I looked around using the only shred of light I had . . .

I sat up fast, breathing hard. Sweat dripped down my forehead. Throwing back the covers, I fanned my legs.

"Hot," I breathed to myself.

My newest reoccurring nightmare was beginning to take shape, and it was really getting under my skin.

Months had passed since the hearing with the elders, yet when I thought back to that day, I could still feel their penetrating gaze as they looked down on me. My mouth still went dry thinking about retelling all the events that led up to that moment. *"And then . . . he threw me from the train . . ."*

My words echoed in my head. I shuddered. Their ruling that day was exactly what I'd hoped for ever since he turned his back on me.

Guilty.

Eli had been stripped of his immortality, and all of his gifts. He was sentenced to working at the elders' compound, a place I hadn't even known existed. I think they mentioned something about cleaning. But I stopped listening after I heard "life sentence." All that mattered was that I never saw him again. Never again would I have to look at the face that deceived me, sent who-knows-how-many goons to follow me, and then tried to kill me.

I walked out that day feeling victorious. He was out of my life for good, and I couldn't be happier. The worry, however, that one of his goons might come out of hiding always tingled in the back of my mind.

I grabbed my bag and headed to the door. If only school could distract me from the nerves in the pit of my stomach. At eight o'clock tonight, I would meet with Lucian—who might be my one chance to fine-tune these nightmares. I could think of nothing else. I feared that my gift wouldn't work the same as his and he wouldn't be able to help me.

Of course, there were good thoughts mixed in there too. With his help, I might stop something bad from happening. Then my anxiety filled me all over again like some never-ending toilet flush of emotions.

Christmas was just weeks away, which also meant finals and study-cram sessions were in full swing. For the first two classes of the day, we studied, making it hard to think of anything except math, science, and my empty stomach. In third hour, Bailey and I were able to collaborate on a book report we were writing together, which really meant we chatted since the report was already done. The hour flew by.

"We need to go dress shopping! The dance is in two weeks! When can you go?" Bailey asked as we gathered our things and left the classroom.

"Ah . . . next weekend." Part of me knew I'd been putting off going shopping because I knew Casey couldn't attend—school rules since he wasn't a student. But I couldn't put it off any longer.

"*Yes*! Finally!" She arm pumped her excitement.

A few people looked our way.

"Shh!" I giggled.

Bailey covered her mouth. "Oops."

Alexis and Breanne joined us just outside the classroom.

"What's *oops*?" Alexis asked.

"Oh, we were just talking about the dance," Bailey said.

"Ooh, are you all going?" Alexis clapped her hands.

"Oh, I am," Bailey giggled. "I just have to make sure Ryan knows."

Listening to the girls talk about their dates made me feel somehow detached from them.

"If I can find a date," Breanne said next, her voice timid.

"You've still got time," I said, hoping to encourage her.

"Just a few weeks!" Alexis said. "I can't wait. I'm so not bothering with a date. Who wants to only dance with one guy the whole time? *Boring*."

We all giggled. *Boy-crazy Alexis.*

"I still can't believe it's already December," Breanne said. "Feels like the school year just started."

"I know what you mean." I ran a hand through my hair.

We walked together to lunch, and my phone rang. I checked the screen. *Casey.*

"I'll meet you in there," I said to them and waved at them to go ahead.

Bailey raised her eyebrows twice and flashed an amused smile.

"Ooooh, the boyfriend!" Alexis sang.

Breanne just giggled, blushing.

I shook my head and turned away. "Hello."

"Hey," Casey's smooth voice came through the phone. "You're at lunch, right?"

"Yep."

"Good. Come outside."

A smile formed on my lips. "What are you up to, mister?"

"Oh nothing . . ."

I burst through the front doors and saw Casey sitting on a blanket in the grass. A small cooler perched next to him.

"Casey! This is so sweet."

I knelt down, threw my arms around his neck, and gave him a kiss, pulling back slowly to stare into his eyes.

"It's nice to see you too." A smile tugged at his lips.

We sat up, and Casey started pulling things from the cooler. Two sodas, two salads, dressing, and cookies.

"I figured since you have the meeting with Lucian tonight, you might be nervous so I thought I'd bring you lunch and maybe help you forget for a while. Plus, I won't get to see you tonight, and I missed you."

"Aww . . . I missed you too. You're the best. Seriously." I picked up the salad he gave me and started eating. "So, what are you going to do tonight?"

"The guys are going to go fishing." He made a face. "Figure I'll tag along. I'm not much for fishing, but it's fun watching them try."

I giggled. "I don't see Ferdinand fishing."

Casey leaned over, "He's part of the reason it's so fun to watch."

I pictured Ferdinand in a fishing hat with lures hooked to it and laughed harder.

"Are we still on for dinner tomorrow night?" he asked, taking a bite.

"Planning on it."

"Good."

I'd finished a little over half of my salad when the warning bell rang.

"Shoot, I've got to go," I said.

"Here, take the cookies with you." He handed me the bag.

"This was the best school lunch I've ever had. Thank you." I gathered up all my things and stood.

Casey gave me a quick squeeze and kiss before he let go.

"Bye," I said.

The rest of the day, all I could think about was Casey and that lunch. The overly thoughtful gesture made my heart melt. Once in a while, thoughts of Lucian popped into my head, making my head a jumble of everything but school. It was hard to focus.

With my change of clothes packed in my trunk, I drove straight to the coffee house from school.

It wasn't long before I stood at the counter, mindlessly wiping it down over and over, the distant hum of Christmas music crooning overhead.

What will today bring?

This could turn out to be one of the best things to happen to me. I could gain control over the dreams or even some insight into how to unlock their mysteries. It would make my life that much easier.

I watched the clock throughout my shift, waiting for the time to come. The second the small hand struck eight, the door opened, and a man walked in. His black hair was slicked back, and the sides were shaved. He looked like he could have just stepped off the runway in his black shirt and designer jeans. He didn't have to introduce himself; I knew it was him right away. The power that emanated from him was familiar, something I'd come to recognize as distinctively Protector. I clocked out and made a beeline for him.

"Hi, you must be Lucian. I'm Abby." I extended my hand, but he embraced me in a big hug. My hands awkwardly pressed into my sides, and my face smashed against his solid chest.

"One thing you'll learn fast about me, Abby, I'm a hugger." He pulled away, grinning at me. "Shall we?"

I led the way out the door, then realized I didn't know where we were going. I turned back toward him to ask, but before I could formulate the question, he spoke.

"Why don't we go somewhere a little more private?" He held out a remote, and an all-black sports car with all-black wheels flashed its lights. My lips curled. It was him in car form.

He opened my door for me and waited until I slipped both feet inside before closing my door and strutting to the other side. The engine revved to life, and I could feel the rumble of the exhaust underneath me. We flew backward, then shot into drive. It didn't take a genius to figure out Lucian liked to go fast. Very fast.

"So, where *are* we going?" I asked, hoping to focus on something else. Anything to keep my stomach from lurching into my throat as we gained speed. I gripped the door handle.

"Somewhere private." He grinned.

It surprised me how comfortable he was making me squirm after meeting me just minutes earlier. I got the impression he was used to getting a rise out of people and enjoyed it.

"People just go wherever you want?" I asked in a teasing voice.

He raised an eyebrow, and a half grin appeared on his face. "Maybe . . "

I sighed, rolling my eyes.

"What? You don't trust me?"

"What is it with you Protectors and blind trust?" I turned to face him. "I mean, seriously, do you know how many Protectors have said that to me?"

"Have any of them steered you wrong?" A cocky smile was still on his face.

I thought for a moment. "No," I said. "Well, yes."

He raised a brow. "Which is it?"

"It's complicated."

"Maybe it's time to uncomplicate things and give blind trust a chance."

I crossed my arms. "Eli tried to get me to trust him exactly as you're suggesting, and look how that turned out."

He stopped smiling. "I'm sorry."

Lucian drove another ten minutes before he turned off into a neighborhood that looked run down. He wound his way through the streets like he could do it with his eyes closed and stopped in front of a house on the end. A chain-link fence separated the neighborhood from an industrial park.

What an eyesore.

He pressed a few buttons on his phone, and the garage door began to lift, slowly at first, then quickly as if a weight had been lifted off of it. He swung the car into the garage and shut the door behind us. He cut the engine before the door closed all the way. The sudden quiet of the garage after the rumble of the exhaust triggered goosebumps on my arms.

I smacked my lips. "So . . . now what?"

"Now we go inside." He grinned. I could sense sarcasm in his voice.

He pressed the unlock button on both our seatbelts and climbed out. When I looked around at the garage, it seemed enormous, certainly not the two-car garage it appeared to be from the outside. I spun around, examining it all.

"This is impressive," I said.

"Eh, it's functional," he said, shrugging.

I shook my head and rolled my eyes. *Modesty.*

"You coming?" He stood in the doorway.

"Ah, yeah." I took one last look and followed him.

He held the door open, leaving a wide space for me to pass through. My jaw dropped the second I was inside. The living room boasted floor-to-ceiling windows, but that wasn't what caught my attention. The view outside the windows captivated me above all else. Waves crashed on the beach as the last of the sun's rays disappeared in the distance. The dull glow that remained in the sky highlighted the white-tipped waves, making the water look as if it were dancing.

Absently, I stumbled to the window, dropping my purse as I walked, gawking at the sandy beach.

"I take it you like the beach?" he said.

I nodded.

"Want anything to drink?"

"No, I'm okay. Is that real out there?"

The beach called to me like a long-lost friend.

He gave me a strange look. "Of course."

This was another amazing Protector endowment—not some smokescreen but a portal somewhere else. I couldn't believe it. Nothing would ever compare to this.

He leaned back against the counter with his arms crossed.

"Where are we?" I asked.

"Florida."

My hand fumbled for the latch to the door. I couldn't resist the urge to go outside. Leaving my flip flops on the deck, I sank my feet into the warm sand and let the cool ocean breeze wash over me. My eyes closed as I breathed in the salty air. *God, I missed this.*

My whole reason for being here was momentarily forgotten as the serenity of the beach relaxed me.

A few minutes later, Lucian sat down on the deck, his chin propped in his hand. He waited patiently with a smirk. My cheeks warmed.

I lifted myself up and pulled my feet from the sand, feeling strange for making myself so comfortable.

"Sorry." Blushing, I stepped back into my shoes.

"Don't let me stop you from your fun," he said.

I was beginning to wonder if his sly grin ever faded or if he just enjoyed teasing me too much.

"Should we get started?" I asked.

"Out here or inside?"

A sheepish smile formed as I turned toward the ocean.

"Guess that answers my question."

He leaned forward to pat the chair next to him. Leaving my flip flops where I stood, I made my way over and sat down.

"Why don't you start by telling me about yourself and your problem."

I fiddled with my hands.

"I'm from California, thus the obsession with the beach. I moved here a year ago when my parents got divorced—my mom's choice, not mine. My dreams started right before I moved here. Of course, I didn't think much of them at the time. My dreams continued through all the drama with Pete and Eli, if you know about that. Three of them have come true. The fourth and most recent started a few months ago."

"From what Edward says, these are bad dreams, is that right?"

"Yeah. Life-or-death moments, at least so far."

"Mine started like that as well. Over time, they evolved to include other important moments. For example, big moments for those around me. As I grew older, they included events that weren't in any way related to me. Those are especially hard because often I haven't met the individuals involved."

"So, what do you do?" I asked.

"Well, in those cases, there isn't a whole lot I can do, but I still try. Just like for the other dreams, I make a list of every detail I can recall when I wake. The lighting. The surroundings. Everything. Sometimes I can figure out the location from memory. Other times, nothing kicks in until right before it unfolds in real life."

"That's it?"

"Well, no. But the rest will take time and training."

"The places you've been are easy to spot in your dreams?" I asked.

"Sometimes." His face wrinkled. "That's not going to work in your favor since you haven't lived here very long."

"Great." I sighed.

"Hey, it may seem like there's a lot stacked against you right now, but you aren't alone. You've got a lot more help than I ever had."

"Really?" I asked.

He nodded. "It's going to take work, but eventually you'll get it."

I sighed and ran my hands through my hair.

"Relax. There isn't a sure-fire trick to get the job done. I'll help you the best I can. If my tricks don't work, I'll keep trying to find something that does."

"Why?"

"Why what?" His brows furrowed.

"Why would you try so hard to help me? You don't even know me." I glanced out at the crashing waves to avoid his stare.

"You say you've been around Protectors a lot, yet you still have to ask?"

I turned back to him, my expression flat. "You could say I have issues believing what people say."

He chuckled. "Edward said you'd been through a lot. I guess I should have known. So, what do you want to know?"

I scrunched up my face.

Lucian couldn't hold back his laughter. "What is *that* look for?"

"Why are you asking what I want to know?"

"How else would we build trust?"

I shrugged.

He looked out at the water. Seagulls squawked in the distance.

"Let's go for a walk." He rose to his feet.

We walked for a while without saying anything, taking in the beauty around us—or at least that's what I did.

"I've got to ask. What's with the secret oasis? I mean it's nothing short of amazing, but what gives?"

"What? You wouldn't want to hide your special place inside a dump?" he asked.

"Well, of course! Who wouldn't? But how?"

A half grin formed once again on his face, and a twinkle shone in his eye.

"That is a question that most Protectors outside of the elders don't even know." ""

"Is there a rule against people knowing?" I asked.

"No." He sighed. "Not really. It's just kind of known to be a secret. Imagine if everyone knew how. Everyone would want to have one. Of course, that wouldn't be such a problem if it didn't draw attention to us."

I walked silently, considering this.

"Maybe I'll tell you someday," he said. "Just give me some time on that one."

"Fair enough."

I strolled onward, trying to think of something else I wanted to know, but nothing came to mind.

A couple minutes later, Lucian broke the silence. "What, cat's got your tongue?"

I laughed. "No, I'm just not sure what to ask."

And I hate to be put on the spot.

"Fine. I'm thirty-one years old. I'm originally from Florida, obviously." He gestured around us. "Umm . . . I come from a long line of Protectors."

I tried to take it all in. Thirty-one? He looked to be twenty, but I'd assumed he was older because of how high in the ranks he was. Maybe he was an exception. Eventually, maybe I'd ask, but I was afraid it was another thing he couldn't answer, so I kept my mouth shut.

"I heard you had a pretty bad fight with Eli Jacobs," he said.

I choked. "Uh, yeah."

"Did I bring up a sore subject?"

"Sort of."

"Why?"

I stopped and looked at him nervously. My eyes flickered back and forth from his gaze to the sand.

"It's a long story," I said.

"It's a long beach."

I eyed him once more, biting my lip. "You've probably already heard it all. News seems to travel fast in your circles."

"Haven't heard it from you. For all I know, what I heard could all be rumors. I don't believe everything I hear." His eyes held mine.

I rolled my eyes and started walking again.

"Eli and I dated." I glanced at him out of the corner of my eye. I figured he probably knew that much. "When we first met, I was interested in Pete Denali."

He blew out a whistle, cutting me off. "There's a family you don't want to mess with."

I rolled my eyes. "Yeah, thanks."

"I take it you figured that out."

"You could say that. Pete's uncle murdered Eli's mother." I paused. "Yeah . . ."

". . . and since I was the one who got involved with Pete, you can imagine who Eli blamed."

"That's ridiculous." Lucian shook his head.

"Not to Eli. After dropping me like a hot cake and ignoring me for weeks, Eli came back. He was amazing, so naturally I thought he had put it behind him. But then he would act distant—not all the time, just sometimes. Of course, I figured he was sorting through his feelings. The joke was on me. In reality, he was having me followed and making me think the threat was elsewhere. Just when I thought we were going to get to the bottom of who was following me, he turned on me. And that brings us to when he ambushed me and threw me off a moving train."

"Whoa, I thought *that* was just a rumor. He actually threw you off a train, and you survived?" Surprise emanated from his words.

My hands shook.

"Oh my gosh," I gasped, tapping my front, patting my arms, and looking over my body. Throwing in a little dramatic flair. "I think I did." I couldn't let the residual anxiety show. It still lingered and reared its head in moments of weakness.

"Ha ha, very funny," he said. "How *did* you survive? According to Edward, you aren't immortal."

"I had a little help."

Then I wondered if Protectors shared their gifts with each other. I figured some probably did, but I decided not to out Casey and his gift of air manipulation.

"So cryptic," he said, his expression amused.

I grinned. "I have to keep some things to myself."

"Fair enough." He shoved his hands into his pockets.

The last rays of sunlight disappeared, and the sky went dark. I thought of Casey, who was probably waiting for me to call, wondering how today went.

"Maybe we should turn back," I said. "It's getting late."

"Aww. Are we scared of the dark?" he teased.

"No." I crossed my arms.

"Come on. There's something I think you'll like. It's not much farther."

I hesitated only a step, then kept marching forward beside him.

"What is it?"

"You'll see."

Again, I could tell that he enjoyed keeping me in the dark. I remained silent and watched the waves as we walked.

Before long, the beach extended out into a peninsula, and my breath stopped when a magnificent lighthouse came into view. The beauty of it made me falter. I stopped, taking it all in.

It was dark enough that the light glowed off the night waters. Floodlights on the ground illuminated the whole building, showing off each and every curve and dip. In the shadows below, I could see planter boxes with flowers peeking out.

"You like?" he asked. I could feel his eyes on me.

"Like? I love. How did you know I love lighthouses?"

"Just a hunch." He shrugged. "Who loves the beach but doesn't have an affinity for lighthouses?"

"No idea." I smiled. "It's magnificent."

"This one is still functional, and the keeper lives there. Maybe one day he'll give us a tour."

"Oh no, I don't do tours."

Lucian's head jerked back to me. "What?"

I gave him a sheepish look, not wanting to elaborate.

"Oh, there's got to be a good story here." He turned his full body to face me, his hands on his hips. "Out with it."

I sighed. How did he drag so much out of me in such a short time? "I'm afraid of them."

"What?"

"I love to look at them . . . from afar. The inside . . . I'm afraid."

He looked at me and then back at the lighthouse.

"I don't get it." The stumped expression on his face made me want to bury my head in the sand. But even in his confusion, he couldn't make his faint smile disappear.

I closed my eyes. "There are ghosts in lighthouses."

A few moments passed in silence. My heart beat loudly in my ears. I opened one eye to peek at him. At that, he started laughing so hard he dropped down on his back in the sand and rolled around, holding his stomach, laughing uncontrollably.

I blew out a breath and stalked back in the direction of his secret hideaway, leaving him behind. I could hear him shuffling to his feet behind me.

"Wait, wait." He sounded breathless through bursts of laughter. "Stop." He grabbed my arm.

My body kicked into gear. Without thinking, I whirled around, pushed into him, twisted my arm, and yanked it free just as Casey had taught me, then side kicked him in the stomach. I took two steps backward before I realized what I'd done.

The dumbfounded look on Lucian's face as he doubled over holding his stomach, trying to catch the breath I'd knocked out of him, promptly morphed into a grin.

"Wow, I underestimated you. You've got some skills," he said.

I looked down at my arm and wondered how they had kicked in. I'd never even remotely had an instinct to fight, let alone someone who wasn't even a threat.

"I'm sorry . . . I didn't mean to . . ." I stammered. I wanted to crawl in a hole.

"Relax. It's no big deal. I'm sorry I laughed. Clearly that wasn't a good idea." He chuckled. "So, you think there are ghosts in lighthouses?"

"Lighthouses are old. It's only natural to have ghosts hanging around, don't you think?"

He considered this. "Well, I guess maybe in some, but not all."

"I'm just not interested in getting up close and personal with one."

Lucian held up his hands in surrender. "Noted. No lighthouse tours. Got it. Just don't beat me up."

I glared at him and his amused expression.

He strode beside me on the way back to his place, and I crossed my arms feeling self-conscious. I yawned and glanced at my watch. Almost 10 o'clock.

"Why is it that I feel you got to know me far more than I got to know you?" I asked.

For once, there was tenderness in his smile. "Because I think that's how today went. That's not a bad thing."

"No, I guess not."

"Maybe it just means you're beginning to trust me."

"Don't bet on it," I said.

He drove me back to work and left me to drive myself home.

As he left, he rolled down the window and called out, "Do me a favor. The next time you have a dream, write down every detail and text or call me if you need anything, even if it's the middle of the night. That's what I'm here for."

I nodded.

I doubted I'd ever call him in the middle of the night. That seemed strange. It's not like he could come over or even do anything for me. No, my problems would wait for the morning.

I dug through my purse for my keys when an unsettling feeling came over me. The hair on the back of my neck prickled. I felt like I was being watched. A chill spread through me.

My eyes roamed the dark parking lot before I caught sight of someone sitting in the chairs in front of the coffee house. I turned my full attention to the dark silhouette almost hidden in the shadows, watching as they stood.

My breath hitched in my throat.

They shoved their hands in the front pockets of a black jacket. The hood covering their head hid any glimpse of their face.

My hands closed around my keys, and I yanked them from my purse.

The dark figure took two steps toward me, and that's where they stopped, ten feet away, staring at me.

I fumbled with my keys, picking out the one I needed. Forgetting all about my remote, I unlocked my door and threw it open. My eyes never left the hooded figure as I threw all of my belongings in the car and dropped into my seat. I slammed my hand down on the lock when the door shut behind me.

From this angle, the light caught their face under the hoodie just enough for me to see a wicked smile creep up on their lips. And just like that, they walked away into the darkness behind the building.

My car roared to life with a flick of my wrist. I threw my car in reverse and sped out of the parking lot.

My arms shook as I held the steering wheel.

What was that?

I breathed deeply, trying to calm myself. In and out.

My first impulse was to call Casey, but then I changed my mind.

Am I reading too much into this?

Nothing had actually happened. The person didn't threaten me or hurt me. They didn't even speak to me. They looked at me, sure, but I was the only person around. Then they walked away. Surely if they meant me harm, nothing was there to stop them.

Maybe they thought I looked like a crazy person fumbling around like I did. Freaking out over what? That there was someone there?

I shook my head.

Nope. I wouldn't be telling Casey, or anyone else for that matter.

*   *   *   *

The next day, Casey and I picked up take-out and went back to his apartment. He wanted to know all about my meeting with Lucian. Though, I had no intention of letting him in on my ghost fears or my unnecessary martial arts. I already felt transparent enough with Lucian knowing.

"You should have seen his place, Casey. It was amazing. To have the beach right out your back door. Gosh, I'd love that."

We sat huddled around his coffee table, the fire unlit. The heat of summer made me not even want to think about turning it on, no matter how cozy it made his apartment feel.

"I know you would. It sounds amazing." He popped a piece of chicken into his mouth. "What did he say about your dreams?"

"Not a whole lot. He wants me to write down every detail when I wake up from one."

He nodded. "Sounds like a good idea."

"I guess."

"You don't sound so sure."

"I guess I'm not. I mean, I can see how it would be helpful. I was just hoping for more."

"You'll get there," Casey said. "Just give it time."

"I hope so."

ABOUT THE AUTHOR

Obscured was C. M.'s debut novel. What began as a way to spend her free time slowly transitioned into a passion for writing. She's currently working on releasing her fourth novel in the *Obscured* series. The best is yet to come!

C. M. is a mother of three. She grew up in the sunshine state of Arizona with a love of reading and an ambition to write. But never took her writing seriously until after the birth of her first child. After that she took up writing more seriously in her spare time and hasn't stopped since.

www.ingramcontent.com/pod-product-compliance
Lightning Source LLC
Chambersburg PA
CBHW070301120726
47910CB00007B/2334